FRAMED

FRAMED

James M. Murphy

iUniverse, Inc.
New York Lincoln Shanghai

FRAMED

iUniverse, Inc.

For information address:
iUniverse, Inc.
2021 Pine Lake Road, Suite 100
Lincoln, NE 68512
www.iuniverse.com

Edited by Margaret Searles. msearles6@netzero.net

ISBN: 0-595-32753-2

Printed in the United States of America

For Joan M. O'Reilly
The Air that I breathe

PROLOGUE

▼

Frank Kendall swapped hands on the steering wheel, fished the buzzing phone out of his inside jacket pocket, opened it and said, "Yes?"

His exhaustion deepened as he listened. He was 67 and he'd put in a day that would have flattened a twenty year old. Now, five minutes from home and bed, he had another crisis to handle. He told the caller, "Of course. I'm in Mission Valley, so it will take a few minutes."

The Interstate 15 interchange was just ahead. He moved the car to the right lane and took the ramp toward downtown San Diego. It was his fault that the long day was stretching into a longer night. When he'd called John McBride from Escondido, he was going to tell his friend and business partner that he was too exhausted to meet him for their usual Tuesday night dinner. He had lost his nerve as soon as he heard Mac's voice. Mac was alone, in poor health, and he eagerly anticipated the night out.

The dinner hadn't been all that relaxing. Frank was cranky, Mac was opinionated, and they argued. As he drove away, he'd even given Mac the finger. He had never done that to anyone.

When Frank returned to the restaurant's parking lot ten minutes later, he saw Mac's Taurus parked in a different space. The caller got out of Mac's car wearing a long coat and a wool cap, his face puffy and shiny. Shocked, Frank pulled the Honda into a parking space, and was out, almost running. "What happened to your face? Are you all right?"

Instead of answering, the man pulled Frank backwards to the fender of the Honda. He fumbled with something inside Frank's jacket, then backed away two steps and drew a large silver handgun.

Then Frank knew. Bitterly disappointed, he said, "This is really dumb."

CHAPTER 1

▼

February 12th, 1997, Wednesday

Gary recognized John McBride from the photo in the police report, a barrel of a man carrying too many extra pounds under a worn, red and yellow plaid, cotton shirt. Too long for his 5–6 height, the shirt hung to his crotch, covering the top of his green work pants. When Gary waved, McBride shuffled over, navigating the maze of tables as if his legs hurt. Perhaps the electronic monitoring anklet was an irritant.

He slumped into the opposite chair at the table for two, dumping the windbreaker he was carrying into a chair at an adjacent table. A faint odor of oil wafted as he reached across to shake hands. His arthritically deformed hand felt like a claw. "John McBride. I go by Mac." His voice rolled out of a barrel chest, deep, raspy and loud.

"Gary Charboneau."

Mac said, "You don't look tough enough to do this kind of work."

Gary liked that assessment. At 31, he could be young or old. His face was nondescript; none of its features drew attention. He kept his brown hair trimmed to a medium length. At six feet, he might be tall or short. Weighing 180 pounds, he could be slim or slightly overweight. People didn't remember meeting him, a huge advantage for an investigator.

Gary smiled. "You look tough enough to eat nails." Mac's square head sat atop the squat block of his body with no intervening neck. Evidently a Catholic, his wrinkled forehead bore crossed ashes from an Ash Wednesday service. His face was all crevices and hillocks sliding away from a heroic Roman nose. The tiny bits of metal embedded in his hair showed that, at sixty-two, he was not a hands-off owner of Framac, his sheet metal business.

Some emotion cracked Mac's deadpan demeanor as he said, "Nah, I'm a pussycat." His deep bass voice projected into the far corners of the restaurant, quieting all the nearby conversations. He winced, then lowered his voice to add, "Used to talking in the shop."

Gary was too warm. The restaurant's windows slanted out at the top. Designed to shade the interior during the summer, the windows let the winter sun flood the room. Gary had dressed for February in Arlington, Virginia. He envied Mac's thin shirt. "Does San Diego ever do winter?"

Mac shifted his body to look out the window. When he faced Gary again, he said, "Kind of chilly today."

Gary laughed, and then saw that Mac wasn't kidding, so he changed the subject. "Why did they let you out of jail? They don't normally do that in murder cases."

"Little lady runs the jail didn't want an old diabetic with a bum ticker in there. Plus I told the judge I'd have to shut the business down, put 180 people out of work, if he sent me to jail. The prosecutor didn't object, so the judge went along."

Gary asked, "You run the business alone?"

"Computers run it; I just work out the kinks. Most of the people got years in; they don't need me to tell them what to do. I hired a salesman to take Frank's place. He'll work out if he stays."

After a moment's pause, Mac added, "Alice shouldn't have asked you to help. I'm tapped out. Been payin' the lawyer and a P.I. named George Martinez, full time."

"This is for Alice. I owe her." That was true. Gary owed his wealth to Mac's foster daughter, but he would have jumped at the chance to work on Mac's case without that incentive. If Mac had been framed, and the justice system in San Diego was the usual screwed-up mess, getting Mac off could launch his career as a P.I. Gary's ace was that his girlfriend was a reporter for *The Washington Post*.

Mac asked, "You gonna work on this for free?"

"If I get you off, you pay the expenses. Is that acceptable?"

"Yeah. If that happens, I'm rollin' in dough." His voice was soft when he asked, "How is Alice?"

It wasn't a rhetorical question, so Gary said, "Like a rattlesnake with a toothache. She's pissed you never told her that Frank was dead and you were accused."

He shrugged. "By the time I got out of jail, Frank's funeral was over. She couldn't do nothin' except worry, so no point in telling her."

"Were you a foster parent for many kids?"

Mac shook his head. "Just the once with Alice. Tore me up bad when she left. I don't see how real parents ever let go of their kids."

"How did you pick Alice?"

"The wife heard about her after Alice put her foster father in the hospital. Must have been a hell of a fight, skinny little slip of a thing was bruised and cut all over. She never said but a doctor thought she'd been raped.

"Same night that happened, me and the wife went down to this office to meet her. Broke my heart, seeing her beat up like that. When I asked if she'd like to come live with us, she said, 'Sure, but let me warn you. You put a hand on me, you'd better be able to defend yourself.'" Mac laughed, a belly laugh that rolled out of his body like a boulder coming down a mountain. "It was a picture, you know?" He paused, perhaps recalling that picture. "So we took her home, and every excuse I could find, I told her that I'd like to hug her but I'd wait until she said that would be okay. Took nearly a year. The chain broke on her bicycle, and I put in a new link. Nothin' really, took me five minutes. No warning, she hugs me. I ended up bawlin'. We was great pals after that."

Gary understood why Alice didn't think Mac was capable of murder.

Mac patted Gary's hand, as if asking him not to be offended. "The P.I. I hired, George Martinez, is sharp. Why do you think you can find stuff he couldn't?"

"George probably obeys the law; respects individual rights, that kind of thing."

"You don't?"

"Not so you'd notice."

"How you gonna help if you find stuff illegal? It just gets tossed out."

"That isn't the real world, Mac. I find out what's true and I pass it to the cops. They figure out a way to make it legal. If they can't make evidence that will stand up in court, the D.A. pretends that it will and plea-bargains. The whole system works on lies."

Mac accepted that with a weary nod.

A sweet-looking blond waitress, whose name tag identified her as Ashley, asked, "You want the usual, Mac?"

The usual was a Ruben and black coffee. Gary ordered coffee.

The conversation lagged. After Ashley brought their coffees, Gary said, "I read the police report." According to that report, Mac had purchased the handgun that was used to kill his business partner, Frank Kendall, outside the Colson's Cavern restaurant. Several witnesses had gotten Mac's license plate number as he drove away from Frank's body. Later, Frank's blood was found on the door of his car.

Mac didn't respond, so Gary said, "You and Frank left the restaurant 24 minutes before the shooting. What happened during that time?"

"We talked a couple of minutes. Frank left before me. We was arguing about somethin' so I walked him to his car. Sonofabitch gets in, closes the door and flips me the bird." He grinned. "That wasn't like him. Kept me laughing all the way back to my car."

"He left before you did?"

"Yeah. My neck don't work. Takes me forever to get out of a parking lot."

He looked out the window, giving an unintentional demonstration as he twisted the upper part of his body to watch a bag lady in the parking lot. She struggled to push her shopping cart over a concrete car stop, oblivious to the clear path around the obstacle.

Mac said, "I figured Frank was home in bed by the time I pulled out of the lot."

"Then why would he come back to the parking lot?"

Mac shrugged. "His kid got him back there some way."

"Who?"

"Frank's kid, David."

"Why?"

"Money." He took another sip of coffee. "The sheet metal business is worth 25 million, give or take a couple. The kid figured out how to get it all. If I'm convicted, Frank's wife, Mary, gets my half. She'll let him run it."

"You think they're in this together?"

He waved that away. "Mary loved Frank. They had one of those great marriages you don't hardly ever see. She's been so torn up since the shooting, she don't come out of the house. Wouldn't surprise me if she dies of a broken heart."

"Did the cops investigate David?"

"That night, I told 'em who did it. They sent guys to his house after they booked me."

"Did they check him for gunshot residue and blood?"

"Checked him and Mary both. They were clean."

The Ruben arrived and Mac just looked at it. "The trial starts Friday, and Julie says we're going to lose."

"Julie?"

"My lawyer, Julie Williams." He took his business card out of a scuffed black wallet and laboriously wrote her name and phone number on the back. His fingers were so deformed by arthritis, he had to use his whole hand to write. When he handed Gary the card, he said, "I told her you'd be around."

Mac took a bite of the Ruben. He stared at the table while he chewed, as if he'd gone off into melancholy. When he could, he said, "I hate handin' the company over to David. Frank and me built it from nothing, like it was our kid we raised. Most of the workers been there a long time, they don't deserve bein' put under David. He ain't goin' to treat 'em right." He winced. "They're good, all of 'em. We're no better than any other fab shop without those people. Won't take David long to wreck the place."

No mention of his coming imprisonment, or the fortune he'd lost, or retribution against the man who had framed him. His sadness was for his employees.

Mac checked his watch. "Can't stay too long. A stamper die broke, and I got a mill tied up machinin' a new one."

"Isn't that kind of unusual? The owner working at a machine?"

"I'm just havin' fun. David's system runs the place, so I don't have a lot to do."

"Frank's kid?"

"Yeah. He ain't short on brains."

Mac looked at his watch again, and then picked up his jacket. He asked, "You like hotels?" His brow furrowed as if he couldn't imagine such a thing. "You could stay with me; get a home cooked dinner most nights. I like to cook. I wouldn't be in your way. Weekdays, I go in early and I'm at the shop all day. The guest bedroom has its own entrance."

Gary shook his head. "Can't do that. Since you're wearing that electronic monitoring bracelet, the police can search any time. I have stuff that could get me thrown in jail."

Mac shook his head. "They couldn't use the bracelet. I have to go to three different doctors, shop for drugs and food; go all over hunting down materials when somebody don't deliver in time. They thought I was going to be at home or at the plant."

"So you're not monitored?"

"Nah. I'm out on bail." His forehead wrinkled. "What illegal stuff you talkin' about?"

"Phony ID cards. Listening devices. Is that going to be a concern for you?"

He looked relieved. "Thought you was talkin' drugs."

"I don't do drugs. I don't even drink."

"Mind I ask somethin' real personal?" Gary used his 'I don't care' expression, and Mac asked, "You risk jail doin' illegal stuff. Why would you do that?"

"Nailing scumbags is fun." Gary wouldn't tell Mac that 'scumbags' included some judges, lawyers, and other political types who abuse the justice system for money. He hated those corrupters with a passion that bordered on homicidal. Screwing with the system was also dangerous, which satisfied his addiction to adrenaline. He did love tweaking the beast.

Mac seemed to be waiting for a better answer, so Gary added, "It's probably the same reason you still run your business. It's more fun than anything else you could do."

Mac looked at his watch. "You want to stay at my place?"

"You're sure it's not an imposition?"

"Alice says you're family. Besides, it's a big place. I rattle around in it."

Gary couldn't see any physical risk. If Mac was the killer, nothing Gary found would hurt him. The prosecution already had an airtight case. And he loved the idea of home cooked meals. "Thanks, I will take you up on that. I've already paid for a motel for tonight, so I'll move to your place tomorrow if that's okay?"

"Come by about nine. I'll fix you breakfast; get you settled." He winced as he added, "After the trial, you might have the place to yourself." He rose, picked up the bill, and tugged the plaid shirt smooth across his belly. He said, "Leave Ashley a good tip. She's got three kids."

As Mac left the restaurant, Gary keyed Julie Williams' number into his cell phone. An answering machine put him on hold. In the parking lot, Mac shuffled to a dark Taurus and got in. Backing out looked like an ordeal. He backed a few feet, then stopped and turned his body to look, then repeated the process. If he had shot his partner, the cops would have been there before he got out of the lot.

When she came on the line, Julie Williams' buttery voice hinted of laughter. If she looked like she sounded, she would be stunning. Mac had told her Gary would call. She listened, gave him George Martinez's cell phone number, and said, "Jury selection starts Friday. With the three-day weekend coming up, the arguments will probably start next Tuesday or Wednesday. That's all the time you have. Appeals based on new evidence are rejected 97% of the time."

After he disconnected, he called George Martinez. George was watching a house, but if Gary wanted to join him, he would go over what he'd found. Gary got the address and type of van, and then asked a waitress for directions to a bookstore. He drove there and bought a Thomas Guide.

George's stakeout was miles away on the northern edge of the city, but the freeways were clear and Gary did the 23 miles in half an hour. He parked a block away from George's white van, walked to it, opened the passenger door and got in before he introduced himself.

George Martinez, a slight Mexican kid in his late twenties, seemed happy to have the company. He offered Gary coffee that was both hot and fresh. In addition to the coffee pot, the van had a refrigerator, a microwave, and a Porta-Potty. George pointed out these amenities, but never looked away from the house where a bail jumper might be hiding. The tour over, he asked Gary, "Mac says you were a Fed?"

"Yeah, but don't hold that against me. I was an electrical engineer creating surveillance devices for the DEA, so I took FBI training to install bugs. I liked the field work better than engineering, but they kept me in the lab. Then a secretary told a buddy about a rumor, so he and I bugged a government honcho. We caught him stealing sixty million."

"Jesus! Sixty million?"

"Yeah. Anyway, we had some trouble, but when it was all over, the government paid us three million apiece. That's more than I need, so I quit the DEA and got a P.I. license."

"Three million must be nice."

"What about you?"

"Used to be a cop. I couldn't stand the fuckin' bureaucracy. For a P.I., I'm doing okay. The department connections help."

George opened a binder. He had everything about Mac's case that the police knew. The San Diego Police Department's investigating detectives, Steve Bacha and Able Mendoza, had both partnered with George during the four years he worked for the police department. Before the detectives were assigned other cases, they hadn't found any concrete evidence of Mac's innocence or David's guilt.

All three men were convinced that the gun salesman had sold the murder weapon to Mac. George handed the binder to Gary and pointed to the open page. "We spent a lot of time digging into this Michael Jank's background, and he is what he is. Family man, a good father, which includes coaching girl's softball. He works two jobs, selling sports equipment nights and Saturdays. His day job is dispatching cement trucks. He hadn't heard about the shooting. He doesn't know anyone in San Diego. He doesn't have any reason to lie, and he's positive it was Mac who bought the gun."

They also couldn't explain how Frank's blood got on the side of Mac's car. George went over the time-line of the shooting. According to Mac, he had returned home twenty minutes later than he should have, so he could have been at the parking lot when Frank was murdered.

After absorbing all that, Gary had to ask, "But you don't think Mac did it?"

"I just don't know."

Gary thanked him and walked back to his rental car. He drove to the motel in Imperial Beach, changed into jeans and a tee-shirt, and went for a walk on the beach. Off to the south, brown smog from Tijuana pushed into a gray fog bank offshore. To the west, the setting sun turned Point Loma into a dark backdrop for the ocean. He'd been too warm in the car, but the brisk wind felt clean and refreshing.

Despite the surroundings, Gary felt depressed. Jet lag, he supposed. Or maybe it was his nagging doubts. Had Mac killed his business partner?

CHAPTER 2

▼

June 26, 1996, Wednesday, eight months earlier

David lay still, closed his eyes and went with the moment, the sun warm on his olive skin, the clean spray-tinted wind a cooling caress as it ruffled the hair on his legs. A seagull's screech was matched by a car's horn from the road above the beach. The noises faded as the roar of the surf built, then returned as the waves ebbed. The warm sand cradled his body in a sensual embrace.

He should have been in L.A. talking to Pitrowski, but if he had gone up to see the guy, the meeting would have turned ugly. Besides, the parts would be there tomorrow; Pitrowski would be happy, crisis averted.

A shadow brushed past his closed eyes. He watched the girl walk away, noting her trim body and long straight hair. From the back, she was essentially naked, her bathing suit bottom almost a thong, and the top held with strings. When she stopped at her towel, she turned and looked at him. Nice looking and so young, she still carried some baby fat.

She had walked by to check him out. He had a male model's hard body and chiseled face. Most women looked, and his dark skin made them imagine him naked.

He waved at her. She blushed; sat on her towel, and looked out toward the ocean.

A noise caught his attention, and he looked toward the road just as John McBride walked into the Dive Inn, an unpainted, cinder-block bar that resembled the adjacent public restrooms. What could Mac be doing there? The bartender was David's connection. Was Mac into pot? David picked up his towel and walked to his car. He put on a tee-shirt and shorts, and then walked back to the bar.

As he plunged into the dim interior, he saw Mac at the bar nursing a beer. He was the only customer. Mac didn't turn to look, so David took a table partially hidden behind the cigarette machine.

The Dive Inn was aptly named. Aside from the liquor, everything in the place should have been trashed. A wooden beam, sandy from the arms of beach-goers and scarred by years of forgotten cigarettes, served as the bar top, its supporting structure hidden behind unpainted plywood. The bar stools had chrome pedestals and padded, purple vinyl seats, relics from a 50's diner. Behind the bar, liquor was arranged on shelves over a scarred mirror. Unlit neon beer signs hung at either end. The bar's other furnishings might have washed up on the beach. Each battered table was unique. The weathered chairs arranged haphazardly around the tables were alike, perhaps throw-aways from a restaurant's outdoor patio. A layer of sand camouflaged the peeling paint on the concrete floor.

Art, the huge, bearded bartender, whose primary job seemed to be chasing non-drinkers away from the bar's restroom, eyed David at the table. In a voice that could be heard at the surf line, he asked, "You just taking up space, or are you gonna buy something?"

Mac turned, glanced at David, and then turned back toward the bar. Wondering if the man was stoned, David moved to the bar and sat down beside him. In the mirror behind the bar, their eyes met, but Mac's face remained expressionless.

Art blocked the image. "Fuck you very much," he said, scowling at David.

David grinned at the linebacker-sized bartender, unmoved. Art's belligerence was an affectation. David said, "Saw my buddy here," he cocked a thumb at Mac, "but he doesn't want to admit that he knows me."

"I know you?" When the man opened his mouth, Mac vanished. The voice was higher than Mac's, and two eye teeth framed a gap where his incisors should have been. When he closed his mouth, Mac reappeared.

David laughed, putting his arm around the stranger's shoulders. "My God, I work with a guy who looks exactly like you. John McBride? Do you know him?"

The stranger shook his head, grinning uncertainly.

"The resemblance is amazing." David looked up at Art. "How about a Bud, and get another drink for this man." David extended his hand toward the stranger and said, "Dan Rhoades," the name on his fake ID.

The man answered, "Ralph Hatch."

His hand felt soft, not at all like Mac's claw. His skin had the rusty pallor of someone who didn't wash regularly. Broken veins on his nose suggested he might be an alcoholic. His clothes did look clean, and he wore a large ring on his left hand. The ring, probably cut from stainless stock by a bored machinist, had no design or jewels. It was the type of jewelry a homeless man could keep, of no value to a pawnshop. Like a worry bead, Ralph Hatch rolled it back and forth with his thumb.

"What do you do, Ralph?"

"I'm on disability." As he accepted the scotch over ice, he added, "Vietnam."

Over the next two hours, Ralph Hatch rendered Vietnam in detail. He described several lifetimes in language that suggested an impressive education. He reminisced about battles survived while grievously wounded; fortunes lost through the stupidity of underlings, and prison escapes in obscure lands, caused or aided by venal bureaucrats. David thought that some of the tales were close to familiar movie scripts, but evidently, Ralph Hatch knew truth was in the details so he supplied local color in abundance. While he consumed an astonishing quantity of scotch, he soldiered on, never slurring or repeating, each tale a carefully woven blend of detail and theme.

David listened only enough to keep the man talking. John McBride had an alcoholic clone! The possibilities overwhelmed his imagination. When the man paused in his narration to go to the bathroom, David decided to give him a ride home. He needed a way to find the man again, and time to digest this incredible development. When Hatch reappeared, clutching the bar for support as he aimed for his perch, David pointed at his empty glass, asking if he wanted another.

"How can I turn down such an attractive offer?"

Art shook his head. "In five minutes, you're going to puke, but you're not going to puke in here. You leave right now, you can walk out. Right now! If you're still here two minutes from now, I'm going to throw you out."

David asked Hatch, "You need a ride home?"

"Thank you for offering, but my lady and I have an RV parked up the street. Normally we reside in a park near Lakeside, but the heat is excruciating there today." As he swung around to get off the stool, he listed and was on his way to the floor when David grabbed his arm.

While he helped Hatch find vertical equilibrium, David's mind raced. The man was a transient; he could be in another state tomorrow. David thought of various ways to find him again, and decided on the surest. He took a hundred dollar bill out of his wallet. With Hatch propped against the bar, David wrote a phone number in the margin at one end of the bill, and then tore it in half. He handed Hatch the portion containing Dan Rhoades' phone number, a number he used for calls he didn't want traced back to him. "If you want the other half, call me next weekend. I'll come pick you up, and we'll find someplace where we can talk."

Staring at his half of the bill, Hatch asked, "Why?"

"I want to hear more about your life, if you don't mind talking."

As if recovering from a face-full of cold water, Hatch blinked his eyes and puffed out his cheeks. "As you can ascertain, I'm fond of the libation. You buy, I'll talk."

"Will you remember to give me a call next Saturday?"

Hatch struggled to remove his wallet, and then placed his half of the $100 bill inside. "An excellent method for insuring compliance. I'm sure thirst will jog my memory."

*   *   *   *

Two hours later, David walked into the office at Framac. His father was sorting purchase orders. The old man was dressed in the same dark blue suit he had worn since David could remember. He looked so natural sitting behind his old desk that the change didn't register for a moment.

David made an effort to look pleased. "Out of retirement so soon?"

"Evidently."

David shook his head in disgust. "Pitrowski called you?"

"And you already know what I'm going to say."

David slumped into a chair. "I should have gone to see him, but what's the point? The parts will be there tomorrow. Let Mac grovel for Pitrowski. He's the one who didn't get the parts finished on time."

"Do you really think that's what I was going to say?"

David repeated the litany in a flat voice. "Business is an intricate balance of possibilities and achievements. My job is to access the needs and capabilities of the producers and consumers; create a contract both participants can accept, and monitor the progress so I can keep the participants informed of the status."

His father searched David's eyes. "Does any of that have meaning for you?"

"I understand it, if that's what you're asking."

"So you choose not to do it, for what reason?"

"I won't waste my life facilitating incompetence."

His father sat back, looking disappointed. David knew the look, and searched his mind for some interesting way to pass the time while the old man vented.

Instead of the usual, his father asked, "Would you care to explain how you do intend to live your life?"

Surprised, David focused on the old man. "Do you have to ask?"

"I'm not as bright as you are. I don't know the answer."

David thought that odd. He had bounced from school to work to school and now back to work, and his father should know by now that he couldn't, wouldn't, be tied to minutiae. "You know I can't stand to be bored."

"You haven't answered the question. How do you intend to live your life?"

"I strive to never be bored."

"You expect to find a job that is never repetitious?"

Irritated, David said, "I control what I do."

The look of disbelief on his father's face faded. "Yes, you do, but for 31 years, I've been shielding you from the consequences." When David made no comment, he said, "I want you to pack your things and leave. I'm going to call a meeting and tell the employees that I'll be back until I can find someone to replace me."

"I'm fired?"

"And evicted. By the end of September, you and Sue are to be out of the house."

David and his father had an understanding. David would supply the reasons why he should not be evicted, and the old man would relent after a few days. To begin the dance, David said, "I'll need some capital for a rental deposit."

"Yes, you will. You've got three months to find a way to get what you need."

"Choosing the tough-love option, Dad?"

His father examined his hands. "You haven't left me any options, David."

*   *   *   *

David was reading a magazine when Sue walked into their bedroom that evening. She closed the door and said in a low voice, "According to your Mother, we aren't going to eat with them any more."

"Dad's pissed. It'll pass."

Sue unzipped her grease-stained coveralls and stepped out of them wearing only a bra and panties. She had a large stain on her stomach where oil had soaked through the coveralls, and her arms were black to her elbows. Her short brown hair was dirty and matted. She wadded the coveralls into a plastic bag. "You didn't go see Pitrowski."

"If I had, I would never have met John McBride's double."

Sue waited for the punch-line with a poker face.

"No joke, I met a guy who looks exactly like Mac. The whole time I'm talking to him, I had this feeling that Mac was putting me on."

A non-event for Sue, she stripped and walked into the bathroom. By the time she had the shower warmed, David was naked. He stepped into the shower with her, closing the clear glass door. As he lathered her hair, she turned to face him, and relaxed against him with her arms around his waist.

He massaged her scalp. "They use you for a drip pan today?"

"Uh-huh," she murmured into his chest. "The lifts were full so I had to use a crawler." She moaned as he worked at her scalp. "It was worth it. I found a corroded connection on an oxygen sensor that had the dealer looking at a lemon-law return. He was so happy, he paid me $700."

David turned Sue around, her back tight against his chest as he washed the oil off her stomach. While he worked on the oil, he almost told her about his plan. She wouldn't take it well, so he concentrated on enjoying her body.

Sue turned and hugged him. Speaking to his chest, she said, "I don't want to live here any more, David."

He felt panic in his stomach. "I do."

Sue turned her back to rinse her hair. "Well, I won't."

"What does that mean?"

She didn't answer. She wouldn't fight, she never fought, but he needed an explanation. He had a nearly irresistible urge to smack her butt.

Sue was the toughest person he'd ever met, an emotional rock. Her attitude had attracted him when he met her at an automotive repair shop. He had charmed her into his bed, and the sex had been great. When he called her again, she turned him down, saying she didn't date egomaniacs twice. Stung, he decided to make her fall in love with him before he dumped her.

She finally did agree to go out with him again; on the condition that the date was over if he told a single lie. It took an effort not to lie when his truth was so banal, but she found something she liked in him. Even more astonishing, by the end of that evening, David needed her.

People he loved never loved him in return, and he had married Sue four months ago knowing that was true of her. She could walk out and never look back. He asked again, "What does that mean?"

"Don't badger me with this abandonment shit. I keep my word. I said for better or for worse, and I meant it. Just chill, okay?" She turned and kissed him. As she wiped shampoo from around his mouth, she said, "I need to be in a place of my own. The tension around here upsets me."

He grinned. "They've been bitching at me forever. Just ignore it."

"It isn't them, it's you. You bait them constantly. I feel like I'm caught in the middle." She kissed him again. "Look at it this way: you're more likely to inherit your Dad's share of Framac if you're not pissing him off all the time." She added, "I make great money. We can afford a place of our own."

David wouldn't leave, so he dropped the argument. Her work as a free-lance electrical systems specialist had driven her income into six figures, but the real riches were here. His parents owed him, and he had to stay in his room to keep that memory fresh.

He was a late-life baby. His mother, worried about her biological clock, produced him and then had second thoughts. From the day he was born, both his parents had mourned the passing of their idyllic lives. When he was four, they were shocked to discover that he knew about their regret. They gave him anything he wanted, but it was too late to give him what he needed. Now they needed his forgiveness, and he was here to deny them any illusion of compromise. His price would be their house and money, and nothing less.

*　　　*　　　*　　　*

The next morning, David stepped from the room just as his Mother walked by in the hallway. He grabbed the tiny woman by the arm and pulled her into a hug. To his surprise, she fought her way out of the embrace and stalked away. He followed her to the kitchen, standing quietly on the other side of the breakfast bar until their eyes met. The fury in her face staggered him.

"Don't be upset, Mom. Dad will get over it."

Normally placid, she was nearly yelling when she said, "He's the calm one. You'd better worry about how long it's going to take me to get over it. You know where he is right now? He's up in L.A. talking to Pitrowski, trying to undo the damage you've done. He's 67 years old, and he had to drive all the way up to L.A. in the morning commute because you couldn't be bothered yesterday."

"Pitrowski is an asshole."

She threw a dishtowel at him, a move completely out of character. She screamed, "You're the asshole, Mister. You begged your father to retire, begged him. In front of all those people, he gave you his job, he told them what a marvelous person you are, that you'd be able to improve the business. Yesterday, he had to tell them that he fired his son. You made him crawl, damn you."

She started to cry, and David moved around the bar to comfort her. She pushed him away. Through her tears, she said, "We were supposed to be retired by now, doing all those things we dreamed about. Now he has to go back to work, and it's your fault.

"We've done everything for you. We paid for you to go to college; we paid for you to start that business, then we paid for you to spend the year in Europe, finding yourself. We would have loved to have gone to Europe, but we paid for you to go.

"You are nothing but a leech, a spoiled-rotten leech. If it had been up to me, you would have been out on the street this morning. *He* wants to give you three months, not me. I want you out of my life now, damn you." She cried harder, asking in a choked voice, "How could you do that to your father?"

CHAPTER 3

▼

February 13, 1997, Thursday

The flatlands of Chula Vista held large tracts of small bungalows built in the 1940s and '50s. Mac's house was in the hilly area to the east, where older, upscale, ranch-style ramblers were set back on large lots. The expansive front yards contained either drought landscaping with rocks and native shrubs, or manicured greenery surrounding crabgrass lawns, evidently the only grass that would grow there. Most of the curb parkways had palm trees as tall as power poles, but huge pines dominated the parkway on Mac's street. The immense trees shared the air space with high voltage lines.

Two gardeners created leaf-blower dust storms as Gary drove Mac's street. His address was a corner house set close to the street, the yard mostly lawn with junipers in the parkway. The faded gray-blue paint on the house, the brown patches in the lawn, and wilted shrubs near the house reflected Mac's troubles.

Mac, in a red bib apron, opened the left side of the double door entry. Gary stepped into an aroma of bacon, potatoes fried with garlic, onions, and green peppers, and the buttery odor of eggs. Mac sounded upbeat as he said, "Good timing. The eggs are about done. Leave your stuff here."

Gary left his two suitcases and tote bag near the front door, and followed Mac to the kitchen. The small round table tucked in a corner was already set with orange juice, plates of toast, and condiments. Judging by the food, Mac loved cooking.

While they ate, Gary asked, "Why did Julie push for an early trial? When bail's been granted, most murder cases take a year or more before they go to trial."

"Wasn't her. I pushed. If I died, David would get away with it."

"Why did you hire Julie? George Martinez said this is her first murder case."

"Talked to five high-priced lawyers who didn't care if I did it or not. She was the first one tried to find out if I killed Frank." Mac scrutinized a potato he'd speared with his fork. "With the case they got, doesn't matter how good she is."

When they finished, Mac took Gary to the master bedroom, complete with a bathroom, king size bed, television, VCR, and stereo in an oak entertainment center. Gary said, "I'm not going to take your bedroom."

"I never use it. I sleep in the bedroom at the front of the house. Little bed suits me better, and that room's usually all I heat in the winter." He indicated the sliding glass door. "That uses the same key I gave you, so you can come and go when you want. There's a gate in the side fence." Mac looked at his watch. "Should get to work, need to finish that die. You need anything else?"

Gary asked him to set up an appointment with Julie Williams. Mac wrote Gary's cell phone number in an address book and gave Gary his private number at Framac. Gary loaded that into the cell phone's memory.

After Mac left for work, Gary rinsed the breakfast dishes, using the time to plan his day. While he ran hot water into the Teflon frying pan, he decided that one way to prevent Mac's conviction was to get David to confess. However unlikely that was, asking might prove helpful. For one thing, he'd see the place he wanted to eavesdrop.

When he had the dishes in the dishwasher, he called Mac at work and asked him for the name of Framac's insurer. Mac gave him the name and said he had made the appointment with Julie Williams. She expected Gary at one that afternoon.

In the master bedroom, Gary unpacked his laptop and connected it to the phone line. He found The Jastillana Group of Insurance Companies on the Internet and downloaded their logo into a file. He moved his picture into the same file, put in the name of Michael Smith, inserted a phony Washington, D.C. address and a fake phone number, and then printed two business cards with his portable color inkjet printer.

*   *   *   *

At 11 a.m., the traffic on Interstate 5 through downtown San Diego ran at an insane speed through some blind turns. Dozens of skid marks, some ending in abrupt changes of direction, indicated that motorists couldn't see far enough ahead. When the Interstate turned north, an airliner skimmed the freeway on its approach to Lindbergh Field. A few miles farther, Gary exited on the Morena Boulevard off-ramp.

He drove through a neighborhood of tiny houses built in the forties. The Kendall house, a newer, two-story Mediterranean, was shoehorned into a narrow hillside lot. The south wall of the house perched on a tall concrete retaining wall. A driveway at the base of the wall led to the garage behind the house.

Gary parked on the street and climbed the stairs to the front door. The house enjoyed a view of San Diego Bay. An aircraft carrier parked at North Island looked like its bow was wedged into a downtown skyscraper.

Mary Kendall opened the door. A short, pleasant-looking woman with dyed auburn hair, she was dressed in jeans, a plaid cotton shirt and fashionable work boots. She seemed distracted. She accepted the insurance company card without comment and invited him in.

The interior reminded Gary of a boutique, crowded with printed fabric and wood furniture; throw pillows, knickknacks and house plants. Mary motioned him to the sofa and asked if he'd like anything. She stood for a few seconds after these pleasantries, and then abruptly sat down as if she'd just thought of it.

Gary took a yellow pad out of the folder he carried. "I understand your son David lives here? Is he available?"

She looked at Gary as if it required some effort to process the question. "He lives here, but he's in Oregon. Corvallis, I think."

"Will he be at Mr. McBride's trial?"

"He'll be back on Sunday. Mac's lawyer called him as a witness, so he doesn't have to be available until she begins the defense."

"Assuming Mr. McBride will be convicted, will you or your son handle the lawsuit to acquire his portion of Framac?"

"He will. I don't..." Tears came, in trickles and then torrents. With a tissue, she dabbed at her left eye, then her right, trying to conserve her mascara, but the tears wouldn't be stopped.

Gary rose. "I'll do this some other time."

As they walked toward the door, she found enough composure to say, "Both Frank and I loved Mac. He was part of our family. I can't believe any of this." That could have been an opening, but she was crying again.

Gary felt relieved to be back in the car. One thing was sure, Mary loved her husband.

Gary's appointment with Julie Williams wasn't until one that afternoon, so he drove out to Mission Beach and found a restaurant with a view of the Ocean. Despite the sunny day, surfers in wet suits were the only people braving the water.

After a clam chowder and sourdough bread lunch, he drove to Hillcrest. The address was a two story professional building housing mostly medical offices. The mission style building, with the mandatory palm trees in the parking lot, held more than 20 small offices, each facing an outside walkway. Near an elevator, he found a directory and took the slow, wheezy-sounding elevator to the second floor.

Inside Julie William's waiting room, two red vinyl couches and three blue vinyl chairs shared the wall space with a tree and two wooden tables holding stacks of magazines.

A door opened, and a petite black woman dressed in a sky blue pants-suit asked, "May I help you?"

"Gary Charboneau."

She held out her hand. "Julie Williams." Her face was enhanced by the braces on her teeth. She wore them like jewels in her smile.

She invited him into an austere office. Steel filing cabinets were hidden by three ficus trees. Philodendrons trailed over the corners of a seven foot bookcase crammed with law books. Two impressionist paintings of rain-soaked Parisian street scenes hung on the wall behind her desk. The steel desk held a tiffany lamp, a telephone, two houseplants, a laptop, and a ceramic teddy bear pen and pencil holder.

Julie motioned for him to sit in one of the three padded chairs in front of her desk. As they exchanged personal information, she seemed gracious and reserved. She referred to Mac as John, and indeed, Gary could not imagine her using nicknames. Despite her warm demeanor and sexy voice, she did not invite familiarity. Gary imagined her response to a sexual proposition might be an apologetic, 'No, but thank you for asking.' A witness might feel that it would be terribly rude not to tell this lady the whole truth.

She gave Gary a typed copy of George Martinez's report. Gary put that in his folder and asked Julie what her defense strategy would be.

"Even if John agreed, which he doesn't, plea-bargaining is out. The District Attorney, Peter Draper, has been in office less than six months, and he's managed to alienate his entire staff in that time. Many of those people are adroit leakers, so Mr. Draper has been ridiculed by the San Diego newspaper for mismanagement and ineptitude. His rebuttal has been that the office staff is largely incompetent. To prove that he is not, Mr. Draper announced that he would try John McBride personally."

Gary wrote the D.A.'s name, pleased to have a deserving target for whatever delaying tactic he could think up. Then he asked, "What will you do?"

"The weakness of a frame is that if you can prove that one item of evidence has been manufactured, then all the evidence becomes suspect. I can establish reasonable doubt with the blood on John's car door, but Michael Jank, the gun salesman, puts the murder weapon in John's hand. If I can't undermine his testimony, the case is lost."

"Was there a tape of Mac's interrogation after he was arrested?"

Julie went to a filing cabinet, opened the bottom drawer, and took out a large padded envelope. She handed the envelope to Gary. "Keep it. There's nothing in there I can use. John's story hasn't changed, and the police bent over backwards to make sure none of his rights were violated."

Gary took the envelope and looked inside. "Does anything identify this as your copy?"

She perched on the front edge of her desk, a smile toying with her mouth. She folded her arms and looked at Gary.

He said, "I might have asked that for any number of reasons, most of them legitimate. Why don't you assume one of those legitimate reasons, and tell me whether anything identifies this tape as one sent to the defense?"

"Not to my knowledge. If there are questions, I will tell them I gave you my copy."

"I'm sure you'll do what you have to do." He closed the envelope. "On a totally unrelated matter, I need an original of any letter Mr. Draper sent you."

Her jeweled grin broadened. When Gary didn't change expression, she pushed off the edge of her desk and walked to the same filing cabinet. She squatted beside the drawer, asking, "Any letter? You don't care about the subject?"

"As long as it's an original."

She returned with a single paper. As she handed it to Gary, she pointed at Peter Draper's signature. "He always signs in blue ink."

Gary stood. "Thank you. I won't take any more of your time."

As she walked him to the door, Julie said, "You will be careful?"

Gary shook her hand. "Careful is overrated."

In his car, driving toward Framac's address in National City, his phone trilled. It was San Diego Police Detective Steve Bacha answering a voice mail Gary had left that morning. Gary introduced himself and said, "I'll buy you breakfast tomorrow if you'll let me pick your brain."

"My partner included in the offer?"

"Sure."

"How about eight at the Carolina Kitchen on Harbor Drive?"

*   *   *   *

Gary expected Framac to be another of the dingy metal buildings that dotted National City. Instead, the new, window-festooned, concrete building sported a brushed metal sign with FRAMAC SHEET METAL imbedded with colored epoxy, the letters glowing with refracted sunlight. The front of the building was lushly landscaped with a mounded lawn that flowed to the curb, and a walkway that meandered through the hillocks.

He parked and walked into the lobby. Behind a Formica counter, a petite lady in her forties, her black hair falling out of a bun, was working on stacks of paper on a large wooden desk. She asked, "Can I help you?" When he asked to see John McBride, she pointed, and then buzzed open the gate at the end of the counter.

The glass wall in Mac's empty office looked into the factory. According to a woman in the next office, Mac was in a meeting. Gary told her that he needed a computer with a scanner and a color printer. She led him to a small room that contained a copy machine, two computers on a metal table, a color printer, and a scanner. Gary placed the letter from Draper into the scanner and made two separate graphic files, one of the letterhead, and the other of Draper's signature. It took some time to match the font used by Draper's office, but once he was satisfied with the typeface, he composed a letter, and inserted Draper's signature at the bottom. When the color printer finished, the letter looked authentic down to Draper's signature in blue ink.

The receptionist gave him directions to a store in a small strip mall that handled FedEx. At a drugstore in the mall, he browsed the magazine racks until five minutes to five, and then he went outside and used a pay phone.

"District Attorney's Office." The woman sounded rushed. Gary visualized a parade of attorneys dumping their last minute requests on her desk.

"This is Roger Danke at Mail Zone. We have a FedEx package here from your office for overnight to L.A., and whoever sent it to us didn't fill in your account number. You want me to send it back to your office? The courier service has already made their last pickup, so it probably won't get back there until noon tomorrow."

"Who is it to?"

"A Mr. Jank, L.A. address."

"Well…I don't know." Gary let the silence stretch and finally she said, "I'll give you the account number. Ready?"

Ten minutes later he left the store, and the tape of Mac's interrogation was on its way overnight to the gun salesman, Michael Jank, courtesy of the District Attorney's office.

CHAPTER 4

▼

June 28, 1996, Friday, eight months earlier

With a lifetime of experience mollifying his parents, David waited two days to approach them. They were usually in a good mood after breakfast, so he stayed in his room listening until he heard Mary pour Frank a second cup of coffee. By their murmured conversation, they were discussing the newspaper, finished with eating the omelets Mary had cooked. All the signs were right.

David used his contrite approach, standing before them at the small round breakfast table in the kitchen, his head slightly bowed, shoulders slumped, voice quiet. "Mom, Dad, I owe you both an apology. There's no excuse for what I did, and I'm sorry. I'll do anything I can to make it up to you."

Mary rose, picked up the breakfast dishes and walked to the sink. Frank said, "David, we have a few new rules we'd like you to observe until you move out. When we're home, we expect both you and Sue to stay in your room. Is that clear?"

"You're going to penalize Sue for what I did?"

"Yes."

David would wait for a better time. "I'll move out as soon as I get some money."

Frank looked disgusted. Did he know about the $32,000 David had in the safe deposit box? Evidently he didn't because he said, "I'll tell you what I'll do. I'll give you $25,000 to integrate the order, inventory, and WIP software in the plant so that we have a seamless system. I'll want each employee to input the data for their portion of any job, and I'll want the most computer illiterate person to be able to call up a report detailing the order status, and the resources still required to complete the order. It should answer the question: what do we need to get this job done in time? If it takes you one day or three months, I'll pay you the money when I'm happy with the system."

"So I'm not fired?"

"I'm not hiring you. It's a contract job. You don't get anything until it's done, and when it's done, you take the money and leave."

"I saw the bids. The lowest was $45,000 to do the system."

"That's right. We save $20,000 if you can do it."

"I'll need to buy hardware and software."

"Yeah, sure, have them invoice us. We'll subtract it from your $25,000."

Even with all the aces, David was losing the debate. "You're saving $20,000 and you won't pay for the software I'll need."

"I may not be as bright as you are, but I didn't just fall off the truck. If I pay for the hardware and software, I get stuck for the $45,000 the other companies want, plus your $25,000 for being stupid enough to agree with you. So that's the deal. You get $25,000, total, to hand us a turnkey system. Up to you. Do you want the job or not?"

The shop was filled with computers he could use, networking hardware was cheap, and the existing software in the plant could be modified to do the job. Worst case, he'd net over $20,000. He accepted the job. It would be a way to stay close to his father and keep a dialogue going. He'd pushed their buttons; it would take time before they recovered, but eventually they would relent and allow him to stay.

*   *   *   *

Sue looked upset when she walked into their bedroom at nine that evening, covered with greasy black dirt. Both hands looked like she'd tried to separate fighting cats, and she was so tired, she groaned when she tried to unhook her bra. As David opened the clasps for her, she said, "Damn Koreans used the letter B for brown, black, and blue on a schematic. Every fucking wire going into the computer module was white with a blue, black, or brown stripe, or blue, black, or brown with a white stripe. I had to ring-out the whole fucking car before I could trouble-shoot it, and for all that, they paid me $150." Naked, she asked, "I don't suppose we have anything to eat, do we? Since we can't use the kitchen?" Without waiting for the obvious answer, she went into the bathroom.

David drove to a nearby fast-food restaurant and bought her a cheeseburger. When he got back, Sue was in bed in the darkened room. He put the cheeseburger down beside her face. She opened her eyes, looked at David, and then back-handed the sandwich off the bed. She glared at him and turned her face to the wall.

✳   ✳   ✳   ✳

Saturday morning, Sue woke up in the same foul mood. She stalked out to her car, David close behind, and she flogged the tiny Geo Metro unmercifully until it bounced into the parking lot at a restaurant.

They were almost finished with breakfast before she made eye contact. When she did, she said, "I'm moving out today. I won't live where I'm not wanted. Come with me."

Sue had always been easy; she had gone along with his plans with only minor protests. As the months went by, she had even stopped asking when he might consider a move to their own place. Evidently, that wound had been festering.

He had to make her understand that he must stay in his parents' house. Words were inadequate; he searched his vocabulary to convey the horror of those nights alone when he was a small child, when he knew his parents would be happy if he were dead. The terror when he learned how easy it was to be murdered. His mother could hold a pillow over his face and all her problems would be gone. She could twist his head and break his neck. She could puncture his neck with a knife and say he'd been playing with it.

As they drove back to the house, David told Sue about the day his father took him out in a boat to fish, a happy outing until he tangled his line and his father swore at the snarl. The next two hours felt like two years as he waited for his father to throw him into the lake. He told Sue about the agony of the countless hours he spent in his room, waiting for punishment that never came, wondering if they didn't hit him because they couldn't bear to touch him. He told her about the day when he was finally ready to die. He broke several windows in the house with a baseball bat, wanting to get it over, knowing that this time, he had made them angry enough to kill him. After that didn't work, he decided that they wouldn't kill him because they wanted him to suffer.

When he and Sue returned to their bedroom, he asked how she could not be happy here. More than a bedroom, it was almost a tastefully decorated apartment; the cherry wood of the queen bed's headboard matched the nightstands and the ceiling coving. Off to the right of the bed, a love seat faced an entertainment center, and the wall beside the couch was a floor to ceiling bookcase. The bed's coverlet matched the printed draperies on the window that looked out toward the harbor and North Island. A walk-in closet edged the full bath. In the bathroom, a glass paneled door between twin vanities led to the rear patio and a hot tub. Except for food, it had everything they needed.

He flung his arms open to encompass the room. "Don't you feel it? This is where I survived. As long as I'm here, they can't forget what they did to me."

Her angry look gone, Sue put a hand on his chest. "It's not yours, it's theirs. They own it, David. If you refuse to go, they probably will have you evicted."

"They won't. They owe me too much."

"Your childhood is a bad debt, David. They can't undo the past."

They had tortured him psychologically. He was due damages. "This house and a few million will do just fine."

Sue hugged him, whispering in his ear, "The money won't solve your problem, David, only time and distance will solve it. Let's go live our lives; try to enjoy ourselves. When they die, you'll get the money and the house."

He shrugged out of her embrace. "They owe me." He didn't know how else to say it, so he repeated, "They owe me."

Her expression looked like resignation, but was belied by the urgency in her voice. "You're like a hamster in a wheel, David. You keep running, trying to make it all come out better. Why can't you bury it and get on with your life?"

David had read that children denied affection before the age of three grew up with no capacity for love. He had no idea if that applied to him, he certainly had feelings for Sue, but in a contest between her and his room, she would lose. He guessed that normal people found security in family and friends, and they could live anywhere. Without his room, David couldn't survive. He could leave it for months and do fine, but only because he knew his room was waiting for him. His room was security in a cold world.

He couldn't tell Sue, so he lashed out. "I'm doing what I have to do."

The tears cascading from her eyes shocked him; he had never seen her cry. She said, "I don't deserve this." She walked into the closet and got both of her suitcases.

As she began to pack, David said, "So you're going to bail?" She upended a drawer into a suitcase, put it back, took the next drawer, and upended that one as well. As she began taking clothes out of the closet, he asked, "Why are you leaving me?"

"I'm not leaving you, David; I'm moving to a place of my own. I want you to share it with me." She watched him for a moment, and said, "If you don't come with me, then we'll both know who abandoned who."

All the words said, he went into the backyard and sat on the swing under the mulberry tree. The swing was like his bedroom, his fortress in a cold world. Now it gave him no peace. The chain caught on a new branch and pulled the swing into an oscillating yaw. The metal ring that held the chain caught on the support bar, moving in jerks.

A few minutes later, he heard Sue's car leave.

*   *   *   *

That Sunday, at one in the afternoon, Ralph Hatch called. He and his girl-friend still had their RV parked in Pacific Beach. "It remains hot in Lakeside," Hatch explained, adding, "We can meet at that same place."

Three hours later, David walked into the Dive Inn. Ralph Hatch, wearing a suit and a white shirt with an open collar, occupied a single table in a dark corner. Evidently he had no money and the bartender, Art, had said he could wait only if he kept his mouth shut. Hatch had opted for distance from the bearded giant, probably unnecessary considering the two young women in skimpy bathing suits who were negotiating with Art for free drinks. David had to wave money before Art got his beer and Hatch's scotch.

Hatch accepted the drink like a man dying in the desert. The ice rattled as he lifted the small glass to his mouth and sipped reverently. At the bar, Art finalized the agreement with the women, and, after some giggles, both bared their breasts. Hatch was awestruck by the display, his mouth open in an idiotic gap-toothed grin.

Hatch's missing front teeth would have to be replaced before he could imper-sonate Mac. By the hungry look he gave his empty glass, he would do anything for alcohol.

At the bar, Art asked the women for their IDs, which drew protests since nei-ther was carrying a purse. "We told you someone stole our stuff off the beach," the redhead said. "Come on. You said you'd give us a drink if we showed you."

Art was the soul of integrity. "And I will. I'll give you any soft drink you want. For liquor, you need an ID."

The dark haired girl asked, "Why didn't you tell us that first?"

"My mistake," Art answered, a wide grin giving lie to the words. "You look so young, I thought you were talking about cokes."

Hatch shook his glass, rattling the ice cubes. "Mr. Rhoades, might I inquire if you have sufficient funds for another?"

David went to the bar, interrupting Art's new round of negotiations. David asked for a bottle of Scotch. Making no move to get a bottle, Art said, "Thirty-five dollars." He looked surprised when David put the money on the bar.

Hatch said, "Oh, my," when David placed the Scotch in front of him. "Daniel—may I call you Daniel?—you are a prince among men."

As Hatch opened the bottle, David unfolded a production contract Mac had signed, and asked if Hatch thought he could duplicate the Vendor's signature.

Hatch looked at the document, laid it on the table, and carefully poured the Scotch into the glass. He sipped the drink, frowning at the paper. "The one on the bottom?"

"Where it says Vendor."

"I'm afraid I didn't bring my glasses." Hatch's nose showed no indentations. When David asked if he ever wore glasses, Hatch said, "Not much need for them. I'm not partial to reading."

Seeing his plan evaporate, David gave him a scrap of paper and a pen, and asked him to copy Mac's name. Hatch wasn't partial to writing either. His labored efforts produced a childlike scribble.

David hated to abandon his plan. He wanted Hatch to open a bank account in John McBride's name, write checks against the business, and put the money in that account. Once presented with the evidence that Mac was embezzling, Frank would have no choice but to bring charges and sue Mac for his half of the business.

If Hatch wanted liquor, he'd learn to forge Mac's signature. Fixing his teeth would probably take a couple of months, time enough to tutor him. He talked like a college professor, so how illiterate could he be?

In case he was sensitive about his looks, David said, "You have a magnificent face. It reminds me of the statues of Roman emperors I saw in Oxford. Just looking at those faces, I knew those men were leaders. They all had strong faces, like yours."

"I have paid some dues."

"I hear that. Your stories about Vietnam kept me awake nights. I think the way this nation treats its Vietnam veterans is shameful." He paused to let Hatch personalize that before he said, "I'm not a rich man, Hatch, but I'd like to do something for all your sacrifices. What would you think if I paid to have your teeth fixed?"

"So I'd more closely resemble the man you want me to impersonate?"

Pleased that he had already considered the idea, David told him that the owner of the shop where he worked had floated a loan to expand his business. In David's story, the owner, Ward Pearcy, was an old man and no longer as sharp as he needed to be. The expansion had been completed but business didn't increase as rapidly as Mr. Pearcy hoped. When Mr. Pearcy failed to cover the premium one month, the people who loaned the money took over to run the shop. "Do you see where this is going?"

"Yes, indeed. A common story. I surmise that the two overseers are proceeding to remove funds from the business?"

"Exactly. And if you haven't guessed, Ward Pearcy is my stepfather. I owe him a great deal, too much to stand by while these men wreck the business he built."

Using Mac's illnesses for detail, David described an imaginary stepfather's tenuous health, and the mounting medical bills. "If things go on as they are, my parents will be bankrupt soon. But if you and I can develop the evidence to put both these guys away, Ward will be very generous."

Hatch didn't react, so David added, "Even if you can't help, at least you'll get your teeth fixed."

"They want to pull the teeth I do have, and replace them with false teeth. I've never met anyone who was happy with false teeth." He listened to David's arguments, but he insisted that his teeth were non-negotiable. They weren't that noticeable, he argued, and he demonstrated by making the argument without showing his teeth. The clenched jaw monologue sounded and looked ridiculous.

It was clear that Hatch would never be able to impersonate John McBride. The whole scenario had been a useless exercise.

"You seem discouraged, Mr. Rhoades. Take a lesson from our time in Vietnam." Hatch hoisted his glass. "Whatever the obstacles, we can upend the rotten bastards."

Hatch had talked about killing in Vietnam. What if Hatch, his mouth set in a grim look, shot Frank in front of several witnesses? Everyone would assume Mac was the killer.

Needing time to consider this new idea, David took out his wallet and handed Hatch a $100 bill. "Keep the half of the bill with my phone number. Call me next Wednesday."

CHAPTER 5

▼

February 14, 1997, Friday

At six in the morning, Gary found the Marina Parkway in Chula Vista deserted. Mac had said it was a place he could do a five mile run without dodging cars and dogs, but he hadn't mentioned the beauty. A four lane road, divided by a landscaped median, edged a park that hugged the shoreline in a lazy turn to the north. Several low, modern buildings hid a marina from the road.

Gary measured a mile and a quarter on the car's odometer, then parked the car along the high curb in front of the Port of Chula Vista office building. A brisk breeze blew off the water, and he decided to wear a sweatshirt for the first lap, then leave it on the hood of the car while he ran the second. The engine heat would keep the sweatshirt warm enough to stave off the chills after his run.

Out of the car, he stretched, set the lap timer on his watch, and ran on the concrete path that snaked through the swath of greenery edging the marina. The breeze was smudged by the rotting smell of wetlands. A power plant to the south belched billowy clouds of steam into the deep blue of the sky.

When the path stopped at the sidewalk, he ran a few more yards to the east, enjoying the sunrise that outlined Otay Mountain in shades of gold. Where railroad tracks ended the parkway, he crossed the street and ran on the sidewalk back to the west, next to an eight foot cyclone fence protecting an industrial complex.

At the end of his measured route, he crossed over the parkway and reversed direction, feeling the effects of the week of inactivity. When he completed the second circuit, he was tired, winded, and queasy.

On the drive back to Mac's, his body heat fogged the windows, forcing him to use the air conditioner. That cleared the windows, but made his damp sweatpants felt like cold metal.

He was late, so he took a quick shower and decided not to shave until after his meeting with Steve Bacha. He dressed hurriedly and drove to the freeway, dreading the twenty miles of commuter traffic. The glut of cars on Interstate Five moved fast, and he pulled into the restaurant's parking lot at two minutes before eight.

The Carolina Kitchen wasn't a place he would have chosen for a leisurely breakfast. Inside, it was a brilliantly lit, rock-video, version of an old-fashioned diner.

With no way to recognize Steve Bacha, he stood in the entryway eyeing the men in the crowded restaurant. Bacha came in a few minutes later, wearing a plastic ID card with his last name in large letters. Tall, with close cut brown hair and a trim brown mustache that accented his round face, he looked far too young to be a detective. His manner seemed relaxed, his eyes taking inventory as Gary introduced himself.

Gary asked, "Your partner joining us?"

"Naw, horny bastard is using this as an excuse to get more saddle time." He watched Gary laugh before he asked, "Do you have a license to do PI stuff in California?"

"Yeah. I needed it for some work I did in the bay area. But Mac isn't paying me. I'm doing a favor for his foster daughter."

"Nobody's paying you?"

"I've got so much money, I can't keep up with the interest."

"Really? Then you'll spring for Eggs-Benedict?"

"I'd be delighted."

Bacha asked, "Why did she wait until now to ask you to help?"

"Mac didn't tell her about any of it until a few days ago. He didn't want to worry her."

"He was probably waiting for sanity to prevail. If you haven't heard, we have a D.A. with an asshole on both ends."

"The case against Mac is a slam-dunk. Why wouldn't he try it?"

Bacha said, "And isn't that a sad commentary on the justice system."

Gary was amazed at the trust Bacha displayed, unusual for anyone employed by the bureaucracy, and inexplicable for a cop. The man seemed to have no fear that Gary might use any of his comments against him. As they followed the hostess to a small table next to the windows, Gary decided Bacha's attitude was beyond weird. When the hostess went for coffee, Gary asked, "Why do I get the feeling that you know me?"

"George knows a cop you know in Washington, and he says you're okay. He also says that you get the job done, whatever it takes. We need that right now."

No doubt about it, Bacha wasn't happy about this case. To establish what he did believe, Gary said, "Mac thinks Frank's kid, David, is the perp."

"I know he is, and judging by his crummy alibi, he did it himself. The asshole knows I know he did it, and he could give a rip. He played the wide-eyed, sincere, respectful of authority, innocent kid during the interrogation. He wouldn't answer any questions, just kept asking if he was under arrest, then he got up and walked out. Like it's all a game and he's in control."

Gary asked, "Why does the D.A. have a beef with Mac?"

"He doesn't. It was just bad timing. Draper's a fuck-up. He'd been in office less than six months when six experienced prosecutors resigned. In the two months after those resignations, three violent perps won acquittals on technical errors. The newspaper went ballistic, so Draper decided to try Mac personally, to show them what he could do."

A waitress brought the coffee and took their orders. As she walked away, Gary said, "But he let you look at David."

"Yeah, before he dug himself into a hole on the nightly news. Three days after the murder, he got us a broad search warrant. We looked for dark clothes, shoes, gloves, knitted headwear, cell phones, car keys, financial records, including bank statements and receipts and safety deposit box keys. We even impounded his car. We didn't come up with a thing, and one thing we didn't find was David. We'd had the house under observation and the shit left without us seeing him."

"What about the gun salesman?"

"Yeah, that's a tough nut. He's reliable and has no reason to lie. He has no record, his bills get paid on time, he works two jobs—the gun selling thing is only part time—he's been married forever, native of L.A., doesn't know any of the principals in the case, and he hadn't heard about the shooting. He didn't hesitate when I showed him a photo line-up, and at the live line-up, he picked Mac out without any waffling. He told me to pound sand when I tried to rattle him, said if I didn't like what he had to say, don't call him to testify.

"From day one, Able, my partner, thought David found a guy who looks like Mac, and the whole thing developed from there. I don't agree, because Jank is just too positive. The perp would have to be an identical twin. But just in case, we gave a bunch of eagle scouts Mac's picture and had them look at all the mug books. They came up with nothing."

"Any ideas on how David got his father to come back to the parking lot?"

"The obvious way would be with a call to his cell phone, but he didn't get or make any calls that day. Maybe David hid in the back seat of Frank's car. No one except Mac saw Frank leave the lot; no one saw him come back, and no one checked to see if his engine was warmer than it should have been."

"You have to assume that David had a car identical to Mac's. Did you try to find it?"

"Yeah. We tried to connect David with a dark colored, eighties Taurus or Sable. Since it's too old to be a rental, we looked at used car sales. In the four months before the murder, 674 fitting that description were sold. Six hundred and forty-one of them weren't sold to David. George investigated the 33 that were never registered to a new owner. None of them were sold to anyone who looked like David or Mac. We checked for traffic tickets. None were issued to David in that period in any car."

"David had to park it close to his home after the murder."

"Yeah, but we didn't think about looking for another car until late the second day. That was the reason we got the search warrant: we knew David hadn't dumped the car because he didn't have time after the murder, and we thought he hadn't been out of our sight. We hoped that he'd be carrying a Ford key.

"By day four, the D.A. had put his foot in his mouth, so he cut us off when we asked for the manpower to canvass the neighborhood for a strange Taurus. Probably would have been too late anyway. George did a thorough job after he was hired, but that was a couple of weeks later. No surprise he came up blank."

Their food was served and Gary mashed his bacon, eggs, and hash browns into a stew he called The Heart Association orgasm. Bacha seemed to be in an incestuous relationship with the Eggs-Benedict. After Bacha mentioned that a .44 magnum, Hydra-shock bullet had exploded Frank Kendall's head, they discussed bullets while they ate.

Later, Bacha said, "There might be a way to nail the kid." Gary raised his eyebrows. Bacha said, "An older woman, June Wilms, lives in the apartments across the street from the shooting scene. The night of the shooting, she saw a man in a long coat checking out a motor home that was parked in the lot; trying to see in the windows. From her description, and by measuring, we figure the guy had to be over six feet tall. She watched him for awhile before she went to bed. The shooting woke her up, and she saw the car drive out of the lot and the victim on the ground. We showed her sketches of the shooter. She said it could have been the same guy."

Gary had seen the sketch, that of the back of a man in a long coat. "Can you make anything out of that?"

"I'm not going to. I've got a pension to protect. The motor home belongs to the owner of the restaurant, and it was empty. But if someone were to suggest to David that the motor home was not empty that night, and if he was the person who looked into the windows, the people inside the motor home would have gotten a close look at him. They would have seen him commit the murder." The waitress offered to refill their coffee cups, but Bacha waved her off as he added, "And if the two people in the motor home were married, but not to each other, they might not be eager to tell the police what they know."

Gary said, "That's a shopworn scenario. Mac tells me that David is not stupid."

"Panic makes idiots out of the smartest people."

Bacha put his napkin on the table and rose. "I like Mac. He's one of a kind. It keeps me awake knowing my testimony is going to send him to jail. Anything you can do to help, do it, and I'll cover your back if I can. But I've spent too many years taking bullshit to give my pension away, so if push comes to shove, you're all alone."

Bacha seemed much too young to be talking about pensions. Gary had to ask, "How old are you?"

Laughing, Bacha held out his hand. "Thanks. This job makes me feel old. I'm 36."

Gary drove back to Mac's. In the bedroom, Gary unpacked a small combination receiver and tape recorder. After removing the base from Mac's telephone, Gary installed a bug. He tuned the receiver until it heard the bug, the feedback drawing a squeal from the speaker. He took the receiver outside and walked to the end of the next block, then used his cell phone to call Mac's house. When the phone machine answered, the recorder in his hand started. The phone pickup was static free.

Back in the house, he removed the bug from the telephone, and then put the bug, receiver, and his tools in a briefcase.

After a leisurely lunch, he shaved, and put on a white shirt and dark gray tie to go with his silver-gray business suit.

He drove through Chula Vista and took Interstate 5 through downtown. When he reached the Kendall's neighborhood, he parked around the corner from the house.

Walking the block, he stopped at an older home across the street from the Kendall's. From the front, it was a perfectly symmetrical house. A sloped roof peaked in the center, and the shape was repeated in a large window over the front door. Interrupting the vertical redwood siding, two small windows maintained the symmetry.

Gary knocked. The front door was opened by a slightly stooped woman in her seventies. Her smock could have doubled for a bathrobe. She looked wary, perhaps prepared to close the door. Gary assessed the odds she would help at somewhere near zero, but he decided to try. "Do you know Mary Kendall?"

She nodded. "She lives across the street."

"I know. I'm trying to find someone who can answer some questions for me." He held up the DEA identification. "Mike Smith, Drug Enforcement Administration. Can we talk?"

She invited him in. The room he entered was narrow, with high walls and a peaked ceiling. The room might have passed for an outsized entryway except for the furniture: two upholstered couches set at right angles, one facing an entertainment center. The only light came from the high central window.

The woman led him to a large dining room. He'd interrupted her afternoon tea, judging by the toast and a steaming teapot.

"Would you like some tea?"

He declined. When they were seated at the table, she said her name was Margaret Deville, and she had known the Kendalls since 1981, the year they moved into their new house. Over the years, she and Mary had shared recipes and samples from those recipes, but no confidences. They were neighbors rather than friends. After Frank was murdered, she had offered Mary any help she needed, but since then, they waved when they saw each other but they hadn't spoken. Part of that was Margaret's reticence to intrude on Mary's grief. "Every person has to find their own way."

From the dozen pictures displayed on a credenza, Gary assumed that Margaret was a grandmother many times over. Wanting to ease into the question about who else might live with her, he pointed at the pictures. "Cute kids."

She talked about her five children, now with children of their own, and her deceased husband. Other than occasional bouts of baby-sitting, she lived alone. It wasn't a long story. She spoke about facts, not feelings.

Gary decided to approach his problem the same way. "I'm here because we think David Kendall murdered his father."

"I thought his business partner did it."

"It was certainly made to look that way. The District Attorney likes the case he has against the partner, and he's going to trial. The DEA thinks the evidence was fabricated by David Kendall. We believe David is running drugs through his father's factory aboard the trucks that bring parts from subcontractors in Mexico.

We think his father found out about it, and David killed him to protect his income."

Margaret hesitated before she said, "David was a teenager when they moved in. He was so different, I never wanted him in the house."

Gary said, "We have authorization to eavesdrop on David, and I'm going to install a bug in his telephone that will record his phone calls and any conversations in his room. Our problem is that we have to have a receiver nearby. We'd like to put it in your house, if you'll allow that?"

"Someone will be here all the time listening to it?" She didn't like that idea at all.

Gary shook his head. "No, it's just a small, voice-activated, recorder." He opened his briefcase, took the paperback-sized unit out, and placed it on the table. "It can be anywhere in your house: in a drawer, in a cabinet, any place at all. Unless David has a radio or television going all the time, it usually takes a week or more to fill up the tape. If you'll watch it, you can call and we'll pick up the tape and put a new one in, at your convenience." Gary paused to give her some chance to digest all that before he said, "If you want to help, you can listen to it and tape over stuff like television programs."

Margaret Deville readily agreed, saying it sounded interesting. Gary taught her how to use the machine. She learned quickly, already familiar with using a VCR. The battery would last for 30 hours of recording, and it would recharge itself if she plugged the line cord into a wall socket for a day or so every week. "If you want to keep it plugged in, we won't have to worry about the battery."

Margaret had an unused outlet near a night stand in her bedroom, which was off-limits to visiting grandchildren. She placed the recorder on an open shelf in the night stand.

Gary used his cell phone to call the Kendall house. When the phone machine answered, he disconnected. He told Margaret, "They're doing jury selection today, and Mary said she would be there. Supposedly, David is in Oregon, so I'm going to go plant the bug now. Do you know where David's room is?"

"It's at the back of the house on the ground floor. It's the only bedroom on that floor."

He handed her the card that had the name Michael Smith and his cell phone number. "Call me at that number if anyone approaches the house while I'm inside."

Margaret stood inside her screen door as Gary walked across the street, up the stairs, and rang the bell at the Kendall's front door. Satisfied that the house was empty, he unfolded the slender steel blade on his automatic lock-pick. The six tines that made up the blade went into the lock silently. When he pushed a button on the box, it shuddered in his hand, making small metallic noises like a mechanism with sand in it. In seconds, a green light came on and the deadbolt opened. He repeated the process on the door lock. The door handle turned and he slipped inside.

He quickly walked through the living area and the kitchen, discovering David's room just off a short hallway to the back door. The room was large, with a sitting area and entertainment center. Opposite the sitting area, a marble-tiled bathroom had a glass paneled door to the back yard.

Picking up conversations in a room that large could be tricky. There were two phones, one on a nightstand, and the other next to the love-seat. Gary wanted the bug to be in the center of the apartment, so he chose the phone beside the bed. With the housing off the phone, the white plastic bug installed like it belonged. Gary replaced the housing, put the tools back in his briefcase, and counted out loud as he walked out of the bedroom and down the hall to the front door, using one count up for each step. At the front door, he peeked out. Seeing no one, he left the house and crossed the street.

Margaret had the door open. "I heard you counting."

She rewound the tape and he heard all 31 counts. It would be great coverage if David left his door open, considerably less when it was closed. He asked Margaret, "Will you give me a call when David gets in?"

She said she would.

Back in his car, he wrote notes. He dated the entry, and tried to remember what was special about February 14th. When he remembered, he groaned. He let the speed dial on his phone call Andrea's number, and looked at his watch. It was 6:30 in the District. Andrea would have opened her mail by now.

When she answered, Gary said enthusiastically, "Happy Valentines Day!"

"My boss gave me candy. Expensive candy: two pounds of chocolate truffles, my favorite. So I rushed home, figuring my boyfriend would do even better, maybe something with diamonds. Did you not get it in the mail?"

He never lied to Andrea, not that he didn't want to at times like this, but her reporter's instincts enabled her to smell a lie over the telephone. "You expect gifts for Valentine's Day?" He tried to sound amazed.

For once, she was at a loss for words. "Oh, you…You think…I can't believe you. Where in the hell is your head?"

"In California, at the moment."

She hung up, evidently in no mood for jokes.

He did feel like a shit, so he drove to Mission Valley and wandered through a mall, looking for a peace offering. He liked Andrea, but he didn't love her. She was aggressive, relentless, pushy, and opinionated. All those traits made her an excellent reporter, but they grated on him. They were a couple because she loved him. He had told her that he would never marry her, and she still wanted to be his lover. Even so, forgetting Valentine's Day was unacceptable.

He found a florist and arranged to have flowers delivered Saturday morning. He had the message read, 'Sorry' and the card signed, 'Idiot.'

∗   ∗   ∗   ∗

That evening, Gary phoned Mac's lawyer at her home, hoping the jury selection was unfinished and that the arguments would be delayed. She told him it had gone badly, but it was complete. "Three women turned out to be emotional adolescents. They practically wet themselves every time Mr. Draper asked them a question."

"Are any of the jurors in love with you?"

"I got three blacks, hoping for sympathy votes, but if I had to guess, I'd say all three will vote the evidence."

Gary said, "I'm going to try an extortion scam on David. Keep your fingers crossed."

She sounded tired. "Whatever it is, it won't work."

CHAPTER 6

▼

August 2, 1996, Friday, Seven months earlier

Creating the software his father wanted was not the simple task David had envisioned. Five weeks into the project, he finally completed the forecast module, but with the booming economy, everyone in the shop was too busy to test the software. His father suggested that he ask Mac. To David's surprise, Mac agreed, and suggested that they use Monday's orders from two weeks before so they could compare the program's forecast with actual data. David got the orders, showed Mac how to edit the input screen, then went to a terminal in the printer room and watched Mac's inputs from there. For a man with arthritis crippled hands, Mac moved a lot of data.

As he watched, David mused about the last four weeks. Sue would not come back, that was clear. She had called him every day for the first week, telling him about her apartment, inviting him over there for dinner, even suggesting he sleep over. She was willing to do anything except agree to move back to his parent's house. Their last conversation had been mostly silence, all the words said. In the three weeks since that call, she had stopped depositing her checks in their joint account and had canceled their credit cards. She might have dropped off the face of the earth for all he knew. He was surprised at how much that hurt.

It had been a month of losses. Despite his coming in to the shop every day at seven and staying until five, Frank wasn't cutting him any slack. Perturbed at being back at work, there was bitterness in his voice when he told David, "With any luck, we'll sell the business, and your mother and I will blow all the money before we die."

That hardened David's resolve. The plan was perfection. No one would look for Hatch after the shooting. A seasoned killer in Vietnam, shooting Frank wouldn't be traumatic for him. With Mac in jail and Frank dead, David's mother would own the entire business. She would ask him to run it, and he would agree.

Engrossed in his reverie, David was startled when Mac came into the computer room and rumbled, "Got the actuals inputted. You ready to run the prediction?"

According to the software's output, the predicted time was twenty-three percent less than the actual time, a huge difference that Mac assumed was a software error. After David showed him the reason, Mac said, "Be dammed. Wouldn't have thought of dividing a job between mills 'cause the setup and first piece inspection add-on time would cost too much." Mac congratulated David, and told Frank about the discovery.

David ignored his father's compliments. Hatch had called last night. The end game was starting.

✴   ✴   ✴   ✴

Saturday morning at nine, David drove to a street in Ocean Beach where Hatch had promised to meet him. Ten minutes later, Hatch waddled around the corner. He ponderously first deposited his butt on the seat, and then coaxed his legs into David's Corolla. David made a U-turn as Hatch buckled in. They were on the causeway to Interstate 5 before Hatch asked where they were going.

"Up to Thousand Oaks to buy a gun."

As if driving 170 miles to buy a gun was normal, Hatch launched into a story about a 280 millimeter cannon the United States used in Vietnam. As Hatch described the involved calculations for the powder requirements of the gun, given the air density, range, elevation over obstacles, and wind, David knew that the information came from a book, but how did Hatch get it?

The question would be impolite, so David didn't ask. Hatch rambled on, and then finally fell silent as they sped through Carlsbad. After a few minutes, he asked, "So, Mr. Rhoades, why do you need me to buy this gun?"

"Dan. Call me Dan." Hatch nodded, somehow managing to convey that he would do no such thing. David handed Hatch Mac's credit card, social security card, and driver's license. Pointing to the picture on the license, he asked, "Look familiar?"

Looking serious, perhaps scared, Hatch nodded and his thumb began rotating the steel ring on his finger. As Hatch's worry bead picked up speed, David explained that John McBride was one of the two men looting the business. The other was Frank Kendall.

Hatch asked, "Are either of these men, ah, to use the parlance, connected?"

"Mafia? No, these men use legal methods to steal."

"Because if using this John McBride's driver's license could expose us to danger, I have a driver's license issued in another name that we could use."

David said, "Using John McBride's license is the point. Beyond that, it's better that you don't know anything else."

"Of course. I don't wish to know why you need the gun. However, I must remove myself from consideration. I haven't disclosed that I have a record. An unfortunate series of DUI's caused me to be incarcerated. They also confiscated my license, hence my need for a license in another name."

"You aren't going to be identified in any way. They don't require fingerprints for the background check; and you look like John McBride, so what's the problem?"

"Not having done time, you might not understand. It's unpleasant and I'd rather not risk it."

David had trouble breathing. He expected Hatch to balk at killing Frank, but the gun purchase? "You trying to tell me that someone with combat experience in Vietnam doesn't have enough guts to go into a store and buy a gun? The salesman won't care who you are, he wants his commission. It's Saturday, so the store will be busy. He has to see three pieces of ID and that's what he'll see. He'll be happy to close the deal and move on to the next customer. Once the store owner has his money; you think he's going to question the sale? And the bureaucrat who looks at the form is going to verify that John McBride doesn't have a record. So where's the risk?"

Hatch seemed to shrivel into the passenger door, whirling the steel ring around on his finger so rapidly his thumb looked palsied. He looked out the window, and the whirling ring slowed. When it stopped turning, he asked, "How do you expect me to negotiate a sale without showing that I lack front teeth?"

"Simple. You don't negotiate. You walk in, point at the gun, and say, 'I want to buy that.' You don't try to be polite; you don't try to make the salesman happy, you wait for him to tell you what he needs and you give it to him: money, identification, and you sign the form when he tells you where to sign it. No negotiation. If he starts a conversation, you look at him like you're pissed and you tell him you're in a hurry. That's exactly what John McBride would do." David added, "Just act like your hemorrhoids are killing you."

After an eternity, Hatch decided that he could buy the gun. He asked David to tell him when the gap showed, and said all the things he might need to say to a salesman. "I'd like to buy a Desert Eagle." "Is that the .44 magnum?" "How much is it?" "I'll want a small box of Federal Premium Hydra-shock." "Where do I sign?" He said them all without revealing his lack of teeth.

David's anger took some time to dissipate. He had taken huge risks to get Mac's ID. Art Garrison, the bartender at the Dive Inn in Pacific Beach, supplied fake licenses and credit cards. Art directed David to scan the documents he wanted into graphic files, and gave him an e-mail address. Within 24 hours of sending the e-mail, he would pay Art $65 for each separate document. Two days later, Art would have the documents, rendered in the same material as the original.

David got a chance to scan Mac's ID when the receptionist, unable to find a replacement baby sitter, brought her two year old son to work. The relentlessly energetic tike bothered Mac. He worked at a Bridgeport mill as an excuse to stay out of the office, and left his coat, with his wallet, hanging on the door to his office. David walked into Mac's office, knocked his coat to the floor, and palmed the wallet as he hung the coat up. If Mac came back before he could scan the cards, David planned to say he had seen the boy dragging Mac's coat and he'd help Mac find the wallet. The plan wasn't needed. He scanned all three cards into graphic files, and replaced Mac's wallet without incident.

Last Tuesday, he picked up the completed duplicates from Art. The magnetic strip on the Visa card didn't scan, and the driver's license holograms were simply printed images, but that was expected. Otherwise, they looked genuine. That Ralph Hatch might be afraid to use the documents hadn't entered his mind.

When they got to the store, David reminded him that he needed to get the job done with the fewest words while looking unhappy. And he evidently pulled it off. He was back in the car, looking relieved, in seven minutes flat. Hatch handed David the receipt. "He said I can pick it up next Saturday."

*   *   *   *

The next Saturday morning, David, carrying $9000 from his stash, was fifteen minutes late when he arrived to pick up Hatch. The rotund man was all nerves. As they drove north, Hatch asked, "What if the store contacted him? They might have had some problem with the paperwork they needed to clear up."

David's stomach flipped. Hatch voicing the concern he'd lived with all week made it seem more possible. Despite that feeling, David managed a contemptuous tone when he said, "I've been working with the guy all week. He would have mentioned it."

Hatch wanted to know all about that, so David told him Mac thought they were buddies. David invented reasons why Frank and Mac needed to be removed from the business, trying to keep both their minds off picking up the gun. If Mac had been contacted, it was likely the police would be waiting, and David would be in deep shit.

At the sports store in Thousand Oaks, after Hatch went inside, the fear was a living thing in David's stomach. Six minutes later, a police car parked in the back of the lot and two uniformed officers got out. As the two approached, Hatch came out of the store carrying a large bag. He saw the officers and stopped, staring at them, a mouse watching a rattlesnake. Would he drop the bag and try to waddle off?

David got out of the car and walked toward Hatch, his back to the officers. Hatch, his attention now divided, stood still until David got to him. Not knowing how close the cops were, David whispered, "Stop staring at the cops. Now laugh and pat me on the back."

Hatch managed a semblance of that, and David said, "Now, let's walk toward the car."

As David turned, the officers reached the end of the row of cars and turned toward a bakery at the far end of the small strip mall. David felt almost giddy as he got into the car. He put a hand on Hatch's shoulder. "Relax, it's all over. No one knows that Mac didn't buy that gun. I told you everything would go all right, didn't I?"

Before heading back to San Diego, David stopped at a restaurant for lunch. He picked up a free publication picturing cars for sale. While they waited for their food, David found several possibilities. Excusing himself, he left Hatch at the table and used the restaurant's pay phone. He talked to three sellers before he found a suitable car. He returned to the table as their sandwiches arrived.

Hatch asked, "You have another purchase you wish me to make in Mr. McBride's name?"

David shook his head. "You said you have a fake ID?"

Hatch looked worried as he worked a driver's license out of his wallet. Rudy Hambly's California license had an El Cajon address. David asked, "Is the address connected to you in any way?"

"My friend and I lived there for a few days some years ago."

"Good. We need to buy a car that can't be traced."

"Now, just a moment, I can't possibly…"

David interrupted. "Sure you can. This time, you'll be Rudy Hambly."

"That isn't what concerns me. The last time I negotiated for a car, the scoundrel discovered that I was arithmetically challenged. Through clever manipulation, he managed to sell me a car for considerably more than the asking price, more than I could afford. They repossessed it and kept my not inconsiderable down payment."

With a mouth full of food, David could only manage a sympathetic look. When he could, he said, "You aren't going to buy it from a dealer. A private party has a dark color, four door, Ford Taurus. You're going to drive it, and if you think it'll keep running for awhile, I want you to buy it with cash."

Hatch looked pleased. "I am quite adroit with cash."

"I'll want you to negotiate the price. I don't want the seller wondering why you paid full price when you didn't have to. He's asking $7000. Since he used the term 'asking,' he probably expects to get about 10% less, say $6300. So you say that the sales tax on the car will be over $500, and the smog certification will add another $50, so would he accept $6600? Since it's more than he expects, he'll accept that."

"And if he doesn't?"

"Then you'll ask what he would accept, and you'll agree to that amount. I'll give you $7000. Whatever you have left after you pay for the car is yours."

Hatch looked interested.

Back in the car, David took the stack of bills out of the glove compartment, and counted out seventy $100 bills. Hatch put sixty of the bills in his right pant's pocket, and the remaining ten in his left pocket.

The seller lived in Simi Valley, a short freeway trip away. David drove by the seller's address, and saw the car parked at the curb. It looked clean and undamaged. David drove a few blocks to a strip mall that had a bus stop at the curb. Hatch was to tell the seller he had come on the bus and walked.

David said, "You'll have to walk the half mile back if you don't buy the car."

He let Hatch out a block from the seller's house and watched as he waddled to the house and up onto the porch. When he entered the house, David drove back to the strip mall. He read the Times while he waited.

An hour passed before Hatch pulled the Taurus into the parking lot, a happy man. "I placed the $6000 on the table so he could see it, and told him that's all I had. He seemed disappointed, but he accepted." Hatch handed David the signed pink slip.

As David trailed the Taurus back toward San Diego, his hopes rose. Promised enough money, Hatch would pull a trigger one more time.

CHAPTER 7

▼

February 15, 1997, Saturday

Still sore from yesterday's run, Gary shut off the alarm when it yanked him from sleep at six. Just after seven, Mac knocked, pulling him away from a restless dream. Julie had scheduled a brainstorming session in her office at nine; Gary was invited.

Gary drove Mac to the meeting. When they walked into her waiting room, Julie, looking like a teenager in a white blouse and jeans, was talking with George Martinez in her usual soft, slow manner. She motioned them to sit anywhere.

Julie opened an overstuffed briefcase and retrieved some notes. Referring to the notes, she gave George and Mac her view of the jury. Judge Lucero had ruled that he wouldn't allow questions concerning David's motive or opportunity for killing his father. She had listed David as a witness to keep him out of the court-room. "I don't want the jury to see a good-looking boy comforting his grieving mother."

She wasn't going to call Mary either. She thought the potential for a scene was too high. She hoped Mary wouldn't attend the trial, but she had attended jury selection.

"In my opening statement, I will tell the jury that some evidence was manu-factured to frame John. Of course, I won't say who might have done that. I want them to try to guess the identity of the killer. I hope they'll be thinking of that while Mr. Draper presents his case. I'll conclude my opening by telling them if they are convinced that any evidence was manufactured, the law says they must assume all of it is suspicious and acquit John. At the start of the defense, I'll put John on the stand. Once they hear the real story, then I can suggest that Mr. Draper is following a path the killer laid out for him."

Julie wanted witnesses to suggest that the evidence didn't look right. She needed some ideas on the questions she could ask to draw out those conclusions. Hoping Michael Jank, the gun salesman, had watched the tape of Mac's interrogation, Gary asked her to examine Jank on his ability to recognize people.

"That could backfire. Suppose he's very good at recognizing people?"

Mac had been sitting quietly, so his bass rumble caught their attention. "You gotta try, 'cause he's wrong."

Julie wrote furiously for a few moments before she glanced up. "If I can get time with Mr. Jank, I'll see how he does on a face recognition test."

George wanted Julie to focus on the gun. He had fired a Desert Eagle, and the recoil was very strong. With his weakened grip from the arthritis, Mac could not have fired the gun with one hand as witnesses said the killer did.

George also thought that the ejection of the distinctive brass, and the noise it made were the reasons David selected that particular gun. He made a persuasive argument that the gun would have been unsuitable for any reason Mac might have had for buying it.

George told Julie about the hunt for the duplicate car the killer drove. When Gary asked, George said, "Twenty-nine of the 33 unregistered buyers were Mexican, so they probably registered the cars in Mexico. The other four were registered in Oregon or Washington."

Gary asked, "So that's a dead end?"

George shook his head. "Not necessarily. For the other 641 cars that were purchased, they verified that the names and addresses on the registrations were legitimate. They didn't verify that the registered owner actually had the car."

"So if David registered the car to someone else's name and address, the police wouldn't have discovered that?"

"Nope. The only way to do that is to call and ask the registered owners if they have the car." He fished in his stack of papers and found a printout. "I've got the list of buyers. You want to divide it up? Maybe we can get lucky."

Gary shrugged. "Why not. I can't think of anything else to try." George gave Gary half the printout.

Julie told the group she needed John McBride's motive for killing Frank. She grinned at the sudden silence. "What will Mr. Draper's psychologist suggest as John's motive? Without knowing that, I won't be prepared to dispute it on cross."

Gary said, "I wondered if we were attaching too much importance to the past 30 years Mac and Frank shared. Mac was depressed, for good reasons, even before Frank's death. His wife is gone. He's been alone for a long time. In constant pain from arthritis, worried about his heart problems and diabetes, maybe he bought the gun to end it all. On that Tuesday night, maybe he was close to that decision when Frank started harassing him. For thirty years, it had been funny, but on that day, it was more than he could take. He resented Frank's good health. He felt scared and trapped by his own failing body, and he had a gun. He fired at his friend, and then blocked that memory."

Julie asked Mac, "How do I respond to that?"

Mac said, "When your body starts to give up, the fear gets bad. But I figured if I spent every day worryin' about dyin', I might as well be dead. So I concentrated on work." Mac looked at his hands as he added, "That was the thing about Frank. He made the work matter, and he was always good for a laugh." Mac's eyes filled. He abruptly got up and went outside.

Julie packed her notes into the briefcase as she said, "Monday is President's day; the courts are closed. Tuesday is the Judge's golf day or something, so the arguments won't start until Wednesday."

Gary waved the printout at George. "Gives us four days to find the car."

George said, "Keep in touch. I'll let you know if I turn up anything."

Outside, Mac was leaning on the high wall, looking down into the parking lot. When Julie touched his back, he shuffled around to face her. Julie asked, "Is there anyone who can testify to your state of mind the day Frank was killed?"

"Yeah. I had lunch in the break room with some people. We had a good time."

"Okay," Julie said. "Get me their names and phone numbers."

Mac and Gary rode down together in the wheezing elevator. Mac pointed at the printout. "I'll help with those. You tell me what to do."

On the way back to Mac's, Gary called his voice mail. Andrea hadn't called. He hoped the flowers would soften her disappointment.

Gary used Mac's phone to call the car buyers, and gave his cellular as the call-back number when he had to leave a message. Mac took half of Gary's printout and went to Framac to use the phone lines there. By five that evening, Gary had called the 158 numbers on his list, but only verified thirty-one buyers. He had left the same message on over a hundred answering machines, 'We need your help with a fraud investigation. Please verify that you or someone in your family purchased a (Ford Taurus/Mercury Sable) last year. Call the voice mail at 555-5183. Give your name and verify that you purchased the car. Thank you.' So far, only four had called back. Perhaps most people were away for the holiday weekend.

To take a break, he called Andrea. When her phone machine answered, he launched into a long, fervent apology, hoping she was screening her calls. She didn't pick up.

He checked his phone mail. Margaret Deville, the lady monitoring the bug in David's bedroom, had left a message that David was home.

Gary drove to a restaurant in National City and called from its pay phone. When David answered, Gary asked, "Is this David Kendall?"

"Yes. Can I help you?"

"Well, it's the other way around, actually. I'm hoping I can save your life."

"Let me guess: a free prostate exam?"

"Well, you're definitely going to take it in the shorts if my clients tell what they saw in Colson's Cavern's parking lot on October 22 of last year." David remained silent so Gary continued, "My clients will testify they observed you shoot your father. You looked in the window of the motor home they were using. They are positive it was you and they will do their civic duty before the end of McBride's trial."

"Unless?" David sounded sarcastic.

"They can be persuaded to be silent by $100,000 in cash before Monday afternoon. This is the only request for money they intend to make." Gary waited, but when David didn't respond, he added, "There is no guarantee that they will keep that promise, of course, but this kind of information does have a limited lifetime. People ask embarrassing questions if an innocent person is convicted."

David said, "That's a great deal of money, but I'll see what I can do. Contact me again Monday morning and I'll let you know how we can settle this thing." He disconnected.

Gary stared at the phone in amazement. Was it going to be that easy?

He called Margaret Deville and told her about his attempt to spook David. "If you hear him talking about it with someone else, be sure to preserve that. It'll have the phone number he calls."

*   *   *   *

Sunday morning, Gary slept late. Margaret Deville had left him a message. She thought he'd want to know that Mary had reported a blackmail attempt to a Detective Bacha. Gary was surprised by his disappointment.

Bacha had left the same message: the blackmail attempt had been reported.

*   *   *   *

In three days, Gary put over a thousand miles on the rental car working his printout on the cars. He eliminated most by verifying that the car was at the new owner's address, and some because the VIN number called for a light color. Sometimes he talked to the owner's neighbors.

On Tuesday morning someone at *The Washington Post* told him that Andrea was in Europe on an assignment. They couldn't say when she might return.

Tuesday afternoon, George called. All the owners on his list were legitimate.

Wednesday morning he waited for Mac in the kitchen's breakfast nook. Gary felt depressed. Mac was going to be convicted, and there didn't seem to be a damn thing he could do to prevent it. The only hope was that Jank would mention the tape of Mac's interrogation. If he did, the judge would have to call a mistrial.

CHAPTER 8

▼

August 13, 1996, six months earlier

In the corner streetlight, a portly gentleman in a silver-gray suit seemed to tilt side to side as he walked, as if doing a penguin impression. With his face in shadow, David didn't recognize Hatch until he stopped beside the Toyota. Dressed for a night on the town, Hatch sported an expensive suit, a white shirt and a solid gray tie. His shoes glistened.

Hatch got into the car as he normally did, by turning away, bending over, and falling backward, blindly trusting that the seat would be there. Safely landed, he hauled his legs into the car, one at a time, making soft sounds as he cajoled his reluctant appendages. He pulled on the knees of his suit, providing slack to retain the sharp creases and looked at David's jeans, polo shirt, and windbreaker. "I haven't participated in an evening's entertainment in ages. Perhaps I over-dressed?"

"You'll do well. Money attracts women, and you look like money."

"Men of my girth tend to expire unexpectedly. In my size, the thrift stores provide a plethora of excellent clothes."

David reached into the rear foot well, and brought out the small ice chest. "There's a glass and ice in there, and a bottle of scotch in the glove compartment. I want to show you something before we hit the bars."

Hatch gently removed the bottle from the glove compartment. "Oh, my, 18 years old," he said reverently. He opened the bottle and passed it under his nose. "Imagine that." He opened the ice chest, put two ice cubes in the chilled glass, swirled them around, and then dumped them back into the chest. His hands shook as he carefully poured an inch of the pale gold liquid into the glass. He sat back in the seat and brought the glass to his lips. He held the liquor in his mouth, closed his eyes and, after a moment, swallowed. "Eighteen years old. A true treasure."

David started the car, and drove toward the causeway. Hatch spun a story about an aircraft factory he'd helped another man start. He described the airplane in loving detail: the Mazda Wankle engine, the sophisticated instrumentation, and the retractable landing gear actuated by a hand pump inside the cockpit.

At Colson's Cavern on University Avenue, David parked across the street and directed Hatch's attention to the rustic restaurant. "This is the only place where John McBride and Frank Kendall meet outside of work. They're inside the restaurant now. You see the Taurus parked about midway up the outside row?"

Speaking precisely, Hatch said, "Mr. Rhoades, you mean these men harm. This is really none of my concern, so why am I here?"

"I think you know why I brought you here."

Hatch sipped the scotch, looking straight ahead. When he lifted the bottle to pour himself another drink, it was half empty. Wondering if Hatch was beyond critical thought, David added, "This will be simple if we keep it between the two of us."

Hatch's eyelids were half closed. "Your plan was rather transparent, Mr. Rhoades. I realized long ago that you want me to shoot Frank Kendall in front of witnesses."

Pleased, David said, "If you look at it logically, comparing the potential reward to the slight risk, it really is a marvelous opportunity." David reached into his windbreaker's pocket, and pulled out a roll of money. "There's $10,000 there. It's yours."

Hatch looked at the fat roll of $100 bills impassively. "I will not sell my life that inexpensively."

David laughed at the droll expression. "You do see the opportunity?" He held up the roll of bills. "This is simply good faith money. If those men are removed, in a few months, the business will be worth $25 million. While my stepfather waits for the factory to sell, I'll put you on the payroll as a machine tool buyer. You'll be in Japan, or Germany, living in five star hotels, wined and dined by salesmen who have large commissions riding on your decisions. When my stepfather gives me my half, I'll give you half of that. That's six million dollars. The bank interest will be a $1,000 a day. You'll have to spend a $1,000 every day just to keep your money from growing.

"And really, when you think about it, there's almost zero risk. If you don't open your mouth, no one will doubt that John McBride shot Frank Kendall. The police won't look for any other person, because all the witnesses will identify

John McBride. Once you leave the restaurant and drive away in the car you bought, we'll both be in the clear."

Hatch looked straight ahead through the windshield. His voice was firm when he said, "I won't kill Frank Kendall, and I'd advise you not to do it either. I'm sure there is another solution to your problem."

David said softly, "I do understand. You are an intelligent man, and I'm sure you know that the moment anyone does kill Frank Kendall, you are in danger because you bought the gun. If the police do learn that it was not John McBride who purchased it, the killer would feel it necessary to eliminate you."

The ring began to rotate. "Threats will not alter my decision."

David put his hand on the man's shoulder. "Ralph, you misunderstood me. I wouldn't threaten you, but the killer might. I can't kill Frank Kendall. I'm the logical suspect, so I need an alibi. I don't have any choice. If you won't kill him, I have to hire someone who will. That person will see you as a threat. You know too much."

"And if I kill Frank Kendall, you will see me as a threat."

"That's true, and in the absence of an unbreakable guarantee of your safety, you should go to the police before any harm can come to Frank Kendall."

Hatch took another sip of scotch. He seemed unable to swallow. When he did, he shut his eyes for a moment and said, "That would be foolish. The police have no sense of fair play. They might incarcerate me for the minor role I did play in your scheme."

With Hatch in the trap, David rushed to his rescue. "What you need is a guarantee that no harm can come to you, regardless of what happens to Frank Kendall. I would be willing to put my promise of six million dollars and the payment of the $10,000 in writing. The note would say I asked you to buy the gun, and you had no knowledge of my intent to kill Frank Kendall. It would say that I forced you to shoot Frank Kendall under fear of death."

Hatch turned to look at him. "You'll do that?"

The sheet of acid impregnated paper, designed to disintegrate in a matter of days, was inside the glove compartment, still sealed in an airtight envelope. David took a pen from his shirt pocket and said, "I'll do it right now. In addition, I'll give you the $10,000 right now. All you have to do is agree to shoot the man. After he's dead and Mac's in jail, and I receive the proceeds from half the business, I will buy your continued retention of that document for six million dollars."

Hatch stared out the windshield. "Murder brings out the best detectives, the best lawyers. Few murderers escape justice."

"If you shot him, the District Attorney would send John McBride to prison. The police would not be authorized to look for another killer."

In an unusually strong voice, Ralph Hatch said, "I will not murder anyone, Mr. Rhoades. I'm afraid that is not negotiable."

Pleading now, David said, "You could live like a king if you found the courage to pull that trigger. It would be so simple. Do you prefer being destitute?"

"I prefer to live life on my own terms. I will not kill anyone."

David recognized the different timbre in Hatch's voice. He would not change his mind. David felt his world disintegrate. All the planning had been for nothing. His future was gone. He hated the toothless bastard; he wanted to smash his face into pulp. David gripped the steering wheel until his hands hurt.

Hatch said, "I'm sure you are deeply disappointed, so we'll part company now." He fumbled with the door handle.

David put a hand on Hatch's shoulder. "Sure I'm disappointed, but I knew it was a lot to ask. I don't have the courage to kill him, so I can't criticize you for feeling the same way. We're still friends. I'll drive you back to your place."

On the short ride back to Ocean Beach, the ring spinning on Hatch's finger might have raised blisters. The man had come to some decision, and David knew what it was. As soon as anything happened to John McBride or Frank Kendall, Hatch would visit Framac's insurance company. With their reward offer in writing; their lawyer at his side, his next stop would be the police station. It was what David would do if the situation were reversed.

At David's urging, Hatch told him about Silverlake Resort in Lakeside, and his partner, Evelyn Nessbaum. The motor home they lived in was cramped, and Evelyn's love for doing cross-stitch taxed the available space with finished and unfinished works of art.

He directed David to the motor home parked on a side street. David pulled up behind it so he could read the license, telling Hatch, "You may be right about another solution. Let's stay in touch, just in case I figure out a way."

As Hatch opened the door and began his ponderous exit, he raised the bottle of scotch in the air. "This will always buy whatever service I am able to provide. I'm quite amenable to any plan that doesn't involve serious crime."

Hatch closed the door, and tottered toward the motor home. David wrote the license number and 'Silverlake Resort' on an envelope.

He drove away. Despair weighed on his chest until he had trouble breathing. On October 1, he would be evicted from his room. His security would be gone. No one would know, or care, if he was sick or even alive. To make his money last, he'd have to live in some dingy apartment. His money would run out, and he'd end up working 50 or 60 hours a week for some power freak. He'd had a taste of that in high school when he got a job parking cars. The lot manager couldn't form a coherent sentence, but he could make David's time at work an endless frustration. David finally told the guy to go fuck himself, and for that he got fired.

And that was probably his future. The first time his manager made a stupid request, David would needle him and end up out of a job. He'd go on to the next job, and the next, until no one would hire him because he couldn't show a resume.

In frustration, maybe he'd do a few lines, maybe drink some, and end up like Ralph Hatch: toothless, living off some mentally deranged woman, too screwed up to find his way out of the gutter.

As he pulled the Toyota into his spot in the garage, a steely resolve replaced his depression. By rights, this garage, the house, everything was his. They owed him.

CHAPTER 9

▼

February 19, 1997, Wednesday

San Diego's courthouse and jail spanned three city blocks, the upper floors bridging the streets. Tree roots had assaulted the sidewalks, so Gary walked close to the buildings. At the Broadway entrance to the Hall of Justice, he found the courtroom on a map, and took the wide staircase to the third floor.

Inside, the courtroom's ceiling was all recessed lighting. A dozen or so spectators sat in rows of pale blue theater seats. Judging by the notepads, three women represented the media.

The business half of the courtroom was crowded. The large defense and prosecution desks were separated by a podium. The narrow isle in front of the desks was bounded by a wide wooden partition that hid the clerk's desk. Because of the size of her work surface, the clerk's chair almost touched the front of the judge's dais. To the judge's right, the witness box stood higher than the court reporter's desk, and only a foot or so separated the two. Both were close to the jury box. The jurors would be able to see a witness sweat.

The judge's dais, the witness stand, and the jury seating area were conservative in size. The only ornamentation in the courtroom, a square, stained glass sculpture, hung on the wood-paneled wall behind the judge's dais. Beneath that, a low, room-width bookcase was filled with identically bound books.

Mac and Julie sat behind the large desk assigned to the defense. Mac looked uncomfortable in a brown suit and tie. Julie looked comfortable in a long sleeved, sky blue, cotton dress that buttoned to the neck. Julie's laptop and some folders occupied a minor portion of the desktop. Two bailiffs sat near the wall, facing Mac.

A tall, blond lady wearing a black suit, and a slim man in an earth-tone plaid suit, stood at the prosecutor's desk sorting documents. Both looked to be in their twenties.

Looking self-conscious, the 14 jurors sat in upholstered chairs in the jury box. Some looked at Mac, who studied his knurled hands.

Mary Kendall, Frank's widow, came in and sat in the spectator section, as far from Mac as the seating allowed. Dressed in a dark pants suit, perhaps trying to disappear into the chair, she seemed lost and lonely. She looked around, spotted Gary, nodded, and then lowered her eyes.

The court bailiff sang his song and the large wooden door at the front of the court room opened. Judge Raul Lucero, a swarthy Mexican in his forties, ambled in, looking over the courtroom as he mounted the steps to the bench. He stood for a moment behind the desk unloading a briefcase, then sat down. While everyone in the courtroom noisily resumed their seats, he opened a laptop computer. When he looked up, he asked the attorneys in turn to estimate how long their opening remarks would take. Draper said, "About half an hour." Julie's opening would be slightly less than an hour. The judge said the court would break after the opening statements, and then asked the prosecution to begin.

Peter Draper told the jury his job was to show that facts proved the defendant was the perpetrator of the crime. Since all the defense had to do was sow doubt in the juror's minds, he told them to cling to the following facts, regardless of the smoke screen the defense planned. He related the events of October 22, 1996, culminating with the arrest of John McBride. He covered the analysis of the shell casings found at the scene which identified the gun as a Desert Eagle, and the gun registration records that indicated John McBride had purchased the same type of gun 10 weeks earlier. The murder weapon was found by a homeowner the day after the murder, in a location on John McBride's usual route to his house. As to the motive, Draper called it a crime of passion. Draper finished his opening remarks by listing the facts he would prove.

Julie scribbled furiously on a sheet of paper, folded it, and pointed the folded paper at Gary. Gary rose and took the note from her. He walked out of the courtroom to open it. She had written, "He didn't mention Jank. Why?"

Why indeed? Gary had Michael Jank's phone number in his notebook. The lady who answered was Jank's wife, Darlene. She said that he had changed his mind. The man who bought the gun looked a great deal like John McBride, but he was now sure that it wasn't John McBride. He had told Draper this, and Draper had said that his testimony wouldn't be needed.

She expected Michael to be at home from five to seven, when he'd leave for his second job. Gary asked for their address, and told her he'd be there at five.

The courtroom door opened an hour later. Julie came out, grabbed Gary and led him and Mac into a small conference room, where Gary blurted, "I talked to Jank's wife. He knows it wasn't Mac who bought the gun."

"Oh, my God," Julie said softly.

"I'm going to talk to Jank this evening."

"No, go now. Find him at work, wherever. We have to know if he's uncertain, or if he is *certain* that it wasn't John. If he knows it was a look-alike, we have to add him to our witness list as soon as possible."

Gary turned to Mac. "I need to talk with Julie privately. Do you mind?"

Mac went out, and Gary said, "Jank may cite a tape of John's interrogation as the reason he changed his mind."

Julie seemed to shrink. She slumped into a chair, shaking her head in despair. Gary said, "The tape came from Draper's office, probably by accident. If Jank told him about the tape, Draper would have arrested the guilty party if he knew otherwise."

Julie looked at him, her eyes narrowed. Her mind must have been racing because she said, "Well, if Mr. Draper knew about the tape, however it came to be in Mr. Jank's possession, he should have made that known to the court prior to trial. And if Mr. Jank is positive that John McBride didn't buy that gun, Mr. Draper has obstructed justice by not making that known to the court. So you have to find out those two things: did Mr. Jank tell Mr. Draper about the tape, and is he certain the man who bought the gun was not John McBride?" She looked at Gary for a moment before she added, "You'll have to be careful how you approach Mr. Jank about the tape."

Which might have been the understatement of the year.

*   *   *   *

While he drove toward Los Angeles, Gary called Michael Jank's wife. She gave him directions to the company in Thousand Oaks where Michael was a dispatcher.

The traffic bunched up around Long Beach, so Gary used the commuter lane. He did the next forty miles without getting a ticket, and when the lane ended near Los Angeles International, he ran into another jam. Between that and the clot in Santa Monica, he took the off-ramp into Thousand Oaks near two that afternoon. He drove three miles into the hills on a gravel road dotted with spilled cement. In the cement company's yard, he parked in front of a manufactured building, the only spot that looked safe. He climbed the steps, assaulted by the noise from outgoing and incoming cement trucks.

Inside, the office area was quiet and clean. He found Michael Jank in a darkened room, seated in front of a monitor covered with lines of data. Jank was handsome, well-built, thirty-something, with Italian looks. Connected to the trucks by a headset, Jank noted Gary's arrival with a nod, spoke to three callers, and then handed the headset to a woman who came into the room. He pointed to a line on the screen, told her the job was a continuous pour, and then hustled Gary out and down the hall.

The tiny break room contained a table, two chairs, and two vending machines. Gary bought a coke and said, "I'm working for John McBride's defense. You've changed your mind about who bought the gun?"

Jank took the coke and pulled the tab. "Yeah." His look suggested chagrin. "The guy was his identical twin. I'm telling you, side by side, you couldn't tell them apart."

"Then how do you know it wasn't John McBride?"

"As soon as John McBride opened his mouth, I could see the difference. The guy who bought the gun had all his front teeth missing, and his eye teeth slanted toward the gap. Reminded me of a vampire. And the voice was all wrong. John McBride has a deep voice; the other guy doesn't. The guy sounded educated, like a college professor, which felt weird coming from a toothless guy. John McBride doesn't use two words if he can get by with one, but the guy who bought the gun never used a short word if he knew a long one. And their hands are so different: John McBride has bad arthritis. The guy who bought the gun had smooth knuckles."

Jank looked out a window and checked his watch as a cement truck rumbled past. He moved to the door and said, "Sharon, tell 517 that he's cutting it close." He told Gary, "Continuous pour."

Gary asked, "If you saw all these differences between the two men, why did you pick John McBride out of a lineup?"

"Because with their mouths' shut and ten feet away, they look identical. I never saw John McBride with his mouth open until the D.A. sent me that tape."

"He what?"

"He sent me a video tape of John McBride being questioned." Jank laughed at Gary's expression. "What's with that tape? When I called and told him I'd changed my mind after watching the tape, he came unglued. He sent a guy all the way up here to pick it up. I had to shovel out the recycle bin to find the FedEx envelope it came in."

Gary's cell phone trilled. He apologized and answered. Julie said, "Talk to me."

"Draper sent a tape of Mac's interrogation to Michael Jank. After he watched it, he's positive he didn't sell the gun to Mac."

"Mr. Draper is rushing his case. Jank has to be here tomorrow morning, and I can't get a subpoena to him by tonight. Offer him anything—anything—if he'll come voluntarily."

*   *   *   *

The next morning when the trial was scheduled to resume, Judge Lucero gathered seven people in a conference room: Gary, Michael Jank, Julie, Draper, Bill Baffert, an investigator from the D.A.'s office, Jenine McKinney, a secretary at the D.A.'s office, and Katie Sanchez, a court stenographer. An open FedEx package, the short letter from Draper's office, a videotape, and a spiral bound notebook were on the table. Judge Lucero waited until everyone was seated before he explained the rules of the meeting: he would ask questions of each person; they would answer under oath, and at the end of the meeting, each would be required to sign a copy of their statements.

Judge Lucero questioned Jank about the tape: when he got it, if it came in the packaging on the table, when he watched it, when he told Draper about his change of mind, and if Draper had requested that he not inform the defense. When Jank told him what Draper had said, Judge Lucero wrote in his notebook. Then he asked Jank why he told Gary about the tape.

"He asked why I'd changed my mind, so I told him the guy on the tape, John McBride, wasn't the same guy who bought the gun."

The judge asked, "Was it your impression that Mr. Charboneau knew about the tape?"

"No. He seemed surprised."

Judge Lucero thanked Jank, and excused him.

After Jank left the room, Judge Lucero asked Julie why she sent Gary to LA. Julie pointed at Draper. "He dropped a witness who could put the murder weapon in John McBride's hand, and I had to know why."

Judge Lucero turned to Gary and asked, "Why did you drive up to Thousand Oaks? Couldn't you have found that answer by calling Mr. Jank?"

Julie answered. "He did phone. Mr. Jank's wife said her husband had changed his mind, but I needed to know the degree of that change. I wanted Mr. Charboneau to see him face to face, so he could determine if we wanted to put Mr. Jank on the stand."

"And you had no knowledge of the tape at that time?"

She neatly sidestepped the question by saying, "Gary told me that Jank's wife didn't say why he changed his mind." She looked at Gary. "That's correct?"

Gary answered, "I didn't ask his wife why he'd changed his mind, and she didn't say."

Judge Lucero turned to Draper and asked some pointed questions. Draper's answers pointed to an office in disarray. The letter included with the tape had been typed by Jenine McKinney, a trim lady in her forties sitting directly across the table from Gary. Draper admitted that he'd evidently signed the letter, but he didn't remember doing it. Ms. McKinney didn't think she'd sent the tape, but she was unable to locate Mr. Draper's copy of the taped interrogation. She also didn't know how many copies of the tape had been made. Draper's investigator, Bill Baffert, added fuel to Judge Lucero's ire when he admitted that he'd told Jank the identification was a moot point, that it wouldn't be used during the trial.

"Did Mr. Draper ask you to tell Mr. Jank that?"

Bill Baffert said, "Yeah. He thought John McBride had fooled Jank."

"And I still think so," Draper added.

"Well, Mr. Draper, that was not your decision to make. That was a question for the jury to decide." Judge Lucero turned to Julie. "I can declare a mistrial, or you can proceed with your defense which will include Mr. Jank's testimony. Your option."

"We'll proceed."

The meeting over, Gary walked with Julie toward the courtroom. He tried to convince her that continuing with the trial was a mistake. "Jank has opened a whole new avenue of investigation. We need to find the guy who bought the gun. We know David's plan to kill his father must have developed after he met this clone, so if we can put them together, David is dust. Since he looks so much like Mac, we can doctor a picture of Mac to show the missing teeth. A mistrial would give us months to show the picture around, maybe find someone who had seen them together."

Julie said, "This is a bird in the hand. At the end of this trial, Judge Lucero will instruct the jury that all the evidence presented by the prosecution is tainted by this conspiracy, and I expect the jury will acquit John."

Why would Julie believe that any jury would follow the law? She was not exceptional in her faith, most lawyers seemed to have that problem. In all the trials Gary had attended, he had never correctly predicted how a jury would rule. Even in the instances where he agreed with the verdict, their reasoning left him dumbfounded. He had once seen an alleged rapist convicted on the size of his fiancée's engagement ring, the jury foreman having convinced the other jurors that a stone that large could only be a payoff for the alibi. And one jury in a civil case assessed a title company millions of dollars for abetting a fraud, ignoring the instruction that the title company had no legal liability.

But it was Julie's call, so Gary asked, "What happened in court yesterday?"

At the courtroom door, Julie told him that Draper had a forensic expert who postulated that the long coat and ski mask explained why Mac didn't have any blood or gunshot residue on him. The wind chill was near 38 degrees, and if John McBride and Frank had been in the parking lot for 23 minutes after walking out of the restaurant, Mac might have gotten cold enough to put on whatever outer garments he had in his car. Then Julie said, "You know Draper rested the prosecution yesterday?"

Astonished, Gary asked, "In one day? How could he do that?"

"The better question is: why would he do that? I think he wanted me to be so busy, I'd forget that he didn't call Jank to testify."

The bailiff came to close the door, so they went into the courtroom. When Judge Lucero declared the court in session, Julie began the defense by calling Mac to the stand. She led Mac through the events of the day of the killing, starting when he got up in the morning. Mac seemed uncomfortable but his answers were short and to the point. Julie was well prepared and established that he'd cooked a large breakfast for himself, that his wife had died some years ago, that he was largely a creature of habit, not varying his routine much from day to day.

Draper objected constantly, citing relevance, and Mac had to wait until the judge ruled before he could answer. After Julie explained, again, that the questions went to motive, Draper having made Mac's supposed depression the motive for killing his partner, Mac turned to the judge and asked, "Don't he remember what you told him last time?"

The spectators and jurors erupted into laughter, and Judge Lucero didn't quite hide a grin. He said, "Mr. McBride is getting impatient, as are we all. One more time: you raised the issue of Mr. McBride's mental state as motive. Therefore, the defense has the duty to establish Mr. McBride's mental state on that day." He stared at Draper, waiting for a response that never came. Finally, he asked, "Do you understand?"

Draper said, "Yes, your honor."

Mac didn't equivocate or embellish. Even on trial for murdering Frank, Mac talked about their differences. Frank bid for jobs that Mac thought they shouldn't take. Mac said he often got mad at Frank. Then, a moment later, his eyes brimmed when he talked about Frank's last day.

Gary watched Frank's widow, Mary, when Mac got choked up. She had tears in her eyes as well.

When Julie finished at 12:44, the court broke for lunch. Jank was waiting outside the courtroom. He seemed to be happy waiting, evidently a marked contrast to his usual day. "My job is where the rubber meets the road. I can use some downtime." He was reading a novel. "Here's hoping I get to finish it."

Gary suggested they walk down to a restaurant fronting the harbor. Inside, they were seated at a window table over the water. They ordered and Jank said, "The cops told me I didn't have to worry about John McBride taking revenge on me. They said if he had killed his partner, it was just a crazy day. But now we know there's a cold-blooded killer on the loose, and no one else has seen him except me."

"You haven't seen the killer. If he had done it, he would have shot Frank Kendall in front of witnesses. As you said, with his mouth shut, he could fool anyone. The guy who planned the murder would have used that."

Jank looked puzzled. "Do you know who did it?"

"Everybody knows who did it. Frank's son, David, is the only one with a motive." Gary locked on Jank's eyes, hoping he might take the hint. "Frank's son probably drove the guy up to your store. You didn't happen to see who was in the car with him, did you?"

"For John McBride's sake, I wish I had, but the store windows are covered with sales posters. I didn't watch him leave the store either time."

*   *   *   *

That afternoon when the trial resumed, Draper confronted Mac on cross. "Was it your testimony that the last thing Frank did in the parking lot was to give you the finger?"

Mac laughed, a rumble that came from his belly, and the laugh continued, tickling most of the people in the courtroom until they joined in. Draper reddened, and Mac put up a hand to indicate he meant no disrespect. "Sorry." Another short laugh escaped. "Guy cracked me up."

"Were you angry with Frank on the day of the murder?"

"Yeah. I got on him pretty good three, maybe four, times that day."

"You testified that you argued with him once a day on average. Was that day worse than normal?"

"Yeah, some. He had to go up to Riverside. I think he was cranky on account of that."

"And was he still cranky when you met him at Colson's Cavern that evening?"

"Nah, the day was over. Besides, we never talked business at dinner."

Draper asked, "Isn't it true you called Frank Kendall a 'damn knuckle-head' that day?"

Mac laughed. "I don't remember, but I probably did. My language ain't the best. Frank was a lot better at it. He used words I didn't know, like he used to call me 'friable.' Still don't know what that means."

"It means brittle; prone to crumbling. Is that what you are, John? Brittle?"

Julie said, "Objection. Conclusion."

"Withdrawn." Then Draper asked, "Why didn't you ever look the word up?"

"'Cause then Frank would have had to find a new word. Guy had enough to do."

At 5:15, Draper finished with Mac. Court was adjourned until nine the next morning. In the corridor, Gary found Mike Jank in the same spot, his bookmark near the end of the novel. Julie apologized to Jank for the delay. She had booked a room for him at a hotel overlooking the harbor, and promised to call him first in the morning.

Gary collected Mac and they walked out to the street. On their way to the parking garage, Gary called Steve Bacha. He was through for the day, but Gary persuaded him to stay until they could get to the police station.

Gary phoned Julie and asked if she could bring Mike Jank to the police station in about twenty minutes, describing what he had in mind. Julie consulted with Jank, who thought it was worth a try.

At the police station, Bacha introduced Gary and Mac to a tall redhead, Helen Pollard, a police artist and photographer. Helen's soft southern accent and gracious attitude charmed Mac. She took several pictures of him with his mouth open. Michael Jank talked Helen through the modifications necessary to create a picture of the gun-buyer, complete to the upper lip slightly folded into the gap between the eye teeth. Helen also made a virtual photograph of the buyer's unadorned ring.

CHAPTER 10

▼

September 11, 1996, Wednesday, five months earlier

David woke late, feeling tired. His entire body ached. Four weeks of intense pressure had taken a toll.

At ten that morning, he put a shovel and a pickax into the trunk of his Corolla, and put an ice chest on the passenger seat. At the small market on Morena Boulevard, he bought ice, six bottles of water, a pint of potato salad, and loaded the cooler.

He drove to the on-ramp to Interstate 5 South. A mile later, he took the climbing ramp that merged into Interstate 8 East, and kicked it up to 75.

*　　　*　　　*　　　*

In Arizona, forty minutes after passing through Yuma, a butte sloped to the edge of the Interstate. Overgrown wheel tracks left the highway and disappeared over the western end of the butte's base. Hoping he could find a spot hidden from the Interstate, David turned and followed the tracks, climbing the shoulder of the butte. Weeds scraped the underside of the car and occasionally, he had to leave the ruts to get around a projection that could do damage. The ascent was deceptively steep, and near the crest, the car was leaned so far to the right that he could see the top of the butte through the driver's side window. Just after the crest, the path abruptly flattened, made a turn to the right, and descended a gentle slope. The path disappeared at a large clearing that edged an arroyo. Glass shards and rusty cans punctured with bullet holes littered the clearing. On the far bank of the arroyo, a riddled fifties pickup sat on its hubs.

When David left the air-conditioned car, the staggering heat urged him to get back in. Waist-high gray scrub-brush edged the clearing, and a dead animal odor fouled the air. The ground felt concrete-hard under a layer of grit that made walking treacherous. He examined the bullet brass that pebbled the clearing. All of it was tarnished. No one had been there recently.

He returned to the car and retraced the path uphill, the wheel tracks fading in the glare, giving the illusion that the road ran to the top of the butte. Perhaps a hundred yards from the clearing, a tall bush grew on the north side of the road. He stopped the car and walked around the bush, finding a patch of short weeds in an area protected from the sun.

Using the shovel, he dug up the patch of weeds. The ground was hard; he had to work the entire surface with the pickax before he could shovel the next four inches away. By the time he had a two-by-three-foot area cleared down to a depth of six inches, he thought he might die of heat stroke before he finished the hole.

In the trunk of the Corolla, he found an old tee-shirt and draped it over his head. He wrapped a bungee cord around the shirt, and then poured the ice water from the bottom of the cooler over his head. His head went numb for a few seconds; he thought he might have given himself a stroke. When that feeling faded, the searing heat seemed to be gone.

He resumed digging. A foot down, he encountered sandy soil that shoveled easily. He dug out the next foot without using the pick. Then he hit another layer of hardpan. He used three bottles of water to keep the tee-shirt wet before the hole was three feet deep. Then he had trouble using the pick, the hole too small for an effective swing. He finally hit sandy soil again, and a few more minutes of shoveling gave him the depth he needed. He stepped into the hole, squatted until his butt touched his heels, bent his head onto his knees, and marked the dirt at the top of his head. The mark was almost a foot below ground level.

David took his time shoveling the dirt back into the hole, letting his muscles cool down before he got back into the air conditioning. He put the shovel and pick into the trunk, brushed the dirt off his clothes and combed his hair. He looked like a hard day, but nothing worse. He drove slowly down the angled track and took the interstate west.

*   *   *   *

Thursday morning, David stayed in bed, working on the problem of how to kill Frank without getting caught. He knew how to get him back to the restaurant, how to keep himself free of blood and gunshot residue, and how to arrange the murder scene so that the blood spatter wouldn't exonerate Mac. Getting rid of the duplicate car would be easy. But there seemed to be no way to contaminate Mac with any physical evidence. If nothing tied Mac to the shooting, the gun and the car might not be enough to convince the police.

As the logical suspect, the police would focus on David. Mistakes were inevitable, and one of those mistakes would convict him. Seeing no way around that, his hatred for Ralph Hatch grew until he felt sick.

* * * *

On Friday the thirteenth, David walked into the 'Meet Market' in Santee just after six. When he'd scouted the place, a dozen singles had been line dancing to country music while perhaps a hundred people watched, some hanging over the railing in the loft above the dance floor. Now, too early for that crowd, the cavernous space was eerily quiet. Next to the massive stone fireplace, at a small table in the corner of the room, Ralph Hatch sat rigidly upright, his hands folded on the tabletop.

David waved and detoured by the bar. He ordered four doubles, put the drinks on a tray, and carried them to the table. Hatch's demeanor improved as he surveyed the bounty.

David sat down. "Are we still friends?"

Hatch put his drink down, shaking his head. "No, I don't think we are. You may think you've got reason to want me dead—you'd be wrong, I don't rat people out—but I didn't get to 61 being stupid. I think it's best if we go our separate ways after today."

David kept his face blank until Hatch looked totally stressed. "Ralph, you've been watching too many cop shows. Why would I harm you?"

"For all the reasons you stated when you asked me to kill that man."

"Since you turned me down, there isn't going to be any killing. You were my one and only chance. I don't have the nerve to do it without you."

"You were extremely upset by my refusal. Perhaps you still are."

David put a hand on Hatch's arm. "I'm sorry I got upset. I just wanted those assholes out. But I'm not sore at you. Like I said, I don't have the nerve to do it either." David sat back in his chair. "Besides, it turns out you were right. There is a better way to help my father." David watched three young women at the bar, deliberately extending the pause before he said, "I intend to pay them off."

Sounding relieved, Hatch said, "That's splendid, Daniel. I assume you asked me here so you could enlist my help with this new plan."

Still watching the women, David said, "I can do it without you, but it would sure go faster if you want to help." He looked at Hatch. "It would involve a lot of traveling. You're probably in no shape to do that."

"That is quite incorrect; my health is excellent. Tell me about this plan."

David leaned in close to Hatch and spoke just above a whisper. "I was trying to sell the gun you bought. I connected with this guy who was in the market for untraceable guns. Turned out he had no interest in buying the Desert Eagle, but he told me he wanted to do one deal for 300 clean handguns. He doesn't want shit, but anything that's serviceable, he'll take. He'll pay $500 each, as long as I have 300 clean guns. That's $150,000."

"Where would you find that quantity at a reasonable price?"

"I already have 80. I found a guy in Nogales who sold me the 80 for $8000. If I can do the other 220 for $100 each, I'll clear $120,000." Hatch sipped the scotch, nodding, so David continued, "The guy will wait for two months. With two of us working together, we can get that many by going to gun shows."

"I do enjoy those shows."

David showed Hatch a map of the circuit they would make through Arizona, Nevada, Utah, Idaho, Montana, and Wyoming. Each city or town where they would stop was marked with the supposed date of a gun show. David concluded his sales pitch by saying, "We can each buy five a day, for a total of twenty at each two-day show, without alerting anyone, but that's all. We'll both use our fake ID's, and we'll get all 220 in a couple of months, even sooner if we stumble across a collection."

"Am I to share in any profit?"

"I'll give you $10,000. I need $100,000 to float a loan to buy these guys out. Expenses are probably going to be $40,000 for the guns and for meals and hotels during the two months on the road, so the $10,000 is all I can afford."

"That hardly seems fair to you," Hatch said. "Why don't we agree to split the portion left over after expenses?"

David raised his hands in surrender. "Great. I'll pick you up Monday morning at nine?"

*   *   *   *

When they met in Santee Monday morning, Hatch was carrying a steel suitcase. David lifted it into the trunk. "Nice suitcase, Ralph."

"It has a good lock. Living as we do, that's a necessity."

David closed the trunk, and got into the car and waited while Hatch went through the cumbersome process of getting in. As David drove, he asked, "What's your partner going to do with you being gone so long?"

"She has activities at Silverlake: sewing circles, a bowling group, friends she chats with. She gets along quite well without me."

✳   ✳   ✳   ✳

In Arizona, the butte loomed like a gravestone as the car climbed the rise, shuddering over the ripples in the hardpan. David eased the front wheels across a small washout, then the car bucked as the back wheels negotiated the ditch, the pick and shovels clanging in the trunk. Hatch had been quiet since they turned off the highway, and now, as the car took an alarming list to the right, he looked worried. David laughed. "I didn't tip it over when I buried the box, and you aren't that heavy."

Hatch didn't comment, so David added, "Shouldn't take more than an hour to get it, then we'll be on our way."

Hatch put both hands on the door to brace himself as the left side wheels went over a hump, tipping the car over so far David had to hang on to the shoulder belt to keep from sliding into the passenger seat. When the car resumed a lesser lean, Hatch cleared his throat several times and said, "I don't mind telling you that I'm extremely nervous. It hardly makes sense, you burying guns."

"It makes perfect sense. Smuggling those guns across the border from Nogales scared me so bad, there was no way I wanted to take them through the California inspection station. I figured I'd dig them up on my way to the gun shows."

David followed the tracks downhill and spotted the bush. His shoulders relaxed. He had worried that it might be gone, perhaps blown away in the constant wind.

He said, "We'll be north of Reno when we finish the gun shows, so we'll go back into California on Highway 50. We'll time it to hit the inspection station in Tahoe when all the gamblers are leaving, and we'll sail through without even slowing down."

Hatch was quiet, perhaps not convinced. David said, "The gun you bought is in my luggage, unloaded. If it'll make you feel better, you can load it and keep it with you. Do that, or whatever else will make you feel better, okay? I don't want to spend the next two months explaining everything I do."

"Since you brought it up, I'd like to keep the gun with me. I don't need the bullets, just the gun. I'd feel so much better knowing where it is."

"Anything you want."

Hatch's stomach was balanced on his lap like he had a sack of cement under his shirt. The man was so badly out of shape that getting him out of the car would take some doing. It had to be over a hundred outside. Hatch wouldn't want to be out in the heat, and he'd never agree to help dig the hole.

David passed the bush and drove down into the clearing, checking for shiny brass. It all looked tarnished. The site hadn't been visited since he'd dug the hole.

He drove back up the hill to the bush and stopped the car. When he got out, the heat staggered him. He could feel his strength ebbing. He walked around to the trunk. Hatch was already there.

David unlocked the trunk. "You could stay in the car if you want."

"You were going to let me hold the gun?"

David used his pain-in-the-ass look, but he opened his suitcase and rummaged under his clothes. Holding the barrel, he handed Hatch the gun, butt first. Hatch took a key out of his pocket, unlocked the steel suitcase, put the gun inside and locked it.

With water from the cooler, David soaked the tee-shirt he'd used before, and tied it to his head with the bungee cord.

"The Arab headwear is very functional in this heat." Hatch observed.

David walked behind the bush and began to dig out the hole. Hatch watched as David made good progress in the loose soil.

Driven by fury, David soon felt the shovel hit hardpan. "Here it is," he told Hatch, boosting himself out of the hole. He sat on the edge, toweling his face with the loose end of the tee-shirt. "You want to shovel out the loose dirt?" Without waiting for an answer, he got up, walked to the car. His pulse was racing, and his stomach cramped. He opened an icy bottle of water, drank some, and then poured the rest over his head. The stomach cramps eased.

David walked around the bush. Hatch was kneeling on the edge of the hole, his back to David, lifting spoonfuls of dirt out with the shovel. He sat back on his heels, looking into the hole. "I don't see the box. How big is it?"

Feeling a weird frenzy, David lifted the pick and brought it up over his head. Pulling hard enough to pierce concrete, he buried the point in Hatch's head. It seemed to penetrate only a short distance and bounced as if the point had hit rubber. The square hole in Hatch's head became a fountain of blood. Hatch rolled to his left onto his hands and knees, then, incredibly, he crawled toward David, grunting hoarsely. David watched in horror as Hatch scurried toward him, his bloody eyes accusing if never quite focusing. When David moved out of his path, Hatch didn't change direction. He crawled on toward the road, his blood covered arms beginning to wobble. The hoarse sound stopped, and he slowly rolled onto his left side and lay still.

Still clutching the pick, David stood next to Hatch, ready to hit him again. Seeing no movement, David pushed Hatch with the pick. The body moved easily. Shifting the pick to his left hand, he reached into Hatch's front pocket to get the key to the suitcase. As if he recognized the contact, Hatch's legs jerked. The harsh grunting sound resumed, more horrible than a scream to David.

David hoisted the pick over his head, and drove the point in through Hatch's eye. The legs jerked once, then slowly extended. The color drained out of Hatch's face, descending until it disappeared into the blood covering his head.

David watched the body for some time, the stillness a living thing. The now dry tee-shirt on his head fluttered like a hand ruffling his hair. He whirled to confront the apparition. He was still alone.

He heard a car. Was it out on the highway? The noise faded. Was the sound of the car coming up the hill masked by the hillside? Paralyzed by indecision, he watched the tracks at the top of the hill, not quite trusting his eyes when no car appeared.

He needed to get the gun. He was about to reach into Hatch's pocket when he heard a motorcycle dislodging rocks as it climbed the hill.

CHAPTER 11

▼

February 21, 1997, Friday

Friday morning on the Marina Parkway, the sunrise colored the trees in varying shades of brilliant green. The Santa Ana wind off the mountains had scrubbed the air clean and lowered the temperature into the forties. As Gary started into the second lap of his morning run, the deep division between shadow and light cleansed the world of ambiguity. Jank would testify today; the newspapers would pounce on the idea of a clone, and Peter Draper would have to drop the charges. All over in less than two weeks.

*　　　*　　　*　　　*

When court convened that morning, Julie called Mike Jank to the witness box. Dressed in jeans and a blue cotton shirt, Jank seemed at ease as he was sworn. He was attentive and his responses were concise while Julie led him through his identification and job history. That done, she asked, "Mr. Jank, you sold the Desert Eagle autoloader, identified as exhibit one, to a man who identified himself as the defendant, John McBride, is that correct?"

"Yes."

"How did he identify himself?"

"With a driver's license and a Master Card."

"Did you look at the picture on the Driver's license?"

"Yes."

"Were you convinced it was the picture of the man standing at your counter that day?"

"Yes."

"On October 24th of last year, from photos of seven men that Detective Able Mendoza showed you, you picked the picture of John McBride as the man who purchased the gun, is that correct?"

"Yes."

"And on October 26th of last year, from five men in a line-up at the San Diego Police Station, you identified the defendant, John McBride, as the man who purchased the gun?"

"Yes."

"Did you have any misgivings about the identification?"

"No, I felt certain it was the same man."

Gary watched the jurors. Most seemed placid and uninvolved, but an older man in the front row looked puzzled by those questions coming from the defense.

Julie continued, "And a week ago, on February 13th, more than six months after the gun was purchased, were you still certain that John McBride was the buyer?"

"Yes."

The juror stopped frowning, his eyes locked on Jank.

"On February 14th, last Friday, did you receive and watch a video tape of the interrogation of the defendant, John McBride, by two San Diego police detectives?"

"Yes, I did."

"Did watching that tape confirm your belief that the defendant, John McBride, was the man who purchased the gun?"

"No, I realized that he was not the man who bought the gun."

Julie moved to the defense table and shuffled through some papers. Jank had tossed a bomb into the center of the jury box, and Julie let them stare at it for awhile.

When she moved back to the podium, she asked, "Mr. Jank, if you look at John McBride now, are you positive he did not purchase the gun labeled exhibit one?"

Mac sat slightly forward in his chair, his hands under the table, his mouth closed.

Jank looked at Mac for a moment before he said, "No."

"Are you saying that now, John McBride looks like the man who purchased the gun?"

"Yes."

The courtroom was silent as Julie moved back to the desk and toyed with some papers. When she returned to the podium, she asked, "What would the defendant have to do before you could tell he was not the man who purchased the murder weapon?"

"Open his mouth; talk, or show me his hands."

Mac put his hands on top of the table. Julie asked Jank, "Can you now say positively that the defendant is not the man who bought the gun from you?"

"Yes. The man who bought the gun from me had smooth joints in his hands." From across the room, the jurors could see Mac's claw-like hands.

Julie asked, "The gun was purchased over six months ago. Why would you remember the purchaser's hands?"

"I want a potential buyer to feel comfortable with me, so I watch for nervous habits."

"Objection, conclusion." Draper said. He remained seated and spoke in a bored voice. "The witness is not an established expert in human body language."

Julie waved her hand, dismissing Draper's objection. "Your honor, Mr. Jank's accuracy in his interpretation of a buyer's body language is not the issue. We are simply establishing Mr. Jank's reason for observing a buyer carefully."

"Overruled."

Julie faced Jank. "Please continue. Why would you remember the buyer's hands?"

"As I said, I look for nervous habits. The man who bought the gun from me constantly toyed with a large steel ring."

From the defense desk, Julie picked up a poster board perhaps 18 inches square, and carried it to an easel against the courtroom wall to the jury's left. In the witness box, Jank had to turn to see it. The drawing of a polished metal, featureless, man's ring was colored a blue-tinted silver. Topped by a large flat surface, the ring tapered into a narrow band.

Everyone in the courtroom had a chance to examine the drawing while Julie threaded her way back to the podium. She consulted a paper there before she asked, "Does this drawing resemble the ring the buyer wore?"

"Yes."

"What did he do with the ring?"

"He spun it on his finger, using his thumb." Jank held up his hand and spun his wedding band around on his finger. "Like this."

"So for reasons which you thought were important to making the sale, you watched his hand because you believed that he spun the ring faster or slower depending on how comfortable he was."

"Yes."

"And that's why you're sure the man had no obvious indication of arthritis, as Mr. McBride does. Is that correct?"

"Yes."

"During the line-up at the San Diego Police Department, could you see Mr. McBride's hands?"

"I don't remember if I could or not. I didn't look at his hands."

"Why not?"

"I took one look at his face, and turned around to tell the Detective which one was the man who bought the gun. He asked me to look again, which I did. There was no question in my mind, so I repeated what I'd said."

"Did the detectives ask the defendant, John McBride, to speak?"

"I didn't give them time to do anything. I'd had a rough commute down to San Diego, and it was late. The detectives weren't in a good mood, and neither was I. On the way into the line-up, Steve Bacha hinted that the guy I had picked out of the photo line-up was the wrong man. So when John McBride walked into the line-up area, I turned around and told Mr. Bacha that he was the gun buyer. He looked irritated, and he told me to take another look. I did and I repeated what I'd said. When he argued that the line-up hadn't started yet, I got mad. I told him that John McBride was the same man who bought the gun, and if he didn't want to hear it, he shouldn't call me to testify. Then I walked out and drove back to LA." He looked at his hands as he said, "It was my fault. I should have been more patient."

"When you did hear the defendant, John McBride, speak on that tape you saw last week, what was different from what you expected?"

"John McBride has all his front teeth, and his voice is deep and quite distinctive."

Julie rummaged on the defense desk, picked up a poster board and made her way to the easel. It was the photograph of John McBride that had been modified by the police artist. When Julie returned to the podium, she asked, "Does this retouched photo show what you expected to see?"

"Yes."

"Was the distinctive gap between his existing teeth visible when the man talked?"

"Not always, but his teeth were visible when he smiled. I tell jokes to put buyers at ease, and he was so nervous, I told him a bunch of jokes. He smiled a lot."

"Were there any other differences between the defendant, John McBride, and the man who purchased the gun?"

Jank said, "On the tape, John McBride seemed confident, and he used simple, direct language. The man who bought the gun seemed timid, and he spoke like a college professor. For example, he said the engraving on another gun was, 'a delicate filigree for so ferocious a weapon.' For someone with missing teeth, the language seemed strange."

Julie consulted her notes. "The gun was purchased from you on August third of last year, and the buyer picked it up on August tenth. That's more than six months ago. How many customers have you met in that time?"

"I'll see maybe 100 people a week. In 26 weeks, it could be a couple of thousand."

"So you've had perhaps two thousand customers in the last six months, yet you can describe the ring this man wore, give a police artist a detailed description of the man's teeth, and remember his exact words about the engraving on another gun. How is that possible, Mr. Jank?"

Jank said, "My salary is minimum wage plus 10% commission on sales. The Desert Eagle at our store retailed for $1,050. The manufacturer was running a promotion on that weapon that included a $150 spiff for the salesman, so I stood to make $255 on that sale."

"You referred to a $150 spiff. What does that mean?"

"It's money the manufacturer pays to the salesman for selling a specific product. Spiffs on guns are rare, and no company had ever offered a $150 spiff before."

"So you remember him because the money involved was unusual?"

"Not just that. I spent the waiting period worried that he wouldn't pass the background checks. He seemed so flaky, I felt sure he'd have a criminal record."

"Why did you say that the man seemed flaky?"

"The usual customer for the Desert Eagle is a gun enthusiast. They're knowledgeable, and interested in handling the gun. This man didn't want to touch the gun."

Julie asked, "Was there anything else that made the buyer unusual?"

"Yes. He knew that the gun, bullets, and taxes would come to nearly $1,200, because he pulled that much out of his pocket in a rubber-banded roll. He didn't count it, he just put the roll of bills on the counter. I opened the roll and counted it, but he didn't watch me. He spent the time looking around the store."

"So, unlike your usual buyer, he seemed disinterested in both the gun and the money he paid for it. Is that correct?"

"Yeah. I assumed he was buying it for someone else."

"Objection." Draper managed to summon some anger. "Speculation."

"Sustained. The jurors will disregard that statement."

"To restate my question, the buyer was unusual because he was disinterested in both the gun and the money, his appearance and his language seemed strange, and his behavior suggested that he was not at ease. Is all that correct?"

"Yes."

"And for you personally, a significant amount of money was at stake, and you worried about the buyer's ability to pass the background checks? Is that correct?"

"Yes."

She said, "No further questions."

Sitting behind his table, slouched in his chair, Draper asked Jank, "Two months after you sold the gun, you picked John McBride out of a live line-up. Is that correct?"

"Yes."

"And you continued to believe John McBride bought that gun for a full six months after you last saw the buyer. Is that correct?"

"Yes."

"And in those six months, you've said you may have seen as many as two thousand customers, is that correct?"

"Yes."

Draper got up, took both poster boards off the easel, and returned them to Julie at the defense desk. At the prosecution desk, he consulted a paper before he moved behind the podium to ask, "Now I know that salesmen often remember customers by the purchase they make. For example, you may remember a person as a handgun buyer even though you don't remember anything else about him. Has that happened to you?"

"Yes, all the time."

"Have you ever had occasion to recall anything else about a buyer, some physical detail perhaps, that turned out to be wrong?"

"Yes."

"Can you describe one such incident?"

"We get people in who use salesmen for their personal puppets. They have a million questions. They'll ask to see every gun in the case, anything to keep the salesman hopping. A man who does that regularly came in a couple of weeks ago, or so I thought. He had a hook nose, bushy mustache, and heavy rimmed glasses. I treated him badly and then realized that it wasn't the same man."

"So you certainly don't claim to be infallible about recognizing people."

"No."

"The Desert Eagle isn't the most expensive gun you sell, is it?"

"No, several rifles cost more."

"Have you had buyers of those guns that you thought might not pass the background checks?"

"Yes."

"Were any of them missing their front teeth?"

"Yes."

"Then let me pose a hypothetical question. Suppose sometime after you saw the person who purchased the Desert Eagle, you had a handgun buyer who had missing front teeth, spoke like a college professor, and had a large steel ring that he twirled on his finger. Could it be possible that your mind merged those characteristics into your memory of the Desert Eagle buyer?"

"No."

"How can you be sure? You could have merged those two individuals in your mind six months ago. You believed that those two individuals were the same because you saw nothing that would persuade you otherwise. You reacted to the tape of John McBride as anyone would who was worried about identifying the wrong man. You didn't want it to be John McBride, and it wasn't. I ask you, Mr. Jank, is that scenario impossible?"

"Yes. Mr. McBride was not the buyer."

"You've said that with his mouth closed and his hands hidden, you can't distinguish Mr. McBride from the buyer. Mr. McBride has a very distinctive face, and you're saying that another individual looks exactly like him. Have you ever seen two unrelated people who look exactly alike?"

"No. That's why I identified him."

"I'd like you to take a little test for me, Mr. Jank."

As Draper picked up a page of photos, Julie was on her feet, objecting. She told the judge that Michael Jank had not testified that he was adept at recognizing faces, only that he had recognized that John McBride's face and the gun buyer's face were similar. The judge overruled her argument, saying the prosecution had the right to test the witness's ability to discern faces. She then objected to the test Draper intended to use. When that argument was overruled, she asked if the jury was supposed to believe that Mr. Jank couldn't recognize anyone if he missed them all? Would the judge, in his instructions to the jury, specify that the test only had relevance to incidental contact? That the test had no relevance to, say, lovers? Or to important financial transactions? That emotional content was the best determinant as to whether one person remembered another? She argued the point until Judge Lucero lost patience. "That's quite enough, Ms. Williams. I have ruled that I will allow this test."

Draper walked to the witness box and handed Jank the sheet of 20 photos, saying, "Look these over for two minutes. After that time, I'll show you another group of photos, and I'll ask you to identify the people you've seen before."

While Jank studied the photos, Gary remembered seeing Julie giving Jank the test the night before. Did she know that Jank would fail the test?

At the end of the two minutes, Draper took back the original photos and handed Jank another sheet. "Now, Mr. Jank, would you tell us which faces were on the first sheet?"

In seconds, Jank handed the sheet back, saying, "Numbers 11, 13, and 18 are the only faces that were on the first sheet."

Draper's stricken look as he turned back toward the prosecution table was clear to everyone in the gallery, and most exploded into laughter. Julie had known how good Jank was, she had argued to interest the jury in the outcome. Gary joined the laughter, admiring the little lady who was good at fighting dirty.

Draper said, "No more questions."

Julie paused for a moment, evidently waiting for absolute silence in the court-room. Then, her voice loud in the silence, she said, "Your Honor, I request the entry of a judgment of acquittal for insufficient evidence. The evidence applying to possession of the murder weapon by John McBride is now known to be the result of a conspiracy, by person or persons unknown, to convict John McBride of a crime he did not commit. In that this evidence was the result of a conspiracy, all the evidence pointing to John McBride's guilt must also be considered tainted by that conspiracy."

CHAPTER 12

▼

September 16, 1996, Monday, five months earlier

David was in the suburbs of El Centro when the shaking started. His index finger quivered, and he took his right hand off the steering wheel to flex it. It seemed all of his fingers were vibrating, his thumb jerking as if seeking some object to curl around. As the car entered a gentle turn, his left hand nearly lost its grip on the wheel, and he had to use his right hand to stay in the turn. When the road straightened, he clasped his hands together with the fingers intertwined, trying to recover their strength. His arms felt unequal to the task.

He knew about stress. As a child, he'd learned to cope with it by exercising. Spotting a small strip mall, he drove in and parked the car. He walked into the residential area north of the mall, intending to hike a mile or so to work off the adrenaline.

Soon, the sidewalk disappeared. At four in the afternoon, El Centro was a furnace, and the black asphalt seared his feet. He felt sick to his stomach as the oil smell from the road mixed with another odor that reminded him of a paper mill. His black hair concentrated the sun's heat on his head. He felt faint when he reversed direction. The strip mall was a speck in the distance, maybe two miles away.

He couldn't afford a heat stroke. The cops would search his car and find a suitcase full of clothes that were not his; a gun, a blood spattered pick and dirty shovel. If the dirt had some unique ratio of elements, they might be able to pinpoint where he buried Hatch.

At a house, he saw a water hose wrapped on a green reel. He staggered toward it, feeling faint. The hose had a triggered spray nozzle. He held the nozzle over his head and squeezed the lever. Very hot water saturated his hair.

The shock cleared his head. He held the trigger until the water was cool, then he soaked himself until he shivered. Dripping, he resumed the walk to his car, his mind clear for the first time since he'd killed Hatch.

He remembered kneeling next to Hatch's body, feeling for the suitcase key. When he heard the motorcycle's rear tire spitting rocks as it climbed the slope, he had grabbed Hatch's feet in panic and pulled him away from the road. At the hole, the body dropped in, head first, but the feet remained above ground level. He heard the motorcycle crest the hill, the engine suddenly dropping to a burbling idle. Standing on the back of Hatch's thighs, he frantically shoveled dirt into the hole.

He heard the motorcycle start down the hill, the engine revving under compression. Trying to look like he'd gone behind the bush to relieve himself, David moved to the road buttoning his pants, sliding his feet to cover the blood trail. The road was empty. The motorcycle had returned to the highway.

Was it possible the rider had seen him bury Hatch? He might be rushing to summon the authorities. Sick with the need to flee, he shoveled the rest of the loose dirt over Hatch's body, and then stamped it down. He tossed the shovel and pick into the trunk and then drove toward the highway, managing to be careful on the steep descent. Once on the highway, he fought the urge to stand on the accelerator and crept along at five miles an hour over the speed limit.

At the California inspection station, he found enough control to use the brake instead of mashing the accelerator to the floor. The inspector asked where he was coming from. He had looked at her as if he might be interested, and said "Yuma. You live there?" The lady inspector had given him a sour look and waved him on.

Now, as he approached his car, a California Highway Patrol car drove into the lot. The patrolman watched David. He did look like shit, his clothes muddy and damp. He got in the car, backed carefully, and then drove onto Interstate Eight and headed west.

A few miles later, the freeway passed over a road that seemed to be the north-south route from nowhere to nothing. He took the off-ramp, and then parked beneath the Interstate. He took the steel suitcase out of the trunk, propped it up on the asphalt, and then hit the lock with the pick. The suitcase dented but didn't open. He hit it again, and the suitcase popped open, just as the Highway Patrolman he'd seen at the mall stopped several feet behind his car. The cop got out of his car, putting his hat on, not in any hurry. The open suitcase had spilled some of Hatch's clothes, but David couldn't see the gun. He tried to look unhurried as he tossed the blood spattered pick into the trunk of the car.

The cop had his hand on the butt of his holstered gun. "Keep both hands where I can see them. Walk out here and lean against the car so I can check for weapons."

David did that. The cop patted him down, then pulled the wallet out of his back pocket and handed it to him. "Remove your driver's license for me."

David pulled his license out, keeping up a running banter about the suitcase from hell. "I lost the key to that thing five months ago on a flight back from Dallas. I've had it in the trunk that long. So I'm driving along just now, and it dawns on me that I've spent more aggravation trying to open it than the damn thing's worth."

The officer radioed David's license number and the car's license.

David continued, "So I figured I'd be out of sight under the bridge here, and I'd bash it open with the pick."

The dispatcher confirmed David's identity and car ownership.

The patrolman opened the back door of his car. "Mr. Kendall, you sit in here while I look at your car. Do I have your permission to look inside?"

Trying to look unconcerned, David said, "Sure."

He waited, his body tensed, knowing his life was ending as the man walked toward the car and the suitcase. He would find the gun; the gun's registration would be checked, Mac would deny buying a gun, the purchase would be examined, and they would discover his relationship with the missing Ralph Hatch.

The cop stopped at the suitcase, and picked up clothes with the end of a pencil, moving them around. Hatch had evidently packed everything he owned, the pile of clothes seemed to be growing. David's heart sank as the cop put on vinyl gloves, then, lifting some of the clothes with his left hand, he probed the bottom of the suitcase.

David finally took a breath as the cop stood up, closed the lid of the suitcase, and then, with a glance at the patrol car, he walked to the Toyota. He lifted David's suitcase out of the trunk, and went through that. Then he took both the pick and shovel out and put them on the ground, then lifted the spare tire cover. He took out the tire, bounced it twice on the pavement, then set that aside. He tapped the trunk walls with his hand, then used a penlight to look into the openings of the trunk lid. Then he moved to the inside of the car, and looked under the seats, then felt up under the dashboard. His search for drugs was thorough, and welcome.

The cop left the Toyota's back seat in the road when he finished. He opened the back door of the patrol car, handed David's license back, and said, "If you're going to assault any other possessions, do it in your own backyard."

David laughed before he walked to his car on shaking legs. He had picked up the back seat when the cop drove around him and made the left turn to go east on the interstate.

Leaving the back seat unsecured, David lifted Hatch's suitcase and dumped it into the trunk. The gun was against the left side, wrapped in a tee shirt. Thank God the cop lifted the clothes from the right side. Leaving it wrapped, David put it under the rear seat, and then secured the seat.

An hour later, as David approached Pine Valley, he saw a large green dumpster behind a grocery store. He left the freeway and parked next to the dumpster. Minutes later, he was back on the freeway, the shovel, pick, and suitcase safely discarded.

He was in El Cajon when he realized that his fingerprints were on the steel suitcase. He should have wiped the suitcase clean, and put the pick in a different dumpster. Suppose someone saw the blood on the pick?

When he got home, he parked in the garage, and then walked into the bathroom. As he took off his clothes, he was amazed at the blood on his white T-shirt. When he held his outer shirt up, he could see the blots on the dark blue shirt. His jeans were stained in the same pattern, and three drops of blood were visible on his shorts. Mixed with the mud, the blood spots hadn't been noticeable.

He emptied the pockets, and then tied his clothes in an old towel. Feeling the threat, he rushed his shower, taking care to scrub his fingernails with the stiff brush. As he toweled off, he walked into the bedroom to get clean clothes. In the darkness of the room, he was startled by a large shape on the end of his bed, bulky in the middle like Hatch. His heart lurched. He strode to the window and raised the shade. A stack of pillows seemed to mock him. He had stacked them while he washed the sheets that morning.

He hurriedly dressed, then took the bundled clothes to his car. With the clothes in the trunk, he drove to a marina near Seaworld, and put the bundle in a trash can.

He returned to the house. Fighting the urge to collapse on the unmade bed, he dragged his heavy body down the hall to the laundry room. His sheets were on the dryer in the laundry basket. Mary used to iron his sheets, but now, she wouldn't even fold them.

He made the bed; found enough energy to hang up his clothes and brush his teeth, then went to bed. His stomach made complaining noises. He hadn't eaten since morning, a thousand years ago. The day replayed itself in vivid detail. As he visualized the blood spattered pick dropping into the dumpster, he wondered if a lab technician somewhere was analyzing the evidence that would kill him?

*   *   *   *

The skinny coyote, his head up, loped down the road. Near the bush, he suddenly froze, his nose sniffing and blowing at the dirt. He followed the scent around the bush. At the disturbed square of earth, he sniffed for a moment, and then began to dig.

The pounding at the door became insistent. David opened it. Two cops were on the front porch, and several police cars were parked in front of the house, lights revolving. The nearest cop, a huge man whose beefy arms strained his short-sleeved shirt, grabbed David's hand and turned him around. As David felt the steel encircle his wrists, the cop said, "David Kendall, you are under arrest for the murder of Ralph Hatch."

David said, "The old bastard was a liar and a bum," trying to make them understand that Ralph deserved what happened to him. The cop laughed.

The knocking came again and David woke with a start. Frank called, "David…, David." Knowing that Frank was standing there with two cops, David struggled out of bed and opened the door.

Frank was alone, in his bathrobe. "Are you going into the shop today?"

"I'm just documenting the system. I don't need to be there."

"I'm going to take the car to get it serviced," Frank said. "I need a ride back."

"Sure. I'll be ready in a few minutes."

"Take your time. I won't leave for half an hour."

*   *   *   *

That afternoon, to keep from thinking about the evidence that was waiting to bite him, David searched the Internet for anomalies in murder cases. He needed some way to tie Mac to physical evidence of Frank's murder.

Nearly three hours later, he found the answer. Where blood evidence was concerned, the killer was the variable. When the police found blood evidence away from the crime scene, they created theories about how the blood had gotten there. All he had to do was to get some of Frank's blood on Mac's car, and the police would generate an explanation.

David estimated that to drive to Chula Vista from Colson's Cavern, spray the blood on Mac's car, drive to back to Clairemont and park, then change clothes and jog to the house, would take about 65 minutes. Adding time to shower, he wouldn't be ready to meet the cops at the door for an hour and twenty minutes after the killing.

He went back to the Internet, looking through dozens of cases. In nearly every murder, it took more than two hours to notify the relatives. The cops secured the crime scene, and took statements from witnesses, and then, when additional manpower became available, they sent someone to inform the relatives. He should have the time he needed.

*   *   *   *

The next morning, he walked to the Hyatt and took their shuttle to the long-term lot at Lindbergh Field where he had parked the Taurus. In his tote bag, he carried a 12 volt coil designed to heat coffee in a car, a small soup thermos, a thermometer, a rubber bulb, a bottle of syrup, and two bottles of water. He drove the Taurus to a spot near Colson's Cavern, boiled water inside the thermos with the coil, and then put the syrup-filled bulb in the water, its spout resting on the lip of the squat thermos. Then he drove to Chula Vista and parked around the corner from Mac's house. The syrup was at 105 degrees. On the night of the murder, the blood would cool as he walked the block to Mac's house.

He drove to National City. In the rear parking lot of an abandoned building, he sprayed hot syrup on the Taurus. No matter where he held the bulb, drops of the warmed syrup landed on the ground. If the police found any drops on Mac's driveway, they would know the blood had been sprayed there. He could use newspaper to catch the over spray, but Chula Vista was often windy, especially in the evenings. Cloth wouldn't work, the blood would soak through.

On his fourth try, he put on the long coat he intended to wear during the shooting, lay on his back beside the car and wedged his body tight against the rocker panel. With the bulb above his chest, he sprayed the side of the car with syrup. The over spray landed on him. He timed the drips off the side of the car. The last one fell three minutes later.

That problem solved, he drove Mac's usual route through Chula Vista, looking for a place to dump the gun. He needed a spot where an adult would find the gun. If kids found it, they'd probably sell it. Once the gun passed through a few hands, it could disappear.

He saw an older home with its front lawn on top of a retaining wall, out of sight from the sidewalk. He noted the address, then drove the Taurus back to the long term parking lot.

When he returned to his parent's house, he used an Internet street directory to look up the phone number at the house. He called, pretending to be taking a survey. He asked for the ages of any children who lived in the house. No children lived there. Good.

David searched for the holes in his plan. It would be better if he could smear some blood inside of Mac's car, but Mac always locked his car and set the alarm. The blood on the door would have to do.

*   *   *   *

The next Tuesday, September 24, David sat in the back seat of the Taurus across the street from Colson's Cavern, his head resting on a large, dark blue pillow placed against the passenger side rear window. The long coat was too warm; the high-top hiking boots suffocated his feet, and the wool cap pulled over his forehead and ears made his scalp itch. While he watched the restaurant's parking lot, David carefully covered his face with petroleum jelly. He unbuttoned the high necked pullover shirt, and spread the jelly on his neck, then buttoned the shirt.

He checked his watch: ten to nine. He leaned forward to look for people near the car, then reached under the front seat and pulled out the cloth wrapped gun. He unwrapped it and wiped the greasy jelly off his fingers with the cloth. Using the cloth to hold the gun, he slid the action back until he could see the bullet in the chamber. He closed the bolt, moved the safety to the firing position and put the gun back under the seat.

It was now or never. By next Tuesday, the first of October, he had to be out of the house, and would have no way to swap phones. Frank put his cell phone on charge on the kitchen counter every night. Last night, he'd removed Frank's phone, and substituted an identical phone registered to Dan Rhoades. It had been nicked and scratched to duplicate Frank's phone. No one had been able to call Frank during the day, but he usually turned off his phone when he was talking to customers, and often forgot to turn it on afterwards.

In the moment before he shot Frank, he would exchange the phones. The police would check the calls to Frank's cell phone, and there would be none.

David would use his modified cordless phone to call Frank back. He had bought the illegal phone in Mexico years before, and used it often to make long distance calls. Unlike the newer phones with security codes, old cordless phone bases usually accepted his phone. Thanks to the number of seniors living in the apartment building near Colson's Cavern, the phone found three unprotected base units.

His pulse quickened as the restaurant's door opened. Mac walked out and held the door. David went numb as another man walked out. From two hundred feet away, Ned Johnson's barrel shaped body was unmistakable. Ned was a sub-contractor for Framac, and a good friend of Mac's. Frank joined the two men, and while David agonized, the three talked for several minutes. If Ned left first, he could still pull it off. Then Frank clapped Mac on the back and walked to his car. As David's heart sank, Frank pulled out into traffic, leaving Mac and Ned behind.

What the hell was he going to do now?

CHAPTER 13

▼

February 21, 1997, Friday

Judge Lucero said he would hear the arguments for acquittal in chambers, and called a two hour lunch break. In the corridor, Gary talked to Jank for a few minutes and thanked him for volunteering to testify. Twenty minutes after Jank said goodbye, Julie walked up, looking glum. "No go. Draper convinced him that the case against Mac shouldn't be decided on one eyewitness." Her face showed pain. "I have to go tell John. I think I got his hopes up."

That afternoon, Julie called Doctor Jurgen Frieze to the stand, and established his credentials as a blood dispersal expert. A trim man in his sixties, his polished demeanor and way of talking to the jury rather than Julie identified him as an expert for hire.

Using an electronic projector, Dr. Frieze displayed photos on a screen placed between the witness box and the jury. The first photo showed dozens of strings taped to the door of Mac's Taurus. He explained that the size, shape, and angle of blood drops on a surface precisely described where the drop had originated. The strings attached to Mac's door showed that the blood came from a single point source two feet away from the door and one foot off the ground. With a laser pointer, he called the court's attention to the one string under the car. He said that the length of the string showed that drop flew in an arc that just missed the rocker panel. Its origin was the same point source as the blood on the door.

He had done a similar analysis on Frank's Honda, which was covered with blood spatter. The strings showed two large sources, one next to the car at about five feet, the other on the ground quite near the car. Where the drops of blood had run, he had measured the length of the runs. For equal size drops, the runs on the door of Mac's Taurus were longer, indicating that the blood that hit Mac's car stayed liquid longer than the blood that hit Frank's car. Dr. Frieze concluded that the blood had been taken from Frank at the scene, kept too warm while it was being transported, and then sprayed on Mac's Taurus as it sat in his driveway.

Using photographs of the shooting scene, and a drawing with hundreds of small dots showing where blood drops were found, he indicted that a large clean area in the center of the drawing was the shadow of the killer. He noted that a significant amount of blood had landed on the killer's clothes and shoes.

Julie led Dr. Frieze through his conclusions with a quick series of questions. The killer couldn't have been inside John McBride's car without leaving blood evidence. The blood spot on John McBride's driveway proved the blood was sprayed there. When arrested, John McBride had oil and metal on his skin, but no blood, so he could not have been the killer. Julie finished her questioning by thanking Dr. Frieze.

Judge Lucero called a break. His body achy from the long period of sitting, Gary took a fast walk down to the harbor. He returned to the courtroom as Judge Lucero announced Draper's cross examination.

Draper rose looking at a sheet of paper. "Several witnesses have said that the killer was wearing a long coat, gloves, and some sort of knit hat. They couldn't see the killer's face even when he turned toward them, so some think he might have been wearing a ski mask. If we assume Mr. McBride was the shooter, would you be surprised to find that he had no blood on the clothes he wore in the restaurant?"

Dr. Frieze said, "He would have had blood on his shoes."

"Yes, we know that, but would he have had blood on his clothes?"

"Not if you assume he was totally covered."

"We know how the killer was dressed. We have to discover if it was Mr. McBride wearing the gloves, coat, and cap." Draper paused to let the admonishment linger. The silence stretched into an uncomfortable length before he said, "And if the cap was also a ski-mask, would you expect Mr. McBride to have blood on his face and in his hair?"

"No."

"Now the witnesses describe the coat and hat as cloth of some type. If we assume for the moment that the coat and ski mask contained a significant amount of wool fiber, as is normal for those types of garments, would the blood that landed on the killer tend to drop off?"

"Assuming wool, it would probably be absorbed."

Draper paused before he said, "So other than the blood on his shoes, the killer might not leave any traces inside the car."

"The blood would still transfer if the cloth rubbed against another surface."

"But it would have to rub. The blood wouldn't just fall off the garments?"

Dr. Frieze shook his head, looking disgusted. "If you forget about the pools of blood on his shoes, and assume he was careful not to rub against anything, perhaps it would be possible that he wouldn't leave any evidence."

Draper used the projector's remote to sort through Dr. Frieze's pictures, stopping at the picture of John McBride's car with all the strings attached to the door. Draper asked, "You said you duplicated this spray pattern to confirm the height and location of the source of the blood?"

After Dr. Frieze said that he had, Draper asked, "When you duplicated the spray pattern, did only one drop land under the car?"

"No."

"In fact, many drops landed under the car, is that right?"

"Yes."

"Since only one drop was found under the car, what did this person use to catch the over spray?"

With his laser pointer, Dr. Frieze pointed at a metal ridge running under the rocker panel. "I would guess some rigid material four feet long and at least three feet wide." Just under the pillar between the front and back doors, the metal ridge disappeared for about an inch. "The drop of blood that landed under the car went through this indentation."

"So this hypothetical person carried a large piece of cardboard, let us say, and the blood in whatever device he used to keep it warm, set the cardboard against the car, sprayed the blood, then waited for it to drip off. Does that accurately summarize your hypothesis?"

"Yes."

"So, to recap the timing, the killer shoots Frank Kendall at 9:33, sucks blood out of the wound, gets in his car and leaves at approximately 9:34. The trip to Mr. McBride's house averages 27 minutes depending on stoplights, so the killer is at Mr. McBride's house by 10:01 if he has average luck with the stoplights. Now you've said he had to wait several minutes for the last of the runs to drop off the door, so at 10:04, we have the killer beside Mr. McBride's car in the driveway holding a large section of cardboard in place. But at 10:04, Police officer Wilson shines his spotlight on Mr. McBride's car to read the plate, and no one is beside the car at that time. And the other Taurus, the one your hypothetical killer supposedly drove, is not in sight. So now we have to say that this hypothetical killer must have parked it around the corner where Officer Wilson couldn't have seen it, so his arrival time at the house would have been a minute or so later. To be gone by 10:04, given a minute to get out of the area before officer Wilson arrived, and three minutes to catch the blood that dripped off the door, the hypothetical killer would have had to arrive at 9:59, making his trip from the scene of the shooting just 25 minutes. He would have had to have better than average luck with the stoplights to do that. But Mr. McBride said he didn't arrive home until after ten, which presents a problem since your hypothetical killer would have had to be set up and spraying by ten. Considering those time restrictions, do you still see your scenario as reasonable?"

"I can't see any other way to explain the blood on the side of Mr. McBride's car."

Draper looked at a paper before he asked, "The blood on the door was DNA matched to Frank Kendall. Why wasn't the drop on the driveway matched to him?"

"It landed on vegetable matter that had attracted ants. There was DNA matter from several sources that masked the blood DNA."

"What about the age of the drop? Where is the report showing that the drop was sprayed at the same time as the drops on the door?"

"Again, the vegetable matter and other contaminates deposited by the ants masked the test results."

Draper looked at a paper on the podium for a time before he said, "You assume that the killer sucked blood from a wound, kept it warm while he drove to John McBride's house in record time, sprayed it while the car sat in the driveway, albeit several minutes before John McBride said he got home, and then managed to leave without the police officer seeing him. The proof of that scenario is based on that single drop of blood found underneath the car. Is that correct?"

"Well, the impact shape shows..."

"Yes or No, Dr. Frieze. You claim that the spraying occurred in John McBride's driveway because of the single drop of blood found underneath the car. Is that correct?"

"Yes."

"But you don't know who that drop of blood came from, or when it was deposited. Is that correct?"

"It isn't that..."

"Yes or No, Doctor. Can you prove that drop of blood came from Frank Kendall?"

"No."

"Yes or No, Doctor. Do you know when that drop of blood landed on the driveway?"

"No."

"So the entire shaky scenario you've built is based on a drop of blood that could have been there for days, and can't even be identified as Frank Kendall's blood. Is that correct?"

"It was primarily based on the impact shape."

"If you assume the car wasn't there when that drop was deposited; if you assume a person standing on the empty driveway might have been shaking a cut finger, could there be several paths that drop might have taken."

"Yes."

"So there is no absolute evidence that the killer sprayed blood on the side of the car while it sat in John McBride's driveway, is there?"

"There is no absolute evidence."

Draper then shuffled through the pictures until he had the drawing showing the blood distribution in the parking lot of Colson's Cavern. He had Dr. Frieze show on the drawing how he came to the conclusion that a great quantity of blood had landed on the killer's shoes. When he finished, Draper asked, "Now, is it possible that Mr. McBride..., ah, excuse me, the killer, as he's walking toward his car, notices this pool on his shoe, and kicks it off, like so?" Draper kicked his leg out, as if trying to dislodge liquid from the top of his shoe.

"Objection: conjecture." Julie's voice penetrated the silence like a knife.

"Sustained."

"Assuming the killer did try to flick blood off his shoe, that would be consistent with a point source about a foot and a half off the ground, would it not?"

"I can't answer that without doing several experiments. It's highly unlikely that the patterns would be similar."

"Oh, yes, you think it's more likely that we have a killer who sucks the blood out of a wound in front of twenty witnesses who don't recall seeing the killer touch the body, transports it twelve miles in a warm bath, gets incredibly lucky with the stoplights so he arrives in record time, sets up some elaborate arrangement to catch the over spray, sprays it and waits to catch the drops of blood that drip off the door, and manages to do all that in the three minutes between the time Mr. McBride said he got home, and the arrival of the Chula Vista police officer. Did I state your case accurately?"

Julie was on her feet. "Objection, argumentative."

Draper said, "Withdrawn."

Using the remote on the podium, Draper cycled through the drawings and photos until he had the picture of the blood runs on the door of Mac's car. He used the laser pointer to indicate one long blood run. "Referring to this run, how long would you say it took for the last of the blood to drip off?"

"The blood didn't drip from that run."

Draper overacted surprise. "There's no blood droplet at the end. What happened?"

"The droplet was removed after it dried."

"Removed? According to the detectives, no one touched the car until after the photos were taken. Are you suggesting someone took it off?"

"It was removed, that's all I can say."

"Could it have been removed by the wind as the car was driven to Mr. McBride's house from the shooting scene?"

"I don't know how it was removed," Dr. Frieze insisted.

"Well, Doctor, you have now said that the single drop of blood under the car, which you previously said proved that the blood was sprayed in Mr. McBride's driveway, could have been deposited by anyone. You've said it could have been deposited in the days before Frank Kendall was shot. You've said a blood run on the door of the car was removed, possibly by the wind as the car was driven away from the shooting site. You've said it's possible that the killer drove the car without leaving blood evidence inside. Has your testimony been nothing but an inept attempt to sow doubt in the juror's minds?"

Julie voiced an objection. Judge Lucero said, "Speeches belong in closing, Mr. Draper. Do you have another question for the witness?"

"No, I'm finished with this expert." He broke the word into two parts, making ex-pert sound like an obscenity.

On rebuttal, Julie led Dr. Frieze through a recap of his earlier testimony. Even so, Gary thought Draper had won that round.

After Dr. Frieze was dismissed, Julie called a succession of witnesses to testify about the bond between Frank Kendall and John McBride. In his cross examination of each witness, Draper focused on the day of the murder. All the witnesses reluctantly agreed that the tensions in the plant had run high that day, that John McBride had been heard yelling at Frank that morning.

The Judge called an end to the day at 5:20 that afternoon. The trial would resume Monday, February 24th.

*   *   *   *

That evening while they ate the meatloaf and cottage fried potatoes Mac had prepared, Gary kept his opinion to himself until Mac asked if something was bothering him. Gary unloaded. "Julie made a rookie mistake. Juries are emotional animals. They aren't looking for facts, they're looking for smoke. Julie created not only smoke, she got fire out of Jank, she had the entire jury in her hand. Jank should have been her last witness. Her blood expert only braided a rope for Draper to use on him. Then she let people testify who would agree with Draper that you'd been angry with Frank that day. The jury is going to spend all weekend thinking about the points Draper scored today. By Monday, they'll have forgotten what Jank said."

Mac shoved a potato around with his fork. "Have to see how it goes."

CHAPTER 14

▼

October 22, 1996, Tuesday, four months earlier

For the fifth consecutive Tuesday, David parked across the street from Colson's Cavern. In spite of his best efforts, his father was in the restaurant eating dinner with Mac.

David had wangled another month at home by 'overlooking' the need to document the diagnostic module in the software, but he'd finished that last Friday. Yesterday, his dad had paid him the full $25,000, ignoring the $3500 Framac had paid for hardware. David had promised he would be out of their house by November first at the latest. After tonight, he would be home to exchange the cell phones on the 29th, but that was it. It was scant consolation that he would have one more chance after tonight, given all that had gone wrong.

On October first, everything looked good. Then, just before Frank and Mac came out of the restaurant, two couples had decided to chat in the parking lot. They continued their conversation until Frank had gone.

The next week, a fire truck had pulled up beside David's car, blocking his view of the restaurant. He wasn't all that concerned until two cop cars and an ambulance came screaming up. While David hid on the floor of the Taurus, they went into the apartment building and stayed for almost an hour. When the fire truck pulled away, both Frank and Mac were gone.

Last week on the 15th, things looked perfect. When both men had driven away, he had picked up the modified cordless to call Frank back. The phone didn't work. He had left it on the previous week, and the battery was dead.

Tonight, things didn't look good either. An asshole in a long black coat was wandering around the restaurant's parking lot, looking into cars. With maybe 400 senior citizens in the apartment building who could see the guy, one was bound to call the cops. The man looked into the motor home parked near the back. What the hell did he think he could see through mirrored windows at night?

David looked at his watch. Almost nine. Frank and Mac usually left about nine. Willing to try anything, David turned on the key and lowered the rear window on the driver's side. He waited for a pause in the traffic, and then yelled, "Get out of there." The idiot whirled around, looked for the voice, and then ran out of the lot. Once on the sidewalk, he stopped for another look, and then walked rapidly west on University Avenue.

A few minutes later, Frank and Mac came out, and they walked to Frank's car. Mac laughed as Frank pulled away. Mac went to his own car, and took his sweet time backing out.

When Mac's tail lights were a block away, David drove into the restaurant's parking lot and parked so that the Taurus straddled two spaces. He pressed the TALK button on his cordless phone. The dial tone was strong. He entered Dan Rhoades' number. He didn't hear a ring, but Frank answered, "Yes?"

"Dad, it's David. I've had car trouble. I made it to Colson's Cavern thinking I'd catch you and get a ride home. Any chance you could come back and give me a lift?"

"Of course. I'm in Mission Valley, so it will take a few minutes."

"Thanks, Dad."

David disconnected. Going through a mental check list, he put the 12 volt coil into the water in the thermos and plugged it in. Methodically, he covered his face with a thick layer of petroleum jelly. When the water boiled, he disconnected the 12 volt coil and continued to work the jelly into his ears, nostrils and eyelids. Dressed in triple layers, he felt too warm, but he shivered.

He loosened the belt on his pants and slid the gun into the waistband. With the gun against his left side, he buttoned the long coat, leaving a single button undone just above his waist. He released the trunk lid and got out of the car. He put the cordless phone in the trunk, and then taped the fake license plate over the existing plate. He shut the trunk and got back into the car.

A moment later, headlights flashed in the trees behind the parking lot as Frank's Honda negotiated the driveway. David got out of the car. As his father drove up, the expression on his face changed to a look of horror. He pulled into the next parking stall, and was out of the car in a rush. His hands on David's shoulders, he asked, "What happened to your face? Are you all right?"

No need for pretense. David took Frank's arm and walked him backwards until he was against the front fender of the Honda. He reached inside Frank's jacket and retrieved the cell phone registered to Dan Rhoades. He replaced it with Frank's cell phone, then stepped back and pulled the gun. He aimed it at his father's face.

Frank looked disappointed. He said, "This is really dumb."

Wanting to erase that look, David pulled the trigger.

The sound numbed his head. In the strobe-like flash, Frank slammed into the Honda. He bounced off the car, half rolled, and ended up face down on the pavement. David fired again and Frank's head collapsed into an oblong shape. Shifting the gun to his left hand, David reached into his coat pocket, grabbed the rubber bulb, squeezed it flat, and pushed the nozzle into a crevice in Frank's hair until it touched something spongy. When he released the pressure, the bulb warmed his hand.

Moving in slow motion, David, keeping his knees bent, hobbled to the Taurus. He opened the door, got in, put the rubber bulb into the thermos, started the car, and backed out in a series of small jumps. Aware that the restaurant door was open, he drove through the lot slowly, then braked to let a speeding car pass. He turned west on University Avenue and accelerated. In two blocks, he turned left, then left again three blocks later, and drove east toward the freeway at twenty five miles an hour. A block before the on-ramp for southbound 805, he stopped, removed the fake license plate and dumped it into the back seat. He drove to the freeway and took the southbound on-ramp.

Unlike the aggressive daytime commuters, the nighttime drivers were erratic. Cars were going 80 in the slow lane, and one was plodding along at 50 in the fast lane. David settled into the flow and exhaled, wondering how long he'd been holding his breath.

He recalled in vivid detail how the body bounced off the Honda, like some giant had tried to drive Frank's head through the metal. With that memory came the realization that his father no longer existed, and that he, David Kendall, had crossed into a new world. Everyone, including the police, would know that he had murdered his father. Whatever the evidence, no one would believe that Mac would kill Frank.

What had he been thinking, killing the man a week before he was to be evicted? Christ, how stupid could he be? What were Frank's last words? 'This is really dumb,' or something like that? Why hadn't he seen the obvious?

He should keep driving south, go into Mexico and drive until his money gave out. When the car quit running, he'd keep going on foot, screaming, feeling them all closing in. He shook inside, as if his nerves were trying to burst through his skin.

As he passed under a freeway light, he noticed spots on his nose. He touched one with his gloved index finger, feeling grit. He looked at the small lump on the glove, wondering how he had gotten dirt on his face. The lights from a trailing car illuminated the red lump. He hurriedly flicked it away, knowing it was a bit of Frank's skull. He could see other dots on his nose, on his cheeks, in his eyelashes. He grabbed the rag that had been around the gun, and almost wiped his face, remembering at the last instant that the rag had to be littered with gun powder. The petroleum jelly on his face was holding the debris away from his skin. Without that coating, he was a dead man.

The close call cleared his head. It didn't matter what anyone knew, it only mattered what they could prove. He had planned this well. That was what he had to remember. He would survive if he just kept to the plan. The bureaucracy of the justice system would pay no attention to what people believed. It would only pay attention to facts. He was going to give them facts.

One thing at a time, he reminded himself. Watch for the connector to Interstate Five. Drop back from the car ahead. Don't follow too close.

He thought about Judy Armbruster, a cute brunette he'd seduced in the tenth grade. She had been a virgin, and on the next date, she had talked marriage, evidently believing that the first was supposed to be the only. When David made it plain that she had been just another romp, she told her older brother. A few days later, her brother showed up with three friends and they surrounded David on the way to school.

David had expected the beating of his life until Frank drove up. A small man, he had walked into the circle and stood beside David, no match for any of the four, but his frailty and age changed the equation. When Judy's brother told his dad what David had done, Frank said, "If you think beating us is going to make the girl feel better, then go ahead."

David was in the fast lane when he saw the connector off-ramp. Somehow, he swerved across two lanes and over the painted island, and just missed the yellow impact barrels. Shaking, he settled into the traffic flow, watching the rear-view mirror, knowing he would be stopped if a cop had seen that move. Bits of gore all over his face, the gun in the car, no cop would miss all that. He would finish his life in jail.

He watched in the mirror as headlights rushed up from behind, seeing death in the white tunnel in his rear view mirror. He would wait until the cop was close behind him, and keep going as if he hadn't seen. Then, just before an off-ramp, he would suddenly brake hard, hoping the cop would swerve into the fast lane while David took the off-ramp. With his life on the line, he had to try every possible way to escape. When all hope of escape was gone, then he would put the gun in his mouth.

The car rushed by, someone in a hurry.

David yelled, "Concentrate on the plan, damn it. Put one foot in front of the other until you're home in bed."

He took the next ramp to Interstate 5 South and waited for the J Street off-ramp. The exit appeared, and he felt he'd never seen it before. He followed J Street east anyway, and soon recognized familiar landmarks. As he neared the house where he planned to discard the gun, he rolled the passenger side window down. It would take some effort to get the heavy gun up to the lawn, some six feet above the sidewalk. As he neared the house, he saw two couples on the sidewalk across the street. He drove by without stopping. What else was going to go wrong?

He parked around the corner from Mac's, in a spot where no houses faced the street. The dash clock said 10:01, too soon for the cops. They wouldn't show up until they had a search warrant. He pulled the bulb from the hot water, and then quickly got out and walked to Mac's, staying in the shadows of the trees. The driver's side of Mac's car faced a street light, so he had no choice but to walk into the glare. He lay down next to the car with his head touching the front wheel, scooting his body until he felt wedged under the rocker panel. Holding the bulb above his shoulder, he squished it flat. As he returned the empty bulb to his coat pocket, taking care to keep it above his body, he watched several runs trail down the car door. The bulb safely in his pocket, he relaxed, putting his head on the driveway, watching the runs as they slowed to a crawl. One drop came to the metal edge, hung there gathering fluid, then fell. He heard it hit his coat. The others were taking their time.

Five drops hit his coat in the next few seconds, but the last run was holding out, the fat drop hanging from the edge, when the world lit up. A spotlight from a car in the street flickered over the house, and then zeroed in on Mac's car. David could feel the muffled rumble of a police car engine. As soon as the cop moved forward, it would all be over.

He steeled himself to run, hoping the surprise would let him get to the car and the gun. Suddenly, the light extinguished, and the cop idled by. Feeling naked in the glare of the street light, David held his breath, hoping, yet not believing, that the cop wouldn't see his dark shape against the dark car. The police car moved beyond Mac's yard and across the intersection. David reached up, plucked the last drop from the side of Mac's car, then rose and moved into the shadow of a pine in the parkway.

At the end of the far block, the cop made a U turn, the headlights trapping David behind the tree. When the headlights shut off, David dared a glance. The cop was parked at the end of the block. Keeping the pine tree between himself and the cop, David backed away. The tree's shadow forced him to back onto a lawn that was edged by a tall hedge. David tried forcing his way through the hedge, but it had grown around a wire fence. With no choice, David crawled, feeling naked in the glare, not able to look toward the cop for fear of showing his white face. It seemed hours before he slithered around the end of the hedge. In the shadow of the hedge, then a tree, then another tree, David made it back to his car.

With his foot out the door, he rolled the car backwards without starting the engine. When he was far enough from the corner, he started the engine and did a U turn, turning his lights on after he'd completed the turn. He drove south to J Street, and then turned west toward the freeway. Keeping the car at thirty miles an hour was difficult.

He came to the house where he wanted to leave the gun. He knew he should go around the block so the passenger door faced the house, where he could use his right arm to throw the gun, but he couldn't spare the time. The cops were moving much faster that he'd expected. He rolled down the driver's side window, drove on the wrong side of the street and stopped. Holding the gun by the barrel, he hurled it with his left hand. He didn't hear it hit; maybe that was a good sign. He drove away slowly, trying to limit any noise.

The lights on J were all red for him, and it seemed years before he was on the freeway pointed toward home. It was 10:17. David had assumed he had an hour and a half before the cops came to notify his mother, but now he wasn't sure.

Just after he went through downtown, a white light flashed across his rear window. He stopped breathing until his side mirror picked up the airliner sinking toward Lindbergh Field. He took the Clairemont Drive off ramp, and made the right turn at the shopping center at the top of the hill. Obeying all the stop signs, he drove to the street where he would leave the car. The clock said 10:37. He opened the trunk from inside, and then got out, locking the door.

Standing at the open trunk, he took off the boots, the coat, cap, and jump suit. He dropped those into the trunk, and then shed the gloves, using his fingers inside the glove that was all but off to remove the other. Rid of everything that could have powder residue, he was dressed in running shorts and a tee-shirt. He put on white socks and tennis shoes with reflector tape on the heels, and then picked up the clean towel the shoes had been wrapped in. He quietly closed the trunk.

He began the downhill run home. He used the towel to wipe away the jelly on his face, careful to fold the towel over after each wipe so his hands never touched the contaminated part. The towel was used up while he was still three blocks from the house. He tossed it into a garbage can on the curb.

Suddenly, he remembered the fake plate on the floor in the back seat of the car. What if it was right side up? Anyone looking in the window would see it. He should go back, but there wasn't time. He padded down the steep hill, slipped through the rear neighbor's yard, and the rotating boards in the fence.

No lights in his parents' bedroom. Relieved, he silently went in through the unlocked patio door. He undressed, dropped the jogging outfit into the hamper, and then took a hot shower, scrubbing his skin pink, breathing handfuls of hot water into his nose, letting water pool in his ears, scrubbing his wrists raw in case the gloves had gapped.

He slipped into bed at 11:05, his pulse racing. It seemed years before the knock came at 12:36.

His mother was descending the stairs as David opened the door. Steve Bacha and Able Mendoza identified themselves, and Detective Bacha told his mother he was sorry but her husband had been killed. She asked how it happened, and refused to believe that someone had murdered him. David sat on the stairs and cried, his nerves a mess. His mother didn't cry. She wilted into the couch. The detectives waited, standing in the center of the room, until David asked what they needed.

Able Mendoza told him Mac had accused him of the murder. He added, "I know its bad timing, but these things become part of the defense if we don't handle them right. We'd like to take GSR swabs, ah, sorry, swabs of your hands and face for gunshot residue. And we'd like to search the house." David agreed. Able Mendoza walked over to the couch and knelt on one knee, bringing his face level with Mary's. "We'd like to take swabs of your hands and face, too. Just to be thorough."

Her hand wave said she didn't care, so Able Mendoza went to the door and waved in a frail-looking older man wearing a police jump suit, evidently a forensic technician. After the technician was through taking swabs from him, David sat beside his mother, his arm around her, while the technician took swabs of her hands and face.

The detectives confined their search to his bedroom and the garage. As the search went on, Mary got angry. David quietly repeated the soothing words. "It's their job, Mom. They'll be through as fast as they can." He said that to comfort her. He wanted to scream at them to get the hell out. Didn't they know how devastating a loss she'd just experienced?

CHAPTER 15

▼

February 22, 1997, Saturday

The picture of Mac's clone appeared in Saturday morning's newspaper, and the reward offer generated dozens of calls into Framac. Most callers claimed to have a friend who had a buddy who knew a guy who looked like the man they were looking for, or some variation of that. By nine, the receptionist called for help, so Mac went in to field the calls. Both George and Gary followed up on the leads as fast as they could, but it was a slow process. Most of the callers lived in homeless shelters, garage apartments, or RV's, and were hard to locate.

Mac began to ask if the person was tall. Eliminating the tall men cut the leads to a manageable number. By seven that evening, Gary had met eight overweight homeless men whose missing front teeth were their only resemblance to Mac's clone. George reported that he had met eleven.

*   *   *   *

At breakfast Sunday morning, Gary bitched about spending another day with the garrulous unwashed. Mac's sympathetic look made Gary feel like shit. The guy was fighting for his life.

To change the subject, Gary said, "I've been trying to figure out how David got Frank to come back to the restaurant without calling his cellular."

Mac frowned and speared an elusive piece of bacon. "Couldn't have got him anyway. I tried to call him twice that day."

"Yeah. The police report said he didn't make any calls on his phone that day."

Mac looked surprised. "That ain't right. He called me, late afternoon sometime."

"On his cell phone?"

"Had to be. He said he was drivin' back from Riverside. He was outside Escondido, so he said we could meet for dinner at the usual time."

"Maybe he'd stopped somewhere to use a pay phone."

"Naw, it was his cell phone. Lots of mountains around Escondido; couple times he broke up." He waved his fork at Gary. "Two Tuesdays in a row, couldn't get him on the phone. Maybe in September. He's drivin' all over, couldn't always make it to the restaurant on time, so I used to call him around five and ask. After I bitched about not getting him those two times, he started calling me to let me know what time."

Intrigued, Gary called Bacha's number, intending to leave a message. Bacha was working. Gary asked, "You have Frank's cell phone listings?" Bacha confirmed that, so Gary asked, "I recall the police report saying that Frank didn't take any calls on his cell phone the day of the murder. How about the Tuesday prior to that? Any calls on his cell phone?"

"Hang on." Gary heard a thump, drawers opening, paper being unfolded, and then silence. The color rose in Mac's face. Bacha said, "Not on that Tuesday and not on the four Tuesdays before that. On every other day of the week for five weeks, his phone was used. I can't believe I didn't notice that."

Gary asked Mac, "Where were you when he called? At Framac?" After Mac nodded, Gary said, "Frank called Framac on a cell phone around five on the day of the shooting."

"I'll see what I can find." Bacha disconnected abruptly.

Gary told Mac that David had evidently stalked them for five weeks before the murder. Mac closed his eyes. After a long silence, he muttered, "Asshole."

When Bacha called back, he said Framac had over a hundred calls that day. He would provide Gary with the list of incoming phone calls for the five Tuesdays. If Gary came up with a few suspected cell phone numbers, Bacha would check them out.

Gary drove to the police station and picked up the listing. By noon, while he was meeting toothless people, Mac resolved the list to four phone numbers that repeated every Tuesday. Three belonged to vendor reps; the fourth was now out of service. Bacha got an address in Julian, a mountain town some 40 miles north of San Diego, for that phone. In October, it had been registered to a Dan Rhoades.

*   *   *   *

Monday morning, Gary drove up to Julian. The address was a remailing service that forwarded Dan Rhoades' mail to a P.O. Box at San Diego Main. Assuming that the box would be registered to Dan Rhoades at the remailing address in Julian, he phoned the details into Bacha's voice mail. Bacha was not scheduled to work until Wednesday.

Gary called George and told him about the cell phone. "I need a listing of calls from Dan Rhoades' cell phone. I've left a phone mail asking Bacha to do that, but he doesn't work until Wednesday. Can you get one sooner than that?"

"Best not to try. People might find out that Bacha is working this on the sly."

"Okay. When we do get a listing, I'll hire you to help me work it. You have the time?"

George's machine gun delivery was nearing unintelligible. "I'll make time. If you do find a person who knows Dan Rhoades, don't volunteer nothing. Be sure you let Bacha show them a photo line-up before you say anything."

"Oh, yeah. We'll do this by the book."

*   *   *   *

After lunch, when Gary arrived at the courtroom, the spectator area was nearly full. The newspaper had published a long article on the trial in Sunday's paper. According to Julie, Draper had taken most of the morning for his closing argument. He subjected everyone to a detailed reprise of the murder, and he concluded by saying all those facts proved that John McBride was the killer.

When court convened, Julie walked to the podium and looked at the jury as if confused. "I'm so astonished that the prosecution continued after Mr. Jank's testimony that I don't know where to begin. The only irrefutable evidence they had was John McBride's alleged purchase of the murder weapon, and Michael Jank was positive that John McBride did not purchase the gun. Since the man who did purchase the murder weapon used John McBride's identification, we have absolute proof that others have conspired to convict John McBride of a murder he did not commit.

"The blood ineptly sprayed on the door of John McBride's car while it was parked in his driveway is further proof of that conspiracy. As the blood dispersal expert testified, the single drop of blood found underneath the car came from the same source as the blood on the door. Obviously, and I do mean obviously, whatever device the actual killer used to contain the rest of the expected over spray had one tiny flaw that allowed that single drop to land underneath the car.

"Mr. Draper contends that the time John McBride reported he arrived at home shows that another person couldn't have sprayed blood on the door before the Chula Vista police officer arrived at 10:04. If John McBride indeed arrived home after ten, Mr. Draper might have a point. The fact is that John McBride doesn't know exactly when he got home. When the officers asked, he gave them the one fact he did have: when he turned on the television, the news at ten was already on.

"John McBride has a picture of his late wife on a stand near the front door. Sometimes he's drawn to that, and spends some time lost in memories. He doesn't remember if that's what he did that night, but he doesn't think he went straight to the television. It's a measure of the man that he didn't make up some excuse to show he was home earlier. After all, no one could have disputed it.

"When the police did arrest John McBride, according to Mr. Draper's experts, he still had traces of machine oil and tiny particles of metal on his hands, face, clothes and shoes, but no blood or gunshot residue anywhere. Mr. Draper explains that by the fact that the killer was dressed in a long coat, gloves, and a ski mask. John McBride has never skied; he hasn't traveled to any part of the country where it snows in at least ten years, and he has never owned a long cloth coat, or a knit cap, or gloves, and certainly not a ski mask. Mind you, Mr. Draper did not say John McBride bought these things for the specific purpose of killing Frank Kendall. He wants to convince you that John McBride happened to have a ski mask in his car, and put it on because he was cold, just before he killed Frank Kendall in a rage.

"And then Mr. Draper wants you to believe that John McBride, dressed in a bulky coat covered with blood and gunshot residue, got into his car without touching any part of the interior, even the steering wheel. He says that John McBride stabbed the brakes in panic several times while he backed out without dislodging the pool of blood we know was on the killer's shoes. He says that John McBride, while he twisted around to see while he's backing, because the arthritis in his neck wouldn't allow him to turn his head, still managed not to rub off any of the blood or gunshot residue on the interior. He wants you to believe that John McBride, while he twisted around to watch for approaching traffic before turning onto University Avenue, still did not contaminate the interior. He wants you to believe that John McBride stopped on a darkened street, and got out to remove all those contaminated clothes, and managed to disrobe without getting any of the blood or gunshot residue on his hands or face. Mr. Draper wants you to believe John McBride dumped his ski mask, special gloves, long coat and shoes in a convenient dumpster, and yet did not remember to throw the gun away until he was four blocks from his house. Imagine that, he didn't remember to throw the gun in the dumpster while he was dumping his shoes. The one thing that can positively connect him to the murder, and he forgot to throw it away. Only a couple of minutes after he fired it at his friend, and he forgot he still had it?

"According to Mr. Draper, that huge gun, covered with blood and gunshot residue, had been rattling around inside the car for 26 minutes before John McBride supposedly threw it into a neighbor's yard. Again, when forensics examined his car, they found no traces of either blood or gunshot residue. If John McBride threw the gun away just before he got home—remember, he'd already dumped his gloves—then he would have had to scrub his hands to remove the residue from the gun. Now recall, John McBride gave the detectives permission to search his house and car as soon as they asked, and they found the showers and wash basins were dry, as were all the towels. To explain that problem away, Mr. Draper conjures up a towel that John McBride carefully wrapped around the gun as he left the scene of the murder in a panic. Minutes later, Mr. Draper wants you to believe that John McBride forgot about this carefully wrapped gun.

"And gloves? You've seen his hands. Unencumbered, they barely work well enough for him to grip items. Now, imagine gloves that would fit over his deformed knuckles. I didn't want you to have to imagine them. I wanted to buy a pair to show you. Guess what? They don't make gloves that large. If they did, the palm section of the gloves would have had to be large enough to fit over his knuckles, leaving loose fabric over his palms. And those gloves would have been covered with blood and gunshot residue, yet none was found on the steering wheel of his car or on the door handle of the car. Did he take them off before he drove the car? Witnesses didn't think so. Did he take them off before he dumped the bloody shoes? He might have had to, gripping shoelaces in the dark might have been impossible for him if he were wearing gloves. And if John McBride dumped his bloody shoes, he carefully selected another pair that had the same mix of oil and metal residue as the rest of his clothes."

She walked over to the exhibit table near the jury box, and lifted the Desert Eagle. She held it up in front of her face, the gun looking huge in her small hands. "This is the best evidence we have to show that John McBride did not commit the murder. Look at the size of this weapon. It weighs almost four pounds when loaded. It fires .44 caliber bullets, very powerful bullets. It's made in Israel, and it's considered a collector's item by people knowledgeable about guns."

She tried to put it down on the table with one hand and the gun fell with a kettle drum sound that echoed in the quiet room. She walked to her spot behind and to the left of the podium before she turned to face the jury again. "The killer selected that gun for several reasons. First, to guarantee that Frank Kendall would be killed, he bought special bullets that open into a propeller shape as they enter the human body. This ensures that all the energy of the massive bullet will be absorbed inside the body, and what that means, Ladies and Gentlemen, is that the body sustains an internal explosion. When the first bullet entered Frank Kendall's head, his brain exploded so violently that his skull was broken into several pieces. The second shot that Mr. Draper described as proof of John McBride's rage was, indeed, unnecessary. Frank Kendall was dead after the first shot. But the killer had another requirement. He needed a second shot for the noise it would make.

"And that, Ladies and Gentlemen, is the second reason the killer selected a gun that would fire a .44 caliber magnum bullet: he needed the noise. University Avenue, where Colson's Cavern is located, is a heavily traveled, four lane boulevard. It is a noisy street. People who live in the apartment building across the street from Colson's Cavern are used to that high level of noise. So the killer selected a gun loud enough to be heard above that din. Because of his arthritis, John McBride can't turn his neck, so he has a unique method of backing out of a parking space. He moves backwards a foot or so, and then he stops and turns his entire body so he can see if it's safe to move back another foot or so. The killer wanted witnesses to see him duplicate that process in a car that looked like John McBride's car, so he needed a gun loud enough to wake up those people in the apartment building.

"Now a true gun enthusiast will see a problem that the rest of us might not. A true gun enthusiast will scoff at the purchase of a massive Desert Eagle to do those two things: fire a .44 caliber magnum bullet, and make a lot of noise, because, Ladies and Gentlemen, there are much cheaper and lighter and easier to handle guns that would fire those bullets. But the killer had another problem. He wanted the police to know which gun had been used. The killer realized that the bullets recovered from Frank Kendall might be too damaged to make a ballistics' match. Now those cheaper and lighter guns are all revolvers, and they don't eject the shell casings when they fire. If he used a revolver, the police would not have a shell casing they could match to the gun used to kill Frank Kendall. When they recovered a gun near John McBride's house, they might not be able to prove it was the murder weapon. So the Desert Eagle was selected because it solved this final problem. It ejected two shell casings at the scene. So the second shot might have had two purposes: to wake up the neighborhood, and to leave a second shell casing at the scene, just in case something happened to the first."

Julie moved to the desk and picked up a paper. "Now, Mr. Draper knows that there was no motive for John McBride to shoot his friend of more than thirty years, so he created this ludicrous theory that John McBride, due to his declining health, had the gun to commit suicide, and, in a fit of rage, used the gun to kill Frank Kendall. Remember, Michael Jank testified that the buyer knew exactly which gun he wanted to buy. If John McBride was looking for a suitable suicide weapon, why would he have chosen a heavy, hard to handle gun that cost twice the price of a more suitable weapon? And why would he have driven 170 miles to buy it? Several dealers in San Diego carried the same gun.

"For all these reasons, I believe that the gun is the best evidence that John McBride has been framed."

Julie took a moment to go through her notes before she turned to face the jury again. "You should be here to decide the fate of the man who killed Frank Kendall. Instead Mr. Draper followed the evidence arranged by the killer, and decided to try John McBride. Michael Jank told you that John McBride did not buy the gun; that someone who looked very similar to John McBride did buy it, using John McBride's identification. If you ignore a faked license plate, there is no credible evidence that John McBride's car was at the scene of the shooting, and there is evidence that someone sprayed blood on the side of his car while it was parked in his driveway, 12 miles away from the scene of the shooting. It all adds up to a conspiracy by someone who had everything to gain from Frank Kendall's death and John McBride's conviction for the murder. So I urge you, Ladies and Gentlemen, find John McBride innocent so that Mr. Draper will be forced to prosecute the actual killer."

After the afternoon break, Draper replaced Julie at the podium. He looked at Julie, and shook his head as if wondering how she could be so naive. When he did look at the jurors, he said, "The reason the prosecutor is given this rebuttal opportunity after the defense makes their closing argument is because the prosecution has the burden of proving the case beyond a reasonable doubt. All the defense has to do is to instill doubt, they don't have to prove what they say is true. Ms. Williams has done her job well. She's taken all the facts in this case, and bent them to suit the will of a mysterious person who she says was the actual killer.

"I doubt she would have taken that approach had Michael Jank not changed his mind. When Michael Jank put missing teeth, a high pitched voice, smooth hands, and a large stainless steel ring into Mr. McBride's visage, the imaginary killer who framed Mr. McBride was born in Ms. Williams' mind. I'm not suggesting that Michael Jank was lying, I believe him to be an honest and honorable man. What I am suggesting is that, in the nearly three months between the time Michael Jank handed the gun to Mr. McBride in the store, and when he next saw Mr. McBride in the police lineup, he had fused two different men into one man. Somewhere around the same time he sold the gun to Mr. McBride, another man with missing teeth and a large stainless steel ring that he twirled when nervous also bought a gun. Three months later, when he's asked to identify the man who bought the Desert Eagle, he identifies Mr. McBride without hesitation. He does not hear Mr. McBride speak, he does not see his teeth, and he pays no attention to his hands, but he continues to carry this fused image of two men because nothing has happened that would make him challenge his memory. Perhaps at less than three months, if he had noticed Mr. McBride's teeth during the line up, he might have resolved his impression into the correct two men. But that didn't happen. Over six months pass before his image of Mr. McBride is shown to be wrong. Six months. How many times have you been shocked to find that something or someone is completely different from the way you remembered, from the way you would have testified in a court of law? Human memory is quite fallible, as all of us know from our own experience. Eyewitnesses are often unreliable.

"When we have no reliable witnesses, we must go back to the facts."

And that's what Draper did. For the balance of the afternoon, he went through the chronology of the shooting, and the blood analysis. Gary was so bored he fell asleep twice.

Just before five, Draper said, "Ladies and Gentlemen, I submit that those all those facts are sufficient to find that Mr. McBride killed his friend. So I ask you to return a second degree murder conviction, to give Frank Kendall's widow, and his son, a measure of justice. Thank you for your attention."

*   *   *   *

Tuesday morning, Judge Lucero began his jury instructions. After an hour of vague verbiage that was supposed to define second degree murder, he read instructions that covered how jurors should regard evidence. "You must determine whether any of the evidence was deliberately arranged by another person to cast suspicion on the defendant. If you believe that any of the evidence was so arranged, then you should regard all the evidence with suspicion." Coming as it did in the middle of three hours of instructions, the statement didn't have much impact.

*   *   *   *

Wednesday, on the first full day of jury deliberations, Gary was driving toward Chula Vista in lock-step with the evening rush-hour traffic when his cell phone trilled. It was Bacha. He had the call listings for Dan Rhoades' cell phone, the phone that Frank might have used on the day he was killed. Gary asked, "Anything interesting?"

"Yeah. The first thing that stands out like a turd in a punchbowl is that the phone was never used again after October 22nd, the night of the murder."

Gary wanted to honk the horn, to let the world know that they had skewered the asshole. David Kendall was Dan Rhoades.

Bacha continued. "And it gets better. The last call that phone received was on the night of the murder at 9:17 p.m., from a tower five miles from Colson's Cavern. That tower overlooks Mission Valley, where Frank could have been if he left the restaurant when Mac said he did."

Gary held his breath.

Bacha said, "The call came from the apartment of a June Wilms who lives across the street from Colson's Cavern. She's 84, and she said she was asleep when that call was made. She has a cordless phone. She keeps the handset next to her bed at night. The base for the handset is in her kitchen. David must have had an illegally modified cordless handset that could use any nearby base."

"Back east, they aren't hard to find on the street."

"Same here. So that's a dead end. But the listing has 158 different numbers that were called from Dan Rhoades cell phone last year. Somebody at one of those numbers must have seen Dan Rhoades."

"Give me ten minutes. I'll come by and pick it up."

CHAPTER 16

▼

October 23, 1996, Wednesday, four months earlier

At noon the day after the murder, Steve Bacha and Able Mendoza were at the door, asking David to come with them to identify Frank's body. At the morgue, they pushed David forward until he was tight against the window in a small viewing room. A body lay on a gurney in a zippered body-bag. A man in a yellow lab coat walked into the room and opened the zipper, exposing Frank's head. The head resembled a squashed mannequin. One eye stared into the open mouth on another part of the shattered skull. David felt nothing. "Yes, that's Frank Kendall. Can I go now?"

Bacha said, "Just thought you'd like to see your handiwork."

They drove David to the police department and put him in a room with a one way mirror. Rather than answer their questions, he asked, "Am I under arrest? Then may I leave?" The third time they didn't answer, he got up and walked out the door.

He took a bus, and then walked the half mile to his street. The detectives were parked in front of his house. Able Mendoza gave him a toothy grin, but didn't get out of the car.

Mary was in the living room looking through the sheer drapes. She pointed toward the street. "What was that about?"

David collapsed in the entryway, crying so violently that he couldn't get a breath. His mother held him, both of them on their knees on the entryway tile. "They think I killed dad," he said through tears that wouldn't stop.

Mary cradled his head. She whispered, "David, people expect the worst from you. They think you're capable of cruelty."

"I didn't kill him, Mom."

She squeezed his face, looking into his eyes. "I know that." Then, with tears beginning to cascade, she choked out the words, "I love you."

The empty words he had heard from her a thousand times finally felt like truth. His mother loved him. Desperate to be worthy of that love, David wanted to say something she had never heard from him. He had used 'I love you' as an insult, so that was out. Then he remembered that both she and Frank often said he only thought of himself. Lifting her hands and kissing them, he said, "You've just lost Frank and you have to hold me up. I'm so sorry. Tell me, what can I do for you?"

She looked at him as if the words hadn't registered. He leaned forward and kissed her cheek, then hugged her. "Just tell me what you need. What can I do for you?"

She sat back on her heels, tears still pouring down her face. In a voice choked with sobs, she said, "Can you handle everything? I want to go to bed and cry."

*   *   *   *

One of the details he had to handle that afternoon was a call from Mary's sister in Atlanta. Vivian didn't like David and, unlike most people, she didn't mind telling him. When she recognized his voice, she said, "Has she found out that you killed Frank?"

"Hi, Viv. I didn't kill Frank, but you are in the majority."

"Let me talk to Mary."

"I just looked in on her a few minutes ago. She's finally sleeping. Viv, is there any way you can come out here?"

Her voice sounded softer. "I want to, but I don't want to be in the house with you."

"I'll move to a motel while you're here. Just come. She really needs you."

"Okay. I'll call when I've made the arrangements."

*   *   *   *

On the news at six, they had film of Mac being taken from his house in handcuffs. He looked downcast. David thought most people would think it was a look of shame, and that raised David's spirits until he noticed that Mac was being led by Bacha and Mendoza.

Since David was their prime suspect, they knew he had a car like Mac's. He planned to drive the Taurus to Tijuana on Friday, during rush hour. Until then, if a cop noticed it, or some nosy person wondered if it had been stolen and called the cops, he'd be dead.

*   *   *   *

David woke, and his first thought was, "Thursday, October 24." Two days into his new and frightening life.

At nine, the morgue called. Frank's body would be released at noon. Which mortuary would handle the funeral? David said he'd call back, and then took coffee up to Mary. She was awake, staring out the window. David felt her loneliness. For the first time in forty-some years, she woke up alone. He handed her the coffee, told her about the call from the morgue, and asked what she wanted. Mary wanted to say goodbye to Frank. She needed one last glimpse.

*   *   *   *

When they visited the Mortuary, the funeral director told Mary a viewing was not possible. Something inside her broke. David could see her folding in on herself. Always a polite, dignified and soft spoken woman, she needed to hide the tears that she could not control. They returned to the house.

Reporters rang the doorbell, agonizingly loud in the house until David disconnected it. The phone rang incessantly so he shut off the ring. He listened to the phone machine and picked up the calls he needed to answer. Violent death inspired lawyers to extend their condolences and their offers of help. News organizations needed comments on Mac's arrest. Two psychologists offered grief counseling. Framac's insurance company wanted to meet with Mary.

At three, Viv called. She would be in at 11:30 the next morning. When David said he would meet her at the airport, she said, "If you aren't there, I'll take a taxi. Are you planning to stay at a motel, or should I get one?"

"Mary needs you, Viv. I'll stay someplace else."

By six, the gun had been recovered. The man who found it was interviewed on the evening news. The newscaster made the point that it was found just blocks from Mac's house. At eleven that night, the news anchor talked about the blood on Mac's car, and revealed that the gun was registered in Mac's name. Someone close to the investigation was leaking developments.

David went to bed at one in the morning. As soon as he shut his eyes, he felt certain he would soon be in prison. The thought was so terrifying, he got dressed, intending to get the car and drive it to Mexico. He changed his mind. It would be much safer driving into Mexico during Friday's rush hour.

He went back to bed. Again, the terror struck as soon as he closed his eyes. How would he survive in prison?

Driven out of bed again, he was into his third glass of scotch when Mary came down. She got herself a glass and they sat together at the table. David slowed his intake until Mary asked for help to get up the stairs, then he went back to bed and finally fell asleep.

*   *   *   *

When he awoke, he thought, "Friday, October 25." How many days until the counting stopped?

Vivian's plane touched down at 11:45 that morning. David was waiting at the gate. The small blond in her early sixties hadn't aged in twenty years. She smiled at David, a first, before she said, "This must have really affected you. You're on time and at the right gate." She added, "I hope you didn't get a motel room. I owe you an apology for thinking you killed Frank." She had seen the news of Mac's arrest.

When Viv met Mary inside the house, they wrapped their arms around each other and cried. They sat on the couch for a long time, crying and passing tissues.

David listened to the messages on the phone machine, called the two that had to be answered, and then walked back to the living room to see if the women needed anything. They had gone up to Mary's bedroom. He knocked softly on the door. Viv opened the door, and he asked if they needed anything. Looking sad, Viv shook her head. He told her he was going out to run errands.

David walked into the backyard, and slipped around the side of the garage to the wooden fence that separated their yard from the Takahashi's. Every day, from ten in the morning until midnight, Lyle and Kim Takahashi were at the restaurant they owned. David had used their yard as a shortcut for as long as he could remember. At first, he had scaled the fence, but splinters were a hazard, so he had removed two boards, rounded the tops and bottoms that were hidden by framing, and used one nail at the top. The boards rotated aside, leaving a gap that he stepped through. He walked the concrete lawn edging and opened the unlocked gate to the street.

Avoiding the thoroughfares, winded from the uphill climb, David reached the block where the car was parked in less than 15 minutes. Approaching the final corner that would give him a view of the car, he understood that he might be about to identify himself as the killer. If the cops had found the car, they would be waiting for him.

Dying inside, he turned the corner. The car was there. He couldn't see anyone. No one seemed to be in any of the other parked cars. His heart in his mouth, he took the keys out of his pocket and inserted them in the door lock.

His body expected an explosion, and the silence seemed surreal. He got in, started the engine, and drove toward Clairemont Drive. At a stop sign, he looked into the rear seat. The fake plate was lying on the floor, face up. Anyone looking into the car could have read it easily. He retrieved it, and as he drove, he shredded the cardboard plate.

Aware that even a minor accident would result in his death, he was hypersensitive to the traffic. It seemed years before he reached the lines of cars waiting to pass through Mexican customs, mostly single men like David, commuters getting an early start on the weekend. He idled along with the slow moving line, approaching the border and safety at a snail's pace. Finally, it was his turn, and the Mexican customs agent asked where he was going. He said, "Meeting some friends for a night out," and the man waved him through.

Three miles from the border, parked on an unpaved street, David opened the trunk, then put the keys back in the ignition and placed the signed pink slip on the seat. In the trunk, he picked up the cordless phone, put it on the ground, and smashed it with his heel. He removed Dan Rhoades' cell phone from the coat pocket, and stomped it, then wrapped both ruined phones in a towel. He folded the clothes, slipped the towel with the phones into the stack, and carrying the clothes, he walked toward the border. He dumped the phones in a trash can, then, a few blocks later, he placed the clothes on a box.

He was back at the border by 4:30. David expected questions; his olive skin and black hair always drew attention at the border crossing, but the harried border patrolman only asked for his birth place and where he'd been in Mexico. David showed his driver's license, and the man waved him into the United States. After the trolley ride to downtown, he took a bus and got off a half mile beyond his normal stop. Feeling safe in the darkness, he took a long route to the street behind his house. He lifted the latch on the Takahashi's gate, walked through their backyard, slipped through the rotating boards in the fence, edged along the side of the garage, and entered his bedroom through the patio door.

When he turned on the bathroom light, his heart skipped a beat. Both rooms had been searched. Everything from the bathroom drawers was piled on the vanity, and in the bedroom, the contents of the drawers were on top of the box spring, which was balanced on the mattress. The empty dresser drawers were on the floor.

Viv was in the living room by herself, watching television. David startled her when he walked into the room. She jumped, then, relief flooding her face, she put a hand over her heart. "You scared the crap out of me."

"What happened to my room?"

Viv went to the kitchen and returned with a search warrant. The police had been looking for dark clothes, shoes, gloves, knitted headwear, cell phones, car keys, financial records and safe-deposit box keys.

He asked, "Did they take all my shoes?"

"Probably. They took your clothes and all the keys they found. They would have taken the keys in your pocket if you had been here."

David felt that bullet whistle by. If they had come earlier, they would now have a Ford key they could trace to a vehicle identification number. His legs turned to water. What else did he have that could kill him? The safe-deposit box key was on his key ring. All Dan Rhoades' credit card bills and checking account statements were in that box.

Viv pointed toward his room. "You need any help putting it back?"

David shook his head. As he turned toward his room, Viv said, "Sue called."

Surprised, David said, "I'll call her." He did miss Sue. While he put his bedroom and bathroom back together, he planned the conversation. He would guarantee to move to her place just as soon as Mary no longer needed him. Sue would agree to that.

With the bedroom restored, David dialed Sue's number. When she answered, he said, "Hi, it's me."

"When's the funeral?"

"Sunday. Can I pick you up?"

"I won't be going. Tell Mary I'm working at a dealership in Tucson this weekend."

"It's a death in the family, can't..."

Her voice sharp, she cut him off. "It's my excuse for not being there, David. Make up a better one if you want, just try to be convincing when you tell her."

David didn't know what to say. She broke the silence. "I'll tell my attorney not to serve the papers until Monday. I'm not asking for anything, and I'm not offering anything. We just go our separate ways. Is that agreeable?"

"You intend to divorce me now? When I've lost my father?"

"Don't try that with me." The contempt in her voice shriveled his resolve. "I told the police that you killed Frank and fixed it to look like Mac did it." Sobbing, she said, "So don't you try that with me, David. Sign the papers, and stay away from me." She abruptly disconnected.

He wasn't surprised that she knew. She had always been able to read him.

He didn't expect to sleep that night, so he watched a movie he'd taped, an action film littered with bodies that never seemed to inspire a police investigation. When that was over, he felt too tired to sleep. A few minutes later, he woke, his heart racing. Hatch and Frank had been propped up on a gurney, both headless bodies pointing at him.

Suppose Hatch's girlfriend, Evelyn, thought it was Hatch when she saw Mac on television. Once she told the police about Dan Rhoades, the police might pressure Art, the bartender at the Dive Inn. If they offered immunity, Art would tell them he had obtained duplicates of John McBride's identification for Dan Rhoades.

He should have killed Art and Evelyn before he killed Frank.

CHAPTER 17

▼

April 27, 1997, Sunday

A half-hour after Gary parked in the cul-de-sac, a light came on in an upstairs bedroom of the house he was watching, and a woman's shadow moved across the blind. The other houses in the upscale neighborhood in Fairfax, Virginia, were dark. Gary picked up a bow made from wide red ribbon and slid it inside his jacket. He left the car and walked quickly to the house. He inserted the tines of his automatic lock-pick into the deadbolt. When the small green light glowed, he turned the box and the deadbolt opened. He withdrew the tines and repeated the process with the doorknob lock. In seconds, he was inside.

To his right, a circular stairway ascended. Through high windows in the living room, underwater lights in the backyard pool projected ripples on the ceiling. Feeling vulnerable in the undulating illumination, he moved behind the stairway column, straining to hear some noise from upstairs. Had she heard the lock pick? Was she waiting with a gun in one of the dark spaces at the top of the stairs? He stood silently, feeling crosshairs on his forehead.

A closet door rumbled, and then he heard her walk into the master bathroom, creaking floor joists marking her movement. Gary eased up the stairs, staying near the wall so the runners wouldn't complain, pulling the bow from his jacket as he moved. A hair dryer started, so Gary ran up the remaining stairs, knowing she wouldn't hear.

Her bedroom door was open. In the closet mirrors he could see her in the bathroom, drying her auburn hair. Through the pale blue peignoir, he could see her thin, medium height body was clad only in nude-colored panties and a bra.

In the hall, he quickly shed his clothes. When she shut off the hair dryer and turned to put it away, he ran to her bed. When she came out of the bathroom, he was lying on her bed, nude except for the red bow he wore like a fig leaf.

Andrea gasped, and then, still clutching her chest, broke into laughter.

Gary said, "Happy Valentines Day."

She walked to the bed and lifted the bow. She pouted. "I wanted a big one."

"He's resting up for his big moment."

"We can always hope." The peignoir, panties, and bra seemed to fall off her body.

*   *   *   *

Later, Gary awoke from a sun-splashed meadow where his mind romped. Andrea was staring at him. "You back?"

"Yeah. Thanks. I love that little nap after we make love."

He pulled her close, and she found a comfortable spot on his shoulder. He traced the scar on her lip with his thumb. Three long scars crossed her face: one on a lower eyelid made her left eye larger than her right, the one he traced started at her upper lip and nicked her nose, and the third interrupted her right eyebrow and extended up into her hairline, all the results of a car bomb in Colombia.

She moved away from his hand. "Don't."

"Scars and all, your face is beautiful."

She misted up, outlandish behavior for this lady. "What caused that?" he asked.

"You're a sweetheart, that's what caused that. Why won't you marry me?"

"Because ten minutes from now, we'll be fighting about something."

"I like a good fight, it gets my heart started." She raised her head to look at him, then she put it back on his shoulder and sighed. "You won't even fight about fighting."

A moment later, she asked, "So, mamma's boy, why are you here?"

"I was horny."

"You're always horny. What was the other reason?"

"I want you to do an article about John McBride. He's going to be tried again."

She propped herself up on an elbow. "With the jury hung 9-3 for acquittal? Did the D.A. find some new evidence?"

"He found a new judge who ruled out letting the gun salesman testify about the clone. That was Mac's only hope."

She left the bed, found a notebook and her glasses, and then got back under the covers. Propped against the headboard, she said, "Talk to me."

Judge Lucero had moved on to a position in the appellate court, and the newly assigned man, Judge Lin Perlin, agreed with Draper that Michael Jank's testimony would be highly prejudicial. Without Jank, John McBride would probably be convicted at the second trial, now scheduled for May 30.

"They scheduled the second trial that soon?"

"Julie Williams, Mac's lawyer, insisted on a speedy trial, thinking that would make Draper decide to drop the charges. Instead, he found a new judge."

"How could this new judge disallow an eyewitness?"

"Before I can tell you that, you need some background." He told her that a lady named Doris Hambly had called about the modified picture of Mac in the newspaper. She got Gary's attention when she mentioned that the man she was calling about used his large steel ring like a worry bead. At a mobile home park in Lakeside, a suburb east of San Diego, Gary talked to Doris Hambly and three other people who agreed that the picture looked like a man named Ralph Hatch. Until late in September of the previous year, he had lived there in a motor home with a lady named Evelyn Nessbaum. In September, Evelyn had told Doris that Ralph had gone off on a job that required two months of travel. By late December, Evelyn was worried because Ralph still hadn't returned. Near Christmas, Evelyn disappeared, leaving her treasured cross-stitched animals behind. Doris didn't believe Evelyn would have done that voluntarily. A month later, the empty motor home was moved to a storage yard. On February 12, it caught fire and burned. The fire department couldn't determine a cause.

Ralph Hatch did have a record: a DUI arrest and conviction in Arizona in 1984. The mug shot of the gaunt alcoholic bore no resemblance to John McBride. According to Doris Hambly, the picture didn't resemble Ralph Hatch either.

Gary said, "So, in answer to your question as to how the new judge could prevent an eyewitness from testifying, he ruled that the picture we are using is a composite that may fit many people. Since we haven't found the buyer, and Michael Jank's memory might be faulty, and his testimony will be highly prejudicial, the judge disallowed all testimony relating to the ownership of the gun."

Andrea puffed her cheeks, wrote furiously, and then asked, "What else have you found?"

Gary talked about Dan Rhoades' cell phone, registered to address in Julian, California. That address belonged to a lady who did remailings. She had never met Dan Rhoades. All their contact had been by phone, and Dan Rhoades had only called her from pay phones. She sent his mail weekly to a post office box at San Diego Main, except for three bills. She paid the bills for both post office boxes and the cell phone from a bank account she opened in Julian under her own name. Once a month, she sent Dan Rhoades the bank statement, and in a week, she received an envelope that contained enough cash to maintain the bank balance at $500, and to pay her fee. All the envelopes she received from Dan Rhoades were addressed with printer generated labels, so she had no document in Dan Rhoades' handwriting.

The only thing she hadn't done herself was to open the post office box at San Diego Main. In the opinion of a handwriting expert, the form used to rent that box a year prior to the murder was not written by David Kendall. No one who worked at San Diego Main recalled seeing David open the box.

Gary had obtained a list of calls from Dan Rhoades' cell phone to 158 different numbers. Of the 122 contacted, most were businesses who didn't know Dan Rhoades, and the people who answered at the remaining numbers wouldn't identify themselves, much less anyone else. They still had no evidence that David Kendall was Dan Rhoades.

Andrea looked at her notes for a time, hummed a few bars of 'I can't get no satisfaction,' and then asked Gary, "I assume the police have looked for this Ralph Hatch and Evelyn Nessbaum?"

"Yeah. Nothing."

"And the car the killer drove? Either David or Ralph Hatch must have bought it."

"Yeah. Nothing."

"No one saw David hanging around the restaurant for all those weeks?" After Gary shook his head, she asked, "I know you've bugged his house. He hasn't said anything?"

"If it weren't for the stereo, I'd think the bug was broken."

She looked at her notes, and then shook her head. "You've got one witnesses' description of a man who looks exactly like John McBride, four people who say there once was a man who matched that description, and a suspicious cell phone record from a cell phone that you can't prove belonged to David Kendall. You don't have squat. Sorry."

CHAPTER 18

▼

November 14, 1996, Thursday, five months earlier

Josh Strahm wanted to meet at Hank's Place, a local tavern that was little more than a bar and six tables wedged into a narrow building. Where the bar ended, a dart board and a pool table gave the drinkers a reason to linger. While Josh finished a dart game with a man lugging an impressive belly, David sat on one of the wobbly wooden bar stools, and sipped his warm beer.

When Josh returned to the adjacent stool, he put a hand on David's shoulder and said, "Sorry to hear about your old man." David examined Josh in the mirror behind the bar. At 31, the blond man still looked sixteen, a baby wearing his hard time like a badge: large tattoos on both arms, dirty long hair, and a steel chain from a belt loop to his wallet.

Josh took the wallet out, extracted two dollars, and motioned to the bartender. When he had his beer, he raised the bottle in a toast. "To Dorothy."

David touched bottles with him. "I don't know how you talked me into that."

At Josh's request, David had managed to get a cute high school junior named Dorothy Lankford to take a drink, probably her first. In a few minutes, she was almost comatose. While they moved her to Josh's car, Josh told him he'd slipped her a roofie, the street name for Rohypnol, a potent sedative that induced amnesia and disappeared from the blood in 24 hours. They both had sex with the unconscious girl, but David found the episode less than erotic. Josh had condoms to contain any DNA, and he used Vaseline so she wouldn't suffer any vaginal trauma.

David said, "Between the condoms and the lube, it was like screwing a can of Crisco, except a lot more dangerous. We could have done serious time."

Josh sneered. "That's no big deal. I did some time." Josh was just out of San Quentin. He was living at home with his 'ass-wipe' brother, a younger sister, and mother, and on welfare since he'd had no luck finding work. Between his mother carping about getting a job, his brother ragging on him about losing the job flipping hamburgers that he had managed to get, and not being able to find another because of his felony record, he was desperate and depressed. The random drug testing by his parole officer meant he couldn't even party to forget about his troubles without going back to San Quentin. "Welfare doesn't give you enough money to buy cigarettes or beer, much less date. The only women I can get now are skags with kids looking for a baby sitter they can fuck."

David eyed his beer bottle. "Duh!"

Josh went so silent, David turned to look at him. His face was in high color. David thought that he was about to get hit with the beer bottle Josh cradled in his hand, so he said, "You're a smart man. How can you bitch about self-inflicted wounds?"

Still ready to swing the bottle, Josh said, "A guy ratted me out."

"I'm not talking about the jail time. I'm talking about now; about the way you look."

Contempt colored Josh's voice. "You want me to dress like a citizen?"

"I don't care what you do, but if you advertise that you're a bad-ass just out of San Quentin, then don't bitch when they lock up their daughters and their cash registers."

"Well, fuck you." David didn't react, so Josh added, "The guy who ratted me out isn't with us anymore. I say that because maybe you'll want to apologize to me."

"I saw that in the paper last week. Overdose, wasn't it?"

"That's what the paper said." Josh's arm remained poised to smash the bottle into David's face.

"I do admire your balls. I apologize if I offended you."

Josh raised his beer and took a long pull.

Still facing him, David said, "I'm just disappointed. I need help, but I can't use you looking like you do."

Josh put the bottle in his lap and grinned as if he'd seen something wonderful. He tilted the bottle a few inches and tapped David's arm with it. He whispered, "You killed your old man." He laughed, finished the beer in one long pull, and then signaled the bartender. "I'll take another. My friend here is buying."

David watched Josh accept the beer from the bartender. Whatever Josh did next would be a complete surprise. The guy was a flawed genius.

Josh leaned close and whispered, "Well, bro, you need help, and I need a future. Just ask, and I'm your man."

"What does that mean?"

Still speaking in a whisper, Josh said, "I do whatever you need done—anything—until all your problems with this thing are gone."

"Not looking like that, you can't. People would remember you."

"Spot me a haircut and some clothes, and you've got yourself a citizen."

✴   ✴   ✴   ✴

The week before Christmas, David sat in a motor home in Lakeside, a suburb east of San Diego. The faded yellow and white motor home Josh had borrowed blended with the neighborhood better than David could have imagined. People walked by without giving it a glance, just part of the scenery. 'Hide in plain sight' was Josh's idea, another in a string of great decisions the seemingly omniscient man had made since they became partners.

Josh had suggested the partnership, two people working together to insure that David became the sole owner of Framac, and Josh became the sole owner of a million dollars. The amount didn't matter. David didn't intend to pay anything. He had to eliminate anyone who knew enough to send him to jail. To his dismay, Josh had insisted on a partnership based on mutual destruction. He would kill people for David, but only after David gave him a videotaped confession describing how he killed his father. Josh would put the tape in a safe-deposit box, and give the key to someone he trusted, who would turn it over to the police only if Josh disappeared. David thought the idea was ludicrous. Josh told him it was that or nothing.

The thought of anyone holding his confession terrified David, but he also fretted that Evelyn might go to the police looking for Ralph Hatch. If she had a picture, someone would see the resemblance to Mac.

Believing there had to be a way to make the tape without leaving any permanent record, David went to the Internet to research methods for erasing tapes. A manufacturer in Hong Kong could supply VHS tapes with a thin film of solvent deposited in a solid suspension on the tape's surface. Each pass of the tape across the rotating heads would release small quantities of the solvent. Two passes would release enough solvent to dissolve the tape in a few weeks.

Three weeks later, they met in Josh's bedroom for the taping session. David handed Josh the tape he'd brought, still encased in the Sony wrapping of a high quality tape. Josh handed it back, saying, "I won't use that." He noted David's alarm, and winced. "I know all about tapes that turn to putty after a few weeks, man. That look tells me that's what this is."

David shrugged. "Had to try. I don't want to hand you my balls."

"Your choice, man. We're in it together, or we're not."

David realized, for better or for worse, he and Josh were partners. To his surprise, that realization brought some inner peace. David motioned to the camcorder and said, "Let's do it."

When David finished the story, Josh replayed the tape. Satisfied, he used a vacuum sealing machine to seal it inside heavy plastic. Several creases appeared where the bag folded at the corners of the tape box. Josh took instant pictures of the packaging, pointing out that the creases were like fingerprints. David could tell that the tape had never been seen or duplicated as long as the creases in the vacuum bag were identical to the pictures.

Since then, David found that he liked the man. Not only had Josh transformed his appearance into that of a model citizen, he seemed to have altered some internal landscape as well, as if the commitment had given his life purpose. He proved to be brilliant at solving problems.

Since Josh's involvement had to remain a secret, David took three meandering drives, following a route that would funnel any tail onto roads that Josh was watching. Someone was following David, and Josh discovered that a private investigator named George Martinez was David's shadow. Josh thought the surveillance was great. If the PI didn't know about David's back way out of the house, he might confirm David's alibi.

Josh obtained all the documents needed to establish a false identity as Gavin Gaither. He found a remailer in Hemet who would accept cash sent by mail, using it to pay her own fee and the bills for two pagers activated for Gavin Gaither. They would communicate by code on the pagers, and from pay phones, rather than risk cell phone conversations.

After Josh picked him up on a motorcycle a few times, David decided they needed a car. He hadn't told Josh about the money in Dan Rhoades' safe deposit box, so when he handed Josh the $4,800 to buy the black, four door Buick, he said the money came from his mother. Josh assured David that he'd be frugal. And he was. When he decided to watch Ralph Hatch's partner, Evelyn Nessbaum, he'd obtained the use of a motor home by promising the owner a full tank of gas.

Now David waited in the motor home because Josh had insisted they learn Evelyn's routine before they made any move. His caution was a total surprise to David. Far from the loose cannon David had expected, Josh was a methodical stalker.

Evelyn's motor home was parked in the first row of Silverlake Resort, her covered windshield facing the street. Silverlake Resort was a slum. Six decrepit trailers and three motor homes in worse condition than Evelyn's occupied the front row. Each was besieged with the overflow from the tight living quarters: furniture, bikes, boxes, tools, car parts, and barbecues. The debris also included trash, perhaps unnoticed in the midst of more valuable stuff. Evelyn's detritus was dotted with potted plants.

David saw Evelyn walk from somewhere inside the park and go inside her motor home. Since the temperatures were in the eighties during Christmas week, Evelyn opened several windows. She emerged with an aluminum pole, closed the awning that had shaded the west side of the motor home from the afternoon sun, and went back inside. David could see her moving around in the kitchen. If she followed the same routine as the previous two days, by six-thirty she would be in an easy chair in front of the TV, and by 9:30, she'd be in bed, still watching television.

A few minutes later, Josh parked his motorcycle behind the motor home. He entered, and raised his eyebrows in a silent question. David said, "Just the same, almost to the minute."

Unzipping his leather jacket, Josh said, "I think she visits another woman, but they don't get together in the evening."

David's stomach fluttered when he saw that Josh was wearing a white shirt, dark slacks, and a tie. Josh loosened the tie and said, "We'll go tonight."

✶   ✶   ✶   ✶

At 8:30 that evening, Evelyn opened her door. She looked a little put out. David realized she probably thought he and Josh were Mormon missionaries in their white shirts and dark ties. He rushed his rehearsed speech. "I'm Dr. Gaither and this is Dr. Sullivan. We're from Standish Lodge, a long-term health-care facility in Ramona. We have a man there who suffered a stroke three months ago, and he's now able to communicate again. His name is Ralph Hatch, and he asked to see you."

As Josh had predicted, everything moved swiftly. When they offered to take her to visit Ralph, Evelyn shut off the TV, grabbed a coat and purse, and then turned off all the lights except for the ones on a fake Christmas tree.

"I should tell my friend where I'm going."

David looked at his watch. "Visiting hours end at 9:30 and it's a 45 minute ride. As it is, you'll only have 15 minutes to visit with him."

She flapped both hands, erasing the request, and locked the door of her motor home. David held the Buick's back door open for her, and she got in.

Josh drove into the mountains toward Ramona. David said, "This Ralph Hatch seems to be illiterate, yet his vocabulary is that of a college professor. Was the apparent illiteracy caused by the stroke?"

"No, he can't read, but he loves to listen to all sorts of books on tape, even textbooks."

That mystery finally solved, David quoted the research he'd done on strokes to keep the tiny woman thinking about Ralph. She was nervous about being saddled with an invalid, too nervous to pay any attention when Josh took a dirt road off the highway. The road was not long, only a hundred yards or so, and she finally glanced around when he stopped and shut off the lights. Outside, the world was deep black, she saw only her own image in the window as Josh opened the door and got out. She asked, "Where's the hospital?"

David reached into the back and unlocked her door. Josh opened it, grabbed the tiny woman by her coat lapels and pulled her from the car. Evelyn's scream stopped abruptly. David got out in time to see her fall. Josh thrust a flashlight into his hand. "Keep it on her head, but don't stand too close."

On her back on pebbly hardpan, Evelyn blinked in the flashlight beam, her broken jaw cocked to the side. Josh had moved away. When he returned, he grunted as he said, "Move back. You're too close." David stepped back and Josh moved into the edge of the beam, a huge rock held high over his head. He dropped it on Evelyn's face. The rock bounced and rolled away from her shoulders, leaving her body flopping as if it had received an electrical shock. Where her head had been, a large patch of pink and white paste vibrated as blood pulsed from the stump. In seconds, all the motion stopped. The paste darkened to a large pool of blood.

Josh opened the trunk and picked up a small hand ax. While David held the beam on the body, Josh chopped off both of her hands and put them into a doubled garbage bag. He got her purse from the car, took out her keys, and then put the purse into the garbage bag with her hands.

They dragged the body to the edge of a brush-choked precipice. Pushing on her feet, they shoved Evelyn's body over the edge, and listened to the cracks and thuds as it crashed through the brush, down a very long slope.

Josh ran back to the car and took a shovel from the trunk. He told David to hold the light on a spot, and he dug furiously for several minutes. He handed David the shovel, saying breathlessly, "Need it a foot deeper." David, feeling Josh's fear, quickly dug the extra foot. Josh slid the garbage bag into the hole, and

David covered it with dirt. Josh jumped on the dirt pile until it seemed level with the surrounding ground, then they worked together to move a large rock onto the spot. Josh took the shovel and the ax to the precipice and threw them into the darkness.

They returned to the car. Josh's voice was weak when he asked David to drive. Lights off, David drove toward the highway and eased the car up to the edge of the road. He didn't see any approaching headlights, so he switched the lights on, and headed south.

Josh held the flashlight between his knees as he scrubbed his blood spattered hands with packaged moistened wipes. His knees shook, and the flashlight beam danced on the instrument panel.

"You okay?" David asked.

"Yeah. Nerves is all."

David patted the man's back. "I am really impressed. That was awesome planning."

Josh continued to scrub. "I should have had the hole dug. It was like digging through fucking cement." Josh inspected his right hand in the flashlight beam. "I didn't expect that much blood splatter after she was dead." The sleeves of his white shirt were dotted with blood spots to the elbows. He unbuttoned the shirt and said, "Slow down when you take the next curve."

Josh threw the balled up shirt out of the window and over the Armco railing. "Go back to Silverlake. I'll shut off the water and electricity to make it look like she intended to go away for awhile."

CHAPTER 19

▼

May 7, 1997, Wednesday

Gary returned to San Diego in the evening, arriving at Mac's in time for dinner. While they ate, Mac told Gary about a new series of tests that Dr. Jurgen Frieze, Julie's blood spatter expert, had done. Mac, dressed in a long coat and sprayed with phosphor-laced syrup, had gotten into a Taurus and backed it up. According to Mac, a black-light photo of the car's interior looked like a city at night. That was the only good news. Julie was pessimistic about the trial, not that she'd said anything, but Mac could tell.

After dinner, Gary caught up on his phone messages. He had hired George to canvass the bars from El Cajon to La Mesa, but George hadn't found anyone who recognized either David or Ralph Hatch. The other message was from Margaret Deville, the neighbor listening to David's bug, asking if they could meet. Gary assumed that three months of listening to nothing had finally gotten to her, and she probably wanted out. It was time to remove the bug. David was not going to talk about his crimes inside his house.

*　　　*　　　*　　　*

At ten the next morning, Gary called Margaret. Twenty five minutes later, he parked around the corner from her house. Carrying his briefcase, he walked the half block, his face turned away from the Kendall's house. When Margaret, slightly stooped, matronly plump and in her seventies, opened the door, she seemed happy to see him. They walked through the living room that felt like a small chapel into her family room. The table was set with tea and scones, perhaps her way of easing into the bad news. He put his empty briefcase on the table, sat down, and sampled a scone. The lemon flavored biscuit with a sugar glaze was delicious, with just the appropriate sweetness to soften the tea.

When Gary commented on the flavor, Margaret said. "Isn't it a marvelous recipe? I found it on the Internet." She patted her stomach. "I had to take up walking to keep my weight down." She added, "I also walked the neighborhood to confirm an impression I had about David."

"Oh?"

"Over the months, I've gotten to know David's sounds, and the sounds of the house. For example, David leaves the things he carries in his pockets near the microphone—his wallet, keys, change, and things like that—and he picks them up when he's preparing to leave. His last stop is usually in the bathroom, and then he goes out the door. If I watch, I'll see his car within a minute. However, perhaps once a week, he makes all the leaving sounds, but I never see his car."

"Any ideas?"

"Well, I thought the only way he could go was through the yard of the house that backs up to theirs. So I went for walk each time I heard him in the shower. On the third day, I saw him come through the gate of that house."

"Do you know where he went?"

"Yes. He walked downhill toward Moreno Boulevard, but he only went a block before someone in a car picked him up." Margaret handed him a note. "It's the license number."

Gary had to laugh. "You are a fantastic detective. How did you get the plate?"

Grinning, she said, "The next time he went out, I drove to the place where he'd been picked up before and parked. When they drove by, I wrote the number down."

*   *   *   *

After he left Margaret's, Gary returned to his car and called Detective Bacha, gave him the license plate number and explained David's route through the neighbor's back yard. Bacha exploded. "God dammit, no wonder the asshole slipped us the day we served the search warrant. We were going to go in Friday morning, but the warrant got held up, then we had to wait until David got back from the airport. I was positive he'd have the Ford key in his pocket. I couldn't believe it when he wasn't home." He paused before he added, "I'll check on the plate and call you back."

Two minutes later: "Joshua Strahm. S-T-R-A-H-M. Did time in San Quentin for dealing. The snitch who put him there died of an overdose shortly after Joshua was paroled."

"Got an address?"

Bacha gave it to him and disconnected.

According to the Thomas Guide, Joshua's house was two miles away. Gary drove to Clairemont, and then walked by the address. Joshua's house was the street-side half of a small duplex probably built in the forties. A badly constructed box, the eves sagged, and ripples marred the thin plywood siding. Only a few homes in the neighborhood looked tidy.

Joshua's black, early-nineties, Buick was parked on the busy, four-lane street. As he walked by, Gary saw the red light of an alarm blinking on the dash.

Gary returned to his car and sat in the back seat for shade. He waited six hours before Joshua emerged. The slight, sharp-featured, blond man had been a spectator at Mac's trial. Gary followed as Joshua drove the Buick to a restaurant on Balboa Avenue. He left the car's windows down to cool the sun-baked interior when he went into the restaurant. Inside the restaurant, Joshua took a window seat, probably so he could watch the open car. After dinner, he drove home.

*   *   *   *

The next morning, Gary read the manual for a car bug he'd purchased but never used. The hard drive in Mac's computer would store the data stream sent by the bug through the UHF transceiver. The sound file was compressed and encrypted for transmission, so he installed software to reassemble the files.

Gary wanted to know where Joshua and David went, so he tested the batteries in four trackers, each a small cube of plastic with a short wire antenna. Since the batteries only lasted for two weeks, he set each tracker's start date to give him eight weeks of coverage. The minuscule power put out by the trackers and the bug required a repeater network of powerful transceivers to extend their range. He called a business radio service and paid for three months of access to their repeaters. He entered the repeater codes in all four trackers, and then had to study the manual before he was able to enter the codes into the bug.

He connected the UHF radio to Mac's PC, and then went out to his car. He put the bug on the rear window deck, attached a tracker to the underside of the car, and went for a half hour drive. When he returned to Mac's house, he listened to the playback. He heard the music he'd played in the car, so the repeaters worked as advertised. The computer had also received and analyzed the tracker's position data, all of it wrong. He discovered that he'd given the software an initialization point in Mexico. He ran the map program again, got the correct position for Mac's house, and then the tracker positions were dead on.

✶   ✶   ✶   ✶

Gary was waiting when Joshua took himself out to dinner just after five that evening. Again, when he parked at the restaurant, he left the windows down. As he had on the previous evening, he sat at a table where he could see the parking lot. He glanced at the car as he ate, until a woman walking by his table distracted him.

A few minutes later, a beautiful girl parked her red truck two spots away from Gary. He was standing beside her door when she got out. Tall, with acres of curly black hair, dressed in tight Levi's and a blouse made from a clinging material that invited touching, she frowned at Gary as he asked, "You see the blond guy at the third window?"

She looked, and then asked, "Why?" Her voice was high and soft, a little girl's voice.

Gary showed her the DEA badge. "I need to look in his car without him seeing me. I'll give you $50 if you can hold his attention for five minutes."

"How would I do that?"

"Mistake him for someone else. Five minutes is all I need. He'll probably take that long trying to hit on you." She looked uncertain until he held out the money. With a 'what the hell' expression, she stuffed the bill into a pocket and walked toward the restaurant.

The girl entered the restaurant, walked by Joshua's table, did a double-take, and said something to him when she had his complete attention. Gary opened the back door of the Buick and knelt on the rear seat to glue the bug to the deck of the rear window. In place, it looked like a stiffener or reinforcement.

He got out, closed the door, and scooted under the rear bumper. He positioned a tracker on the left side of the Buick's bumper mount, feeling the magnet suck it onto the metal. He placed another there and two on the right bumper mount.

That done, he slid out from beneath the car. The girl still had Joshua's head turned. Gary gave her a thumb up. She put her hand over her mouth as if she were embarrassed, said something, and then moved away.

Gary returned to Mac's house at 6:30 that evening. He brought up the software to unscramble the first sound file from the bug. He and Mac both listened to the segment the bug had recorded, compressed, digitized, and then transmitted.

The bug eliminated all silences, so the playback sounded like a stream of car engines, mostly indecipherable chatter from people walking by the car, and then wind noise as the car was driven. It had recorded seven minutes of sound in the 30 minute segment. Happy with his new toy, all Gary needed now was Joshua and David together in the car.

CHAPTER 20

▼

January 12, 1997, Sunday, four months earlier

During the drive to Pacific Beach, Josh asked about David's week.

David waved a hand. "All quiet. I don't think the investigator's watching anymore. What did you find out at Silverlake?"

"I saw the manager—I'm still using the line that I want to move in there when he has an opening—and he said he's going to move a motor home into storage at the end of January. So she either hasn't been found, or they haven't identified her."

Josh grabbed David's arm. "No worries today, my man. Today is party time, and I am so ready to party." Josh had learned that his parole agent had the schedule for drug tests in his computer. The man also had his password taped to the monitor, so Josh had hacked his own file. He wouldn't be tested again until March 17, plenty of time to get clean.

In Pacific Beach, Josh waited in the car while David walked to the Dive Inn. Inside, his shoes crunched in the sand on the concrete floor. The bartender, Art, looked at him, but continued to hit on a redheaded teenager wearing a thong and a string top. In a minute, she headed for the door, mumbling something that included "asshole."

Art brought the beer he'd ordered and David put a hundred dollar bill on the bar. "And I'll have three of the usual."

Art looked at the bill, a sour expression on his face. "That won't do it, David Kendall."

David's muscles froze. If Art knew his name, he knew everything.

Art added, "I'll need a hundred of those every month for a year."

"I don't have any money."

"You're a fucking millionaire. You own a successful business now."

"My mother will own the business if John McBride is convicted."

"Then get the money from mommy."

Thinking Art might be wired, David asked, "What would I be paying for?"

Story-telling was Ralph Hatch's life, and after constructing so many imaginary tales, David's unfolding true story had inspired him. Art had heard everything. When David ordered duplicates of Mac's ID, Art had proof the stories were true. Then Hatch disappeared and John McBride's picture was in the newspaper when he was arrested for killing Frank. In mid-December, when a woman came in looking for Hatch, Art knew that he was never coming back.

Just in case he was wired, David said, "You should have reported all that to the police. What you have now is an extortion attempt, which is a felony in California."

Art folded his arms. "I can go to the cops if that's what you want. Your choice." When David didn't respond, Art said, "In case you're thinking of doing me, I've got the whole story down on paper, and someone will deliver it to the cops if anything happens to me."

Still concerned that Art might be wired, David said, "I have been thinking about a deal we could do. When mom inherits the business, I might get a million. I could use it to buy merchandise that you and I could turn into several million in profit."

"Fuck you very much," Art said amiably.

"Think about it. I know my way around Mexico. I can find a dealer. You know the market here, so you could find a way to unload one big shipment. We could make one big score, and both of us would be set for life."

"I don't partner with killers."

"You've got your letter. I don't care what you think you know. It's all bullshit from a drunk." David paused before he said, "But I am serious about the deal. After that guy who murdered my father is convicted, we could be set for life. And while we're doing the deal, you call the shots. The only way I'm going to get paid is if you feel like paying me. It's a win-win for you, and I take all the risk."

Art leaned on the bar, his face close to David's. "I'm going to find out if you have money. If you don't, maybe we'll work something out."

David pointed at the hundred on the bar. "Can we do some business now?"

Art took the hundred, walked into the back, and reappeared clutching three baggies. He put them on the bar. "These are for medicinal purposes only."

David didn't laugh; he felt dead inside.

*   *   *   *

Parked next to the cross on Mt. Soledad, overlooking the city and the ocean beyond Coronado, Josh rolled two well-packed joints, handed one to David, and then lit his own. He inhaled deeply, reclined his seat, and reluctantly released the smoke. "Awesome shit," he said reverently.

David was into his second toke before Josh said, "The letter is bullshit." David looked at him, wondering if the dope was talking. Josh pointed the burning cylinder at David. "Does a drug dealer trust anyone enough to let them hold a letter like that? Not on this planet." Josh took a hit and tried to talk without releasing the smoke. "Your problem is that he can put you and the guy in Arizona together. He put the fake ID in your hand. He can fucking hang you a dozen ways. We have to take him out."

"He's big and he's armed. Taking him out won't be easy."

Josh lazily waved a hand. "Not true, my man, not true at all."

CHAPTER 21

▼

May 11, 1997, Sunday

George called Gary on Sunday. He ran through the litany of dead ends before he said, "I did set up a date tomorrow to meet some guy who says he was at Colson's Cavern the night of the murder. You want to take it?" Before Gary could answer, George added, "Guy lives in his car. I wouldn't have agreed except he told me he eats there regularly."

"A homeless guy? How does that work?"

"He says their dumpster is especially sanitary."

Gary sighed. "What the hell, it'll be a new perspective. Where do I meet him?"

*   *   *   *

The next morning, Gary located the late seventies Ford Thunderbird in a shopping center's parking lot. The yellow car had once sported a vinyl covered roof, traces of glue lingered in strips on the roof's black primer. Mud streaked the scarred yellow paint on the lower body. Looking through the grime encrusted windows, the tops of the seats were islands in a sea of the man's possessions, with just enough clear space for a driver.

Gary waited in his rental car for the Thunderbird's owner. Minutes later, a slight, gray-haired man, in his late forties or early fifties, left a nearby thrift store and aimed for the Ford. His khaki pants and red pullover shirt looked too clean for a homeless guy.

He was the owner. Gary intercepted him after he unlocked the car. His face slid through wariness, irritation, and hostility before Gary showed him the flyer.

The man tapped it with an index finger. "This is the guy supposed to look like the guy who killed his partner?" He watched Gary carefully as he talked.

Pissed about the long wait for another bullshit artist, Gary turned to walk away.

"Seen it happen. Wasn't that guy who did it."

Gary walked back. Standing close, he asked, "You were there when the shooting happened?"

"Yeah."

"Why didn't you tell the police?"

The man looked embarrassed, but his eyes remained focused on Gary's face when he said, "No point. Got a record, so they wasn't going to believe me."

"What do you remember?"

"It was a young guy who killed him."

The man looked thin and malnourished. Gary pointed at a fast food restaurant. "Can I buy you some lunch, Mr...?"

"Fred Ehmer. Sure, I haven't eaten yet."

He turned to walk to the restaurant, but Gary motioned to the rental. "We'll use the drive-through so we can talk in private."

After they'd ordered, they waited to get to the window. Gary asked, "How long have you been an alcoholic, Fred?"

He gave Gary a weary glance. "What's that have to do with the price of rice?"

"I don't want to waste my time."

Fred watched Gary's eyes. "I've been off it about seven months now."

"Would you take a blood test today to confirm that?"

"Sure."

The car ahead moved away from the drive-up window. After the food was delivered, Gary drove into the parking lot and parked next to Fred's car.

Fred unwrapped his sandwich. "Had to get off the stuff, because the car's the only home I've got. I get another DUI, they'll take the car and I'm on the street."

Fred looked at his car and spoke to the window. His speech pattern changed. "Almost killed myself last year, I was that down. That's when I quit drinking. I figured if I wasn't afraid of dying, I shouldn't be afraid of living without booze. It was hell for the first three months, but it's easier now. Nothing's really turned around yet, but I don't feel sick all the time like I used to, so I figure I'm on the way up."

"I'll buy you two fifths of anything you want if you'll admit you're still drinking."

Fred looked at Gary, agony on his face. "You think I'm made of steel? As long as I've been off it, my heart took a leap when you offered that." He examined his sandwich and said, "Don't offer again, okay? I don't know if I'd make it, somebody gives me a bottle."

After a moment, Gary asked, "You say you saw this young guy shoot an old guy?"

Between chews, Fred managed a muffled, "Yeah."

"Shot the old guy right in the face, then put another in the back of his head?"

"Didn't see him shoot the old guy again. After the first shot, I've got my head down. When I heard the second shot, I bailed down the other side of the restaurant."

Gary showed Fred a picture of David. "That the kid?" Fred glanced at Gary, a question on his face. Shaking the picture, Gary asked, "Did you get a good look at him?"

Fred tapped the picture with his sandwich. "Yeah, I'm positive, that's him. That's the guy who did the shooting. Who is he?"

"He's an asshole. He's a big guy: 6-2, olive skin, great build."

"Yeah, no doubt about it, the guy was big."

"Have you talked with anyone about why you quit drinking?"

"No one gives a shit. Boozers are always saying they're off it." Fred wiped mayonnaise from the side of his mouth. "Why?"

"It might help if you were too scared to drink after the shooting, maybe afraid you'd talk about it and the guy would find you."

"Now that I think about it, that was the reason I quit. Scared the living shit out of me."

Gary said, "The man on trial doesn't deserve to be in prison. I'm not going to promise you anything, but if you can get him off, I'll do right by you."

Fred winced. "It's a long shot. The cops aren't gonna believe me."

"You get the facts straight, they might."

*   *   *   *

Gary rented a motel that afternoon. When he saw the bed, Fred wanted to take a nap. Then he saw the bathroom, and he stayed in the shower for half an hour. He came out of the shower with a towel wrapped around his middle, then abandoned the towel to climb into bed. "Ah, man, you have no idea," he said reverently.

He pointed at the garbage sack that contained all his clothes. "Everything in there is dirty. Maybe we can find a Laundromat later?"

"You enjoy the comforts. I'll do your wash at my place while I'm getting some stuff together. I'll be back in a couple of hours."

Fred's clothes were on the bathroom floor. Gary emptied the pockets on the nightstand, and then stuffed those clothes into the garbage bag. Fred looked worried. "I really hope you're coming back."

Gary shouldered the bag. "You think I rented the room so I could steal all these valuable clothes?"

Fred winced. "You don't understand. When it's all you have…"

Fred did look relieved when Gary returned three hours later. He got out of bed and sorted through the folded clothes, put on underwear, then selected a pair of khaki pants.

Gary stopped him. "Wear dark stuff. I want you to show me around the parking lot at Colson's Cavern tonight."

*   *   *   *

At nine that night, Gary parked across the street from Colson's Cavern. He asked Fred, "Where were you when the shooting happened?"

"See the dumpster?" At the rear of the parking lot, the dumpster was in an enclosure surrounded by cyclone fence with imbedded lattice. "When I'm short on money, I can find a good meal there. It's sanitary; you hear what I'm saying? They put all the food in plastic bags. Usually everything in the bag is good food. Come away so full, I don't need to eat for days." He added, "Course, they call the cops if they catch you, so it's got to be done real quiet after dark."

"Like around eight?"

"Don't have a watch and the clock in the car don't work, but you have to wait for a couple hours after the restaurant gets busy."

"Why is that?"

"So they have time to throw things out. You don't want to be eating stuff that's been cooking in there all day."

"Oh, right. So you were in the dumpster when you see the kid looking around?"

"Yeah, he's right by that motor home, watching the parking lot."

A bus roared by, rocking the car with a blast of wind, the noise so loud Gary had to repeat his question. "How many cars were there?"

Fred squinted with the effort. "Ah, five I think."

Gary showed Fred the photos taken the night of the shooting. "One car is missing in this picture. Were the others like that?"

Fred shook his head. "No. There were two down at this end." He pointed at the street end of the parking lot. When he pointed to the rear of the parking lot, he said, "These three were there, but this one wasn't." He pointed at Frank Kendall's car in the picture. "This space was empty."

"Are you sure about that? There are four witnesses in the apartment building who saw some guy looking around the parking lot earlier. They didn't say anything about the cars being in different places later."

Pointing at the photo, Fred said, "Yeah. They was two cars at this end, and nothing until these cars here."

"OK, if you're sure that's where they were when you first got there." Fred looked confused, so Gary repeated, "That's what it looked like when you first got there. This picture was taken after the shooting." Fred didn't say anything, but he kept looking at Gary expectantly. "The killer's car was here." Gary put his finger on the space next to Frank's car.

"I wasn't there after the shooting. I don't know what it looked like. Those spots were empty when I got there." He tapped the photo as he added, "And two cars were here."

They walked into the parking lot and Fred showed Gary where the two cars had been parked when he first came into the lot. Gary stood on the spot where Frank Kendall was shot, again using the description, 'the old guy about your size wearing a suit.' He showed Fred where the killer's car had straddled the next parking space, far enough away to not be spattered with blood during the shooting. "Both the old guy about your size wearing a suit, and the short chunky guy who came out of the restaurant with him, talked for a couple of minutes and drove away. A few minutes later, the young kid drove into the lot in a car that looked like the one the chunky guy drove. About fifteen minutes later, the old guy about your size wearing a suit drives came back into the lot, and parked in the next space over from the kid's car."

"Yeah, I guess."

Almost shouting, Gary was in his face. "Don't guess."

Fred didn't flinch. "I was in the dumpster. I see one car come in, I duck down. Another car comes in, I duck down. I didn't pay no attention to where they parked."

Gary put his arm around Fred's shoulder, trying to apologize. "Good going, that's the way you need to be. You tell me when I'm off base. You know your story, I don't. If you say it was a certain way, that's the way it was."

The owner's motor home was parked in its usual place. As they walked to Fred's vantage point, they had to squeeze between the motor home and the dumpster enclosure. Solar film on the motor home's side windows reflected the parking lot's lights.

They moved around to the back of the dumpster enclosure. Fred lifted the latch, and disappeared inside. The lattice cut off most of the light from the parking lot and from a floodlight over the rear door to the restaurant. In the darkness, Gary bumped into Fred, who whispered, "If somebody comes out, duck down inside. You don't get hurt when they throw the bag in, 'cause nothing's heavy." Using only his arms, Fred silently hoisted himself up over the edge into the steel bin. For a malnourished small man, the move showed years of practice. When Gary tried to follow, his feet banged on the metal side, a loud kettle drum sound in the stillness. They listened for a moment, expecting some reaction. When nothing happened, Fred examined the contents of a plastic bag.

Gary asked, "Are you hungry?" Fred had finished dinner just two hours before.

"I could handle some dessert."

Standing on piles of garbage, the view of the lot through the lattice was much better than Gary had expected. "Where was the kid when you first spotted him?"

Fred indicated the motor home. "He looked in the window, then he leaned against the fence. While he was there, I couldn't move."

"Was he wearing a long black coat and a knit cap?"

"Yeah. It was a witch's tit that night. I was wearing my own long coat to keep my teeth from banging."

"What happened then?"

"Somebody came out and dumped some trash. When I poked my head up, the kid was gone. So I started looking through the bags again."

At Gary's request, Fred got out of the dumpster and stood between the motor home and the fence. Looking down from the dumpster, Gary could see Fred's face in the mirrored window on the motor home. Forced to remain quiet, Fred would have had enough time to memorize David's face.

Gary got out of the dumpster without making too much noise. "If you want to judge how tall he was, get back inside while I look in the windows. He's a couple of inches taller than me."

When he heard Fred in the dumpster, Gary looked in the motor home's window, holding his hand over his head to suggest David's height. Fred was grinning when he joined Gary again. "Guy stood there for a long time. I got a damn good look."

Leaning against the latticed fence, Gary talked to Fred's reflection in the window of the motor home. "So then the old guy who was killed walked out of the restaurant with a short chunky guy. They talked for a few minutes, then the old guy about your size pulled out. Did you see him leave?"

Fred whispered, "Yeah, I seen all that. I was standing up, going through a bag looking for tiramisu. This place makes it real good. It doesn't have any particular smell you can go by, so you have to taste everything to find it. So I'm doing that while they talk. Same time the old guy leaves, the bag's empty, so I go back to looking."

"The chunky guy pulled out a minute or so after the old guy left. He has trouble turning his head, so he backed out in a series of short moves. Did you see that?"

"Like I said, after the old guy left, I didn't watch no more."

"Some time after the chunky guy's car left, an identical car drove into the lot and parked in that spot I showed you. How soon did that happen?"

Fred was watching Gary in the mirrored window. "Wasn't long, a couple of minutes maybe. I didn't know it was the same kind of car, just saw the headlights. I watched to make sure they went into the restaurant, but nobody got out. A couple of minutes later, the old guy comes back."

Gary turned and put his face close to Fred's, and said in an angry sounding whisper, "That's not right, Fred. Shit like that can make you look like you're lying. The old guy didn't get back for at least fifteen minutes." After he was sure Fred had that message, Gary asked, "Then what happened?"

"So the old guy parks beside the other car, and gets out. He walks around the back of his car, and about the time he gets to the rear fender, I see the kid get out."

"The man fell near the front of the car. How did the kid get behind him?"

"Oh, yeah, that's right. He was standing beside the door when the kid got out. He had to move to the front."

On the other side of the dumpster, a door opened. Fred put his hand on Gary's arm as if to tell him not to move. Light spilled through the lattice work, something thudded into the dumpster, and then the light cut off. A moment later, the restaurant door closed.

Gary looked around the corner to make sure no one was outside. Then he leaned against the motor home, and asked Fred, "When did the kid exchange cell phones with the old guy?"

Fred paused for a long minute before he asked, "Is that what they was? I saw them hand each other something. Couldn't see what it was."

"Yeah, you wouldn't be able to tell from this distance. Did the kid shoot him then?"

"Yeah, he comes out with this big silver gun. Shit, I see that, my feet want to run inside the dumpster, but the old guy didn't move. Thing goes off like a flash bulb, all I can see is this big purple spot. I'm scared shitless he knows I'm there, so I duck down, and then I hear it go off again. Well, I'm outta here. I run behind the place and down the other side. My car's parked just around the corner."

"Did the kid drive by you as he left?"

"Shit, I'm moving flat out, I ain't looking. Once I get to my car, I drive away."

Four people came out of the restaurant and walked to a car that was parked a space away from where Frank Kendall had been shot. Fred and Gary watched in silence until the car started. As it backed, Gary said, "Of course, you can't identify the old guy or the chunky guy. It was too dark to see them clearly."

"Well, I think it was the same guy in the newspaper picture."

"You don't read newspapers, Fred. You never even heard about this guy being accused. You saw a murder, and you're afraid the killer is still loose, so you thought you'd better report it." Gary motioned toward the car. "Let's leave before somebody spots us."

Fred said, "I'll just check that last bag for tiramisu."

Gary grabbed his arm. "Go back to the car. I'll get a take-out order of tiramisu."

"Oh, Jesus, that'd be so nice."

✳   ✳   ✳   ✳

In the morning, after a restless night of listening to Fred talking in his sleep, Gary had him replay the shooting several times. Gary pushed Fred to visualize the scene. "Can you see those two men talking? Can you see them, really see them?"

Fred was sweating when they broke for lunch. After lunch, they returned to the motel and ran through the scene two more times. At three, they took an hour break, and then Gary asked him to tell the story from the beginning. Gary tried to trip him up, accusing him of making mistakes when he hadn't. By that evening, Gary thought Fred was ready.

✳   ✳   ✳   ✳

When he returned Fred to his car the next morning, Gary gave him $500. As Fred looked at the money, Gary told him, "That's yours. If you get to testify, you get $4,500 more when it's over. If you get him off, it'll be a lot more." Gary held Fred's arm until their eyes met. "Do your best, okay?"

"They ain't going to believe me."

"You were there, Fred. Make them believe you." Fred looked frightened, so Gary added, "And remember, we never talked; we never even met. You never called George Martinez; you never talked to anyone connected to us, you never saw the flyer about the chunky guy, and you don't know anything about a trial. Whatever happens, you stay with that, even if they threaten to throw you in jail, even if they do throw you in jail. You okay with that?"

A quick nod and Fred was out of the car. Gary watched him drive away, nervous that he might fold under questioning and spill the story.

Too late for second thoughts, Gary called George. George told him that he still hadn't raised anyone at the 36 phone numbers left on Dan Rhoades' cell phone records.

Gary said, "They must not be in use anymore. Can you find out who the numbers belonged to?"

"Yeah, but it won't come cheap. Probably a $100 a number."

"Do it. We need a break. You got enough to cover it until we get together?"

"I'll let you know."

"Come by Mac's when you have time. We can settle up, and I've got some things to show you." George agreed and Gary asked, "That guy who said he preferred the dumpster at Colson's Cavern?"

"Yeah?"

"He never talked to you."

George said, "Man, I gotta get more sleep. I'm hallucinating all over the place."

CHAPTER 22

▼

February 14, 1997, Friday, three months earlier

As the brightly lit Mormon temple in San Diego came into view, David had to pull over to the shoulder on Interstate 5. He could hear his heart pounding, a live thing trying to break through his chest wall. Flushed, sweating, short of breath, he had all the signs of a heart attack. Too hot, he rolled down his window. The traffic noise was excruciating, but he desperately needed the air. The pressure in his chest wouldn't let him breathe.

He knew why he was having a heart attack. Reality had faded during the two weeks in Oregon. He'd connected with Jessica the day after he got to Corvallis. A freshman at the university, she was smart, funny, and a reluctant virgin from a strict southern family. On the long drive to San Diego, he built a future with Jessica and his mother, a loving unit that would nurture all its members. Then, in sight of the city, reality crushed that dream. The shock had been too severe, more than his heart could take.

Josh had insisted that David leave town, pointing out that he would need the alibi in case anyone connected him with Art's murder. But if Art had caught Josh setting him up, Josh might be dead, and David's confession could be in police hands by now. Or if Josh had been caught burning Evelyn's motor home, he would have told them that David had killed Evelyn, and that he had only been hired to torch the trailer.

A semi roared by just inches away, the heat, smell, and dirt exploding into the car, the impact from the air so violent that David wasn't sure the truck hadn't hit his car. It took a few moments to clear the dirt from his mouth, but the activity calmed him. His heart kept beating, the sweating stopped, and he felt cool again. He found a gap in the traffic and pulled back onto the road, the steering wheel gritty in his hands.

When he got home, his mother was standing outside the back door. It was almost 11:30. She was usually in bed by nine. His voice trembled as he asked, "Are you all right?"

Tears brightened her eyes. She took his arm and they walked toward the house. He held the door for her. In the hallway, he put his suitcase and overnight bag outside his door and followed her into the kitchen. Could she hear his heart hammering? He nudged her toward a chair at the small breakfast table and asked, "Can I make you some tea?"

"How about one of those White Russians?"

He rummaged through the bottles in the cupboard and mixed her drink. He poured himself a water glass full of scotch. At the table, she pointed to his drink. "Did you have a bad trip?"

"You're scaring me. What's wrong?"

"I watched jury selection today." She sighed, and then took a deep breath. "Get my mind off of this. Tell me what you did in Corvallis?"

He changed Jessica into a 26 year old graduate student, but otherwise described the affair accurately. His mother seemed happy for him, so he added, "I've done a lot of thinking. I'm sorry I was so selfish."

She said, "A man from Jastillana Insurance came by. He wanted to know if I'd be handling the lawsuit to remove Mac as a partner. I told him you would. Will you do that?"

"Sure. Do you want me to hire someone to run the business?"

"Mac sent me a letter through his lawyer. He recommended that we put Ricardo Ruiz in charge of in-house operations. Do you know him?"

"Yes, he's very knowledgeable. He would be a good choice."

"Do you have any interest in running the business?"

David could feel the hairs on his arms stand up. He searched for the right response. "Do you want to keep it?"

She shrugged. "Frank always said it would take two years to sell the business for what it's worth. Dissolving the partnership could take a couple of years, so it may be four years before the business sells. If you don't want to run it, we'll have to find someone right away."

"Then I'll be glad to manage it for you."

*   *   *   *

David paged Josh at eight the next morning, sending him the code for a pickup at ten. Josh returned the 10-4, but changed the time to 11. That was a relief. To Josh, it was just another Saturday and he liked to sleep in on the weekends.

Near eleven, David had walked almost to Moreno Boulevard before Josh wheeled the Buick onto the street. He turned into a driveway and David opened the passenger door and got in. Josh said, "Problems are gone."

David said, "How about we go up to Del Mar. I'll buy you brunch at the hotel."

As Josh drove toward Interstate 5, David said, "Mom asked me to handle the lawsuit to get Mac's half of the business. She also asked me to run it."

"Does that put you in a position to move money?"

"Oh, yes, indeed. I think your services as a consultant will be required immediately. What do you think, 125 large to start? That should help until we sell the business."

Josh accelerated down the on-ramp to Interstate 5 north. "Remember, my man, don't count it until you're walking away from the table."

Judging by his grin, Josh wasn't taking his own advice.

David said, "Tell me about the motor home."

As he looked toward the fast lane, Josh said, "I put on a great show for the old folks at Silverlake Wednesday." He grinned. "I used a cigarette with matches rubber-banded around it for a timer. I put that inside a paper bag, so the bag would be fuel when the matches went up. I ripped up two cushions, put the paper bag on the bed, and piled this mountain of foam over it. About 30 minutes later, the thing blew up. Bam!" He slapped the steering wheel with his palm. "All the windows blew out; flames 20 feet high, noise like a jet taking off, it was fuckin' spectacular. Burnt it down to the frame in nothing flat."

Josh pretended to be busy watching the traffic at the off ramp to Pacific Beach. David waited as they entered Rose Canyon, knowing Josh was teasing him, waiting to see if he'd blink. The minutes stretched. David blinked. "What about Art?"

Josh looked disdainful. "Piece ah cake. It did cost us $400 for the heroin."

"Heroin?"

"Yeah. You want to hear about it?" He noted David's expression and laughed, and then he said, "I pretended to be a citizen with several kilos of heroin I wanted him to move, and he asked me to give him a demo that night after the bar closed. Same night I torched the motor home, I went to the bar. I shot up in front of him to let him know I wasn't a cop, and while he sampled it, I slipped roofie into his beer. So he's feeling fine; he finishes the beer, and the roofie put him on his ass. Then I hung a needle into a vein, and filled him up with the rest of the heroin."

"Have they've found the body?"

"Thursday morning. A story in the local section of yesterday's paper had a caption that read: 'Bartender found dead, apparent drug overdose.'"

"I guess we'll find out if he had a letter to the cops."

Josh waved a hand. "I tell you, man, isn't a drug dealer living who would write stuff down and hand it to someone for safe keeping. Just doesn't happen in the real world."

*   *   *   *

David lay on his bed to watch the evening news. His phone rang. An unfamiliar voice asked, "Is this David Kendall?"

"Yes. Can I help you?"

"Well, it's the other way around, actually. I'm hoping I can save your life."

"Let me guess: a free prostate exam?"

"Well, you're definitely going to take it in the shorts if my clients tell what they saw in Colson's Cavern's parking lot on October 22 of last year." David went cold. Somebody was about to tell the cops what they knew over his bugged phone. His brain churned, trying to come up with a way to stop the conversation before the caller revealed too much. He took too long; the voice filled the silence. "My clients will testify they observed you shoot your father. You looked in the window of the motor home they were using. They are positive it was you and they will do their civic duty by the start of McBride's trial."

Relief flooded his body. Whoever it was hadn't been there. Wondering if a cop was trying to trip him up, he asked, "Unless?"

"They can be persuaded to be silent by $100,000 in cash before Monday afternoon. This is the only request for money they intend to make."

David decided that he couldn't get in trouble if he stayed quiet. He let the silence stretch until the guy added, "There is no guarantee that they will keep that promise, of course, but this kind of information does have a limited lifetime. People ask embarrassing questions if an innocent person is convicted."

No matter whom it was, the cops knew or would know about the conversation. David realized he'd have to report the call, the sooner the better. He told the caller, "That's a great deal of money, but I'll see what I can do. Contact me again Monday morning and I'll let you know how we can settle this thing." He hung up abruptly.

He was about to call the police, but then he realized he'd been handed a gift. He found his mother in the kitchen, drinking tea while she worked a crossword puzzle. He sat down opposite her, trying to look frightened. She looked up, caught her breath, and asked, "What's wrong?"

Holding her hand in both of his, he said, "Someone just called. They want $100,000 by Monday or they'll tell the police they saw me shoot Dad."

His mother reacted as though he'd asked for the money. She withdrew her hand and her face clouded. Before she could speak, David said, "Would you report the call to the police? They don't believe anything I say."

Relief flooded her face. She now knew her son was innocent.

✳   ✳   ✳   ✳

The defense had subpoenaed David, so he wasn't allowed to attend Mac's trial. He was told he would be contacted by phone, and would have two hours to report to the courtroom. He waited three days for a call that never came.

It was not quite five on Friday when Josh paged him, using the code for a pick-up at six. David showered and dressed, then went through the Takahashi's yard. He waited a half a block from Moreno Boulevard until Josh arrived.

Josh looked grim. He took the steep hill up to a church's parking lot that overlooked the city and parked. He turned to face David. "McBride came within a hair of getting off."

"Are you shitting me?"

Josh shook his head. "You made a major mistake using that guy to buy the gun. The salesman knows the buyer wasn't McBride. Your man had missing teeth and smooth knuckles."

There it was, the mistake he hadn't seen, the one that would kill him. When Hatch refused to kill Frank, he should have bought a gun off the street. Of course the salesman would remember Hatch. How many Desert Eagles are sold in a year? Now that they knew about Hatch, it was only a matter of time.

David turned to Josh. "But McBride didn't get off?"

"No, it goes on, but you can see the jury doesn't much care what comes next. The defense showed that blood was sprayed on the door of McBride's car while it was in his driveway. Those two things probably convinced them all that McBride was set up."

"How did they know I sprayed it in his driveway?"

"One drop landed under the car."

His coat must have bunched up and left an opening. He told Josh about the scare as the cop's spotlight caught him lying beside the car.

Josh said, "Actually, that helped. The D.A. used that timing to show that the blood couldn't have been sprayed there."

*   *   *   *

Saturday, David went numb when he opened the newspaper and found Hatch staring at him from a large ad. Under the picture he read, "$3000 reward for information that leads to the identification of this man." They would find someone who knew Hatch. They might find someone who had seen them together.

Sunday morning, the picture was in the paper again, inducing a fresh jolt of panic. On Monday he opened the paper and again, Hatch's face stared out at him.

Monday evening, he listened to Josh's gloomy assessment of the judge's instruction to the jurors. "He fucking *told* them that the evidence was planted and they should ignore it."

Tuesday morning, he woke feeling that this would be his last day on earth. Again, the ad was in the paper. That evening, he found some relief in the report that the jurors had reported a deadlock, even though Judge Lucero had sent them back into deliberations.

Wednesday he decided not to look at the paper. The balance of the day crawled as he waited for a verdict that never came.

Thursday, on the news at six, the verdict was announced: a hung jury, voting 9-3 for acquittal. Draper appeared bleary eyed, saying he would, 'evaluate his options' before making any decision about a retrial. David suspected that he was the option.

That night in the car with Josh, they couldn't find much to talk about. Josh was positive Draper wouldn't retry the case. "Nine to fuckin' three is a ball game. Draper has to know Jank is going to fry him again, no way around that."

"Could we take Jank out?"

"Wouldn't help. They'd use his testimony from the first trial." After a moment, Josh added, "If you're right about the bartender being the only person who saw you with Ralph Hatch, then even if they do find out who Hatch is, it ain't going to mean diddly-squat. I think you're covered pretty good."

*   *   *   *

Three weeks later, an overweight woman rang the bell at nine in the morning. When he opened the door, she held out a pudgy hand. "You're David Kendall?"

As he shook her hand, her cheeks puffed up to accommodate her smile. For her size, her dark blue pants suit fit very well. The tailored coat accentuated her bust and hid the size of her hips. He asked, "And you are?"

"Terry Jastillana, of The Jastillana Group of Insurance Companies. My father, J D Jastillana is the CEO of the group. He asked me to speak with you. Perhaps we could be assured of privacy in my car."

She waited in the entryway, and David got his keys and wallet, his mind in turmoil. Why would Mr. San Diego send his daughter to speak with him privately? One thing for sure, Mr. Jastillana hadn't become a multimillionaire worrying about nits.

In her Lincoln Town Car, she drove at a leisurely pace. She talked about the trial, and the hung jury. David understood that she wanted to know what he thought, but he wasn't sure how to respond. Finally he said, "Ms. Jastillana, I'm sure you have better things to do than tour Clairemont. Why don't you tell me what you want?"

"I need to know your true feelings about Mr. McBride."

"The man murdered my father and he's going to get away with it. That's how I feel."

She seemed happy with that answer. She said, "I can't help thinking that Mr. Jank has earned some serious money. It was outlandish testimony, but my father thought it was predictable. For two and a half million, I'd lay in the middle of Broadway stark naked."

"You think someone paid Jank two and a half million to change his testimony?"

"Mr. McBride knows that if he's exonerated, we pay him five million dollars. I'm guessing he promised Mr. Jank half to see those missing teeth and smooth hands."

"Wouldn't the insurance have to be paid anyway?"

"No, there is an exception when one partner causes the death of the other. If Mr. McBride is convicted, we have no liability."

David talked to the passing houses. "Then we both want Mr. McBride convicted." He looked at her. "Did you think I could help with that?"

"No. Framac has faithfully paid premiums over many years, and we would like to retain the business. If you are put in charge after Mr. McBride's conviction, you can be assured we will make some settlement to compensate you for your loss."

With no further explanation, she returned him to the house. Two weeks went by with no news, and he decided that whatever the plan was, it had failed. Three days after that, Judge Lucero was appointed to the Appellate Court. A week later, Peter Draper asked Judge Lin Perlin to set a date for Mac's second trial. It was scheduled for May 30, 1997.

On April 24, 1997, almost two months after David's conversation with Terry Jastillana, Judge Perlin ruled that Michael Jank's testimony would not be allowed in Mac's second trial. John McBride couldn't be identified as the registered owner of the murder weapon, but the court would allow testimony about where the gun was found after the murder.

In late May, as the date for John McBride's second trial neared, David and Josh were cautiously optimistic that, this time, there would be no surprises.

CHAPTER 23

▼

May 20, 1997, Tuesday

Judge Lin Perlin asked Julie, "Why have you included Mr. Ehmer, a known perjurer, on your list of witnesses?"

The dark wood paneling and bookcases seemed to absorb the late afternoon light filtering through a dusty window in Judge Perlin's chambers. Three officers of the court, in somber suits, sat at the massive wooden desk. Julie's pale blue pants suit provided the only color in the room, identifying her as the interloper. A small lady dressed in black sat next to the Judge's desk, typing on a court reporter's machine. Gary had chosen a chair out of the line of fire.

Julie said. "Detective Steve Bacha has stated that Mr. Ehmer's account of that night contained two facts that were previously unreported, and therefore constitute new evidence. My investigator, Mr. Charboneau, has questioned other witnesses who agree that Mr. Ehmer is correct. Mr. Draper has not allowed the police to question the other witnesses, or to interrogate David Kendall, to corroborate or dispute Mr. Ehmer's recollections. And after Mr. Ehmer picked David Kendall out of a photo line-up, Mr. Draper prevented the police from putting David Kendall into a physical line-up."

Draper looked outraged. "Your Honor, she's trying to put David Kendall into this trial. This is Mr. McBride's trial."

Judge Perlin's face reddened. "Good God, Sir, if the man can prove he was there, he becomes an eyewitness. You must, at the very least, explain why the new evidence does not change the facts of the murder, and you must provide proof that Mr. Ehmer is lying." Judge Perlin shook his head. "I'll have your balls if you make me declare a mistrial."

"Yes, Sir. I'll ask the police to investigate."

At that, Perlin declared the hearing over.

Julie and Gary walked out of the courthouse and began the three block hike to the parking garage. Gary asked, "Was there some reason you wanted me at that hearing?"

Julie said, "I thought I might need you to testify. And there was another reason, but let's wait until we're in the car."

In the car, as Gary sparred with the afternoon commuters on the streets leading toward Hillcrest, Julie said, "I would never suggest that you coached Mr. Ehmer. I certainly hope you wouldn't have committed that grievous a felony, and certainly not with an alcoholic who might give you up for a pint of scotch. But that aside, I do think you might have considered that a witness like him makes the defense look desperate. It could lose the case for us."

Gary stopped at a red light. "As a matter of fact, I have thought about that problem. I assume that you'll take the steam out of Draper's cross by asking all his questions first, so you'll establish that Mr. Ehmer is an alcoholic, a liar, a man with a police record, and so on, before you ask any questions about what he saw."

The light changed and the traffic moved sluggishly. Julie said "That would be the standard approach, yes. And in the standard cross, Mr. Draper will repeat every sordid detail before asking why the jury should believe anything Mr. Ehmer has to say."

Gary allowed the rental to coast up to the next red light. "If you carefully avoid any questions about Mr. Ehmer's recent drinking…while referring to him as an alcoholic…Draper might not notice." He glanced at the light and then back to Julie. "According to someone who knows, Mr. Ehmer quit drinking as a result of the shooting. It might impress the jury if Draper brought that out on cross."

"And how will Mr. Ehmer prove that he is no longer drinking?"

Gary suggested a way to do that. It was such an excellent ambush, Julie was still laughing when she got out of his car at her office.

Gary drove to the Dive Inn in Pacific Beach. Its phone had the only number that Dan Rhoades' had called three times. Gary wanted to see if money might jar someone's memory.

When he opened the bar's door, the sunshine blasting through the doorway spotlighted a dingy room. David didn't frequent the place for the ambiance. When the door shut, the bar darkened and Gary had to wait until his eyes adjusted.

The tall, cadaverous bartender, perhaps in his eighties, asked, "What'll it be?"

Gary opted for a bottle of beer. "You worked here long?"

"February."

"You know where I can find anyone who worked here last year?"

The bartender pointed at the door. "We scattered his ashes in the ocean."

Gary leaned forward. "What happened?"

"You a cop?"

"Private investigator."

The man's sunken cheeks seemed to suck in. "Found him with a needle in his arm. Heroin overdose." His face showed contempt. "Art been around shit a long time, so he wouldn't have done that by accident. Couple of hours before he died, he made a date with me to go shooting the next day. Why would he call me if he planned to off himself? Far as I'm concerned, he didn't do it accidental; he didn't do it on purpose, so that means he didn't do it."

"When did this happen?"

The man looked at the calendar hanging beside the ruined mirror. "February 13th."

The day after Gary had arrived in San Diego. David had been in Oregon. Regardless, the bartender's murder was a huge coincidence.

The man asked, "What you workin' on?"

"A murder case. A guy plans a murder, I go where he went, try to find something that fits. If your bartender was murdered, maybe he knew too much."

"Have to do with drugs?"

"No, nothing to do with drugs." Gary took the picture modified to look like Ralph Hatch out of his notebook and put it on the bar. "Ever seen him?"

"No." He reached over and swirled Gary's bottle to see how much was left. It was still full, so he put it back down. "We got some regulars been coming in here for years. You could ask one of them." He brightened. "One of them works here emergencies. You offering some money? I could get him down here."

"Would fifty get him here?"

"In a flash." He turned, lifted the handset on a dirty phone and punched two buttons. He leaned back against the liquor cabinet. "Smitty, private dick down here wants to give you fifty to pick your brain. Told him you didn't have one, but he wants to try anyway." He laughed. "Hell, tape it. You know how to do that, don't you?"…"Okay, I'll tell him ten minutes, but don't blame me he decides to leave."

He put the handset back and told Gary, "He's so broke, I'd give him four minutes."

Smitty missed that time, but not by much. He shook Gary's hand. A short, pudgy man, with buzz-cut black hair that was growing out unevenly, he seemed nervous and timid, yet he spoke with confidence. "You said something about fifty? How can I help you?"

Gary showed him Mac's modified picture. "Ever see a man who looks like this?"

"Ralph? Yeah. He was a fixture in here last summer. Haven't seen him in months, though. I can tell you some of Ralph's stories."

*   *   *   *

At noon the next day, Smitty met Gary and Steve Bacha at a restaurant in Pacific Beach. Over hamburgers, Smitty repeated the story he'd told Gary the day before.

Ralph Hatch had regaled the regulars in the Dive Inn with frequent updates about a plan to embezzle from one business partner and pin it on the other partner who looked like Ralph. As the story evolved, Ralph was asked to kill a guy, so Ralph's look-alike would be arrested for the murder. For proof, Ralph had shown Smitty half of a hundred dollar bill with a phone number written on the margin.

Smitty never saw Ralph with anyone, and he couldn't pick David out of Bacha's photo line-up. Other regulars at the bar had no doubt heard Ralph's stories. He gave Bacha the names of two other men who could identify Ralph Hatch. At Bacha's urging, Smitty called both men and asked if they'd ever seen Ralph with a kid. They hadn't. He promised to keep asking that question as the regulars came in.

After Smitty left, Gary and Bacha did a recap. Three men had heard Ralph Hatch talking about some kid's plan to kill one business partner and blame it on the man who looked like Ralph Hatch. The content of the story was hearsay, but the story could be used to show knowledge of a crime. It also placed Ralph Hatch in a bar that Dan Rhoades had called, and that was circumstantial evidence if David was ever identified as Dan Rhoades. The bartender who worked there when David and Ralph Hatch met in the bar had died under suspicious circumstances. Again, circumstantial evidence.

Including Michael Jank, eight people now agreed the composite was an accurate picture of Ralph Hatch. As Bacha put it, "Draper hadn't shot his mouth off about convicting Mac, the kid would be toast by now."

Bacha rose to go. "By the way, we got a hit on a ring similar to the one Hatch wore, on a body found buried in Arizona carrying ID for a Rudy Hambly. H-A-M-B-L-Y."

The Hambly name rang all of Gary's bells. "Hang on a second." He found the number and then called Doris Hambly, Evelyn Nessbaum's friend at Silverlake Resort. Bacha sat down and watched as Gary talked with Doris. She confirmed that her late husband's name was Rudy Hambly. When Gary told her about the body that might be Ralph Hatch's, she asked him to hold while she looked for her deceased husband's wallet.

After a short pause, she said, "The wallet isn't in the box. Ralph Hatch was in my home several times. He could have taken it."

Bacha said that the ring was being sent to San Diego along with dental x-rays. Due to the advanced state of decomposition, no prints were available. The cause of death had been the result of a large square hole in the skull. The Arizona medical examiner had given the most likely cause as a pick to the brain.

Gary asked, "What about the ring? What if Jank identifies that?"

"It's a plain piece of polished metal. There's nothing distinctive about it." He tapped Gary's watch. "It would be like trying to identify someone by a black plastic watch."

"Could Draper charge David with Ralph Hatch's murder?"

"That won't fly until someone connects David to Ralph Hatch."

Gary said, "Look at what we've got. Ralph Hatch and his girlfriend, Evelyn Nessbaum, both disappear, Ralph in September and Evelyn in December. Ralph is found murdered, so that means Evelyn was probably murdered too. The motor home they lived in burned in February. The bartender at the Dive Inn, who was working at the time Ralph told his stories, died the same night the motor home burned. So we know David was eliminating witnesses."

Bacha shrugged. "I'll pass it by the man, but don't hold your breath."

Bacha was ready to leave, but he said, "By the way, we're going to do a line-up for this homeless guy who said he was there when Frank Kendall was shot. We will invite David to participate. I'm hoping he won't volunteer, because then I get to arrest the shit. That'll be fun."

"Any chance the arrest could be delayed a couple of days?"

"It will be delayed for two days. I'm going to schedule it for ten p.m. this Friday evening. The guys who work at the jail hate Friday nights. The place is usually ass deep in drunks, and it gets really tense. Since it's the Memorial Day weekend, it'll be even worse: severe overcrowding and lots of puking. Tuesday's the soonest we can put a line-up together, so David will get to sample the accommodations for three whole days."

"If you talk to David while he's under arrest, telling him what we know might be a good move."

Bacha shook his head. "That'd tell him what we don't know."

"I'm hoping he'll talk about that with a trusted associate."

"Oh, yeah?" Bacha looked at Gary as if he could read his face. "You wouldn't get anything we could use."

"We would know the truth. Usually there are legal ways to discover the truth, once you know what the truth is."

Bacha said, "You've been hanging around cops," as if that were frowned on. "Okay, let's give it a shot." He rose.

Gary said, "Don't let on we know about Joshua."

He put a hand on Gary's shoulder. "Yeah, I figured that out all by myself."

Back in the car, Gary listened to his phone messages. The first was from Julie. Gary had told her about Smitty. "Judge Perlin won't allow any line of questioning that goes to circumstantial evidence for David's guilt. He'll only allow those facts that go to establishing John's innocence. We can use the phone calls to show Frank may have had Dan Rhoades' phone that day, and that phone could have been used to call him back to the lot, but since no facts tie David to that phone, we can't infer that David called him back."

The second message was from George Martinez. "Gary, my source came through on the 36 Dan Rhoades' phone numbers. Thirty-three of them belonged to businesses that closed. The other three are private individuals who changed numbers. The new numbers are 555-2703, 555-5291, and 555-1097. She didn't charge me for the 33 closures, so all you owe me is $300 bucks."

Gary called the first number. A woman picked up almost immediately. Stunned, Gary stumbled his way into the rehearsed pitch. "Ah…This is an official call…ah…regarding a case being investigated by the San Diego Police Department. Your phone number is among a group of phone numbers called by a man named Dan Rhoades. Do you know anyone by that name?"

"I haven't seen him in over a year."

Expecting any response but that one, Gary was momentarily stumped. Finally, he asked, "Would you recognize him?"

"Yes. We dated for a month or so."

"Could you describe him?"

"Very good looking. Black hair, white even teeth, dark skin, a weight lifter's body. He looked like a male model."

"Tall, short?"

"I'm only five-two and he's at least a foot taller than me, around six-two."

"Would you be available next Tuesday to look at a police line-up?"

She worked second shift, but if the lineup were held in the morning, she could be there. After he got the necessary information, Gary disconnected, his ability to plan confused by this new reality. He put her name, address and number into a database in the laptop, and then decided to complete the calls while he considered what he should do.

He dialed the next number on the list. The evidence was strong that Frank had used Dan Rhoades' phone on those five Tuesdays. With further police investigation, the locations of the calls could be matched to Frank's itinerary for those days.

He gave up after the tenth ring, and then dialed the third number. Gary thought that David had made a fatal mistake. Dan Rhoades' cell phone was used to call Frank back to be murdered, and the phone was never used after October 22. Both those things established a firm connection to the murder. Although this evidence was circumstantial, murder convictions had been obtained with less.

The phone was answered on the fifth ring. The woman sounded out of breath. Gary said, "This is an official call concerning a case being investigated by the San Diego Police Department. Your phone number is among a group of phone numbers called by a man named Dan Rhoades. Do you know anyone by that name?"

"I did. I haven't heard from him for maybe a year."

"Can you describe him?"

"He's a manipulative, lying, son of a bitch."

Gary laughed. "I hear you. How about his physical appearance?"

"Tall, dark, and handsome. Six-pack abs, shoulders that don't quit, buff chest, and dark skin all over."

"Would you be available next Tuesday to look at a line-up at the police station?"

"I live in Poway. With the trip down, that's going to be hours away from my job that I won't get paid for. Can you reimburse me for that and the trip?"

"Would a hundred dollars cover it?"

It would. She gave Gary her name and address, and he told her he'd be back in touch Monday night to tell her where and when.

He called Bacha and gave him the news. Bacha said, "I think we may have the asshole by the short hairs."

CHAPTER 24

▼

May 23, 1997, Friday

Thursday, Detective Steve Bacha had called and invited David to appear in a line-up. David had refused. Now, at ten Friday evening, the doorbell rang. When he came out of his bedroom, two cops were standing in the entryway with his mother. They both walked over and grabbed him. One cop turned him around, the other handcuffed and searched him, then put his belt and pocket contents into an envelope. "David Kendall, you're under arrest for the murder of Frank Kendall." David had been expecting to hear those words for so long, he experienced a sort of relief. The cop took a card out of his shirt pocket and read the Miranda warnings as they led him outside to the police car.

The cage in the police car smelled faintly of vomit and reeked of pine-scented cleaner. Once they were underway, both cops rolled their windows down. That didn't significantly affect the strength of the pine cleaner, but it did make their conversations mostly unintelligible. What he did hear suggested two bored men passing the time. They were transporting garbage, just another odious task during a routine work shift.

At the jail, the car went down a ramp that ended with the top of the car at sidewalk level. The cops got out; one opened the back door on the passenger side and motioned David out. Outside the car, both held an arm as they faced the brightly lit double doors. David had trouble breathing, fearing those doors as if they were the gates to hell. The cop pushed a button on the wall and looked up at a monitor. The motor opening the doors completed its spastic cycle and they pulled David into a wide hallway. They pushed David face-first into the wall on the right, and then one cop went outside, evidently to move the car. When he returned, both cops removed their handguns and locked them into small boxes built into the wall. David was hustled through a metal detector, down a corridor, through another set of double doors, and into a large waiting room.

Inside, he saw three rows of comfortable-looking steel seats, painted dark blue. All the support structure for the seats, including arm rests, was welded metal tubing anchored to the floor. Two men lay on the floor in unnatural poses, each with a leg chained to the steel supports. They seemed to be dead. Two men slumped in the chairs also looked dead, their heads draped over the chair backs as if their necks were broken. The chains on their ankles were the only evidence that someone thought they might be alive.

David was pressed against a thick glass window, which pissed-off the woman in the room behind the glass. "You keep him the fuck away from the window."

"Easy," the cop said soothingly. "He's in for murder. Sober as a pilot."

The woman slid a drawer through to David's side. "Last asshole threw up in the tray."

The cop put the manila envelope with David's pocket contents into the tray, and after she pulled the drawer through, the woman did an inventory for the camera above the shelf. Then she took out David's driver's license and did some laborious hunt and peck typing on a machine. The machine spit out a plastic card. She put that in a red plastic holder attached to a plastic tie, and slid it through. The cop attached the red tag to David's left wrist with the plastic tie.

The cops hustled David to another door, opened it, and shoved him inside. The narrow room held a bench and a metal toilet which was currently in use by a bleary-eyed man without any teeth. He turned to look at David and his body followed his gaze, the stream of urine splattering the bench. A man in an expensive suit jumped to his feet, the next man did the same, until all four men were standing, watching the yellow puddle meander toward David's end of the bench.

As the offender stuffed himself back in his pants, a cop opened the door. When he saw the problem, he said, "Bring him here." David and a short black man led the drunk to the door, David almost gagging. The man's stench made normal body odor seem like perfume. The cop said, "Sit him down." They parked him on the bench. "Now push him to the other end." David and the black man looked at each other, shrugged, and then David pushed on the man's shoulders and waist while the black man kept his legs from dragging, and they slid the uncomplaining drunk the length of the bench. "Now all of you sit the fuck down."

The officer ignored the chorus and shut the door. No one sat. David, willing to solve the problem, mentioned the obvious solution. The black man agreed. Each taking one of the offender's arms, they laid him on his back on the bench, and then pulled him the length of the bench. Other than fluttering his hands and making a happy noise, the drunk didn't seem to mind. They rotated his reclining body, then pulled him back to his original spot near the toilet, and sat him upright. The bench looked dry, so David moved away. The drunk began to lean as if he might fall over, and the black man nudged him upright. When it seemed the drunk had grasped the concept of vertical, the black man released his arm. A moment later, the drunk vomited, splattering the wall, and his own pants and shoes. The odor from incompletely digested wine added a moist bouquet to the stench in the room.

Over the next three hours, the drunk passed out and slid into his vomit. David and another man hauled the unconscious man to the waiting area. A cop chained the drunk's ankle to the chair supports, making five apparently dead bodies littering the room. The well dressed man was given a mop and a bucket of soapy water and told to clean up the holding cell. Two more drunks and one belligerent short guy replaced the four original occupants of the cell. Both drunks vomited, and the short guy spent his brief stay shouting insults at any cop who came within hearing. He wasn't angry. He explained his tactics as a way to get rushed through the process. It worked, he was gone in minutes.

David felt dazed when he was brought out to complete the booking process. At another window, he was fingerprinted by a tense man who was willing to break David's fingers to get an acceptable print. Then he was taken to a small room where an angry cop, pissed at David's height, adjusted his camera and took his mug shot, complete with numbered sign. Then he was sent into the jail where two tense cops wearing white rubber gloves watched while he stripped. He had expected the body cavity search to be embarrassing, instead he obeyed each command as if walking a tightrope, surprised by the intensity of his fear. When he was through the process, wearing an orange jumpsuit and elastic banded slippers, he felt like a survivor.

Because of his height, he was assigned the top bunk in a three tiered bunk bed. His bed stack was wedged beside another stack in a brightly lit, day use, area. Eight seats were anchored to the metal table in the center of the small room, indicating the surrounding cells were designed to hold perhaps sixteen men. Including David's tier of bunks outside the cells, the area now housed 54 men. All the cell doors were open. David was expected to use a toilet in one of the cells.

David climbed into the top bunk and watched a spider traversing the high ceiling. With the lights on, steel doors slamming, and men talking in the bunks around him, sleep seemed unlikely. He felt sick. Was this the first day of the rest of his life?

He didn't recall any time when he wasn't aware of the jail's noise, yet he did manage some sleep. He suffered diarrhea during the night, and had to cope with the anger of the six residents of the cell where he used the toilet.

✳   ✳   ✳   ✳

Saturday afternoon, he was called out, led through three sets of doors to a small room where a tall, young man in a business suit was waiting. Victor Massey was a criminal lawyer from the firm Mary had hired to defend David. He told David there would be a line-up Tuesday morning, and if he was identified by the witnesses, he would be arraigned on murder charges. He would plead not guilty. Victor Massey's message was the Miranda warning simplified. "Keep your mouth shut."

✳   ✳   ✳   ✳

By Tuesday morning, David was so tired he was hallucinating. He heard music as if he had a radio inside his head, tuned to a station playing eighties music. The beat made him feel jumpy. At nine, he was called out and led to the same small room, now occupied by Steve Bacha and Able Mendoza. David felt the danger. "You can't talk to me without my lawyer present."

Steve Bacha pushed him into one of the molded plastic chairs. "Your lawyer is coming, shithead. He's signing in now." Both men pulled chairs close to David's and sat down, their knees almost touching his. Bacha leaned forward, close enough to nauseate David with his coffee breath, and said, "We aren't going to ask you any questions. We're waiting for your lawyer. We want him here so he can talk to you later, tell you about the penalties for first degree murder; tell you how close you are to a dirt nap. That's all we're here for, just to tell your lawyer what we've got and watch you squirm."

Victor Massey was clearly annoyed to be back in the jail. He surveyed the three men with a look of disgust and announced, "I have an appointment in a half hour."

Bacha pointed at a chair. "Sit down and listen. You'll be out of here fifteen minutes tops." The tall lawyer sat down and Bacha turned to David. "Last summer, you met Ralph Hatch at the Dive Inn in Pacific Beach. He looked so much like John McBride that you knew right away he would be useful. You bought him drinks and then you tore a $100 bill in half, wrote Dan Rhoades cell phone number in the margin, and asked him to call you. When you met again, you suggested a plan to embezzle money from Framac and blame it on John McBride." Bacha grinned. "Stop me if you've heard any of this before."

David looked at Victor Massey, who was examining the ceiling. Bacha continued. "Ralph couldn't pull that off, so you had him buy the gun and the car, and then you tried to get him to shoot Frank. When he refused to do that, you took him to Arizona, killed him with a pick, and stuffed his body in a hole.

"You stalked your father for five Tuesday nights at the restaurant where he and John McBride met for dinner, but something screwed up each time. You exchanged cell phones every Tuesday, and on October 22nd, it all came together. After John McBride drove away from Colson's Cavern, you called Dan Rhoades' cell phone on a modified cordless unit, and got your father to come back to the lot. You made a mistake when you drove your car into the lot. You didn't park where John McBride had been parked. When your father came back, you exchanged cell phones with him, and then you shot him.

"That wasn't the end of the murder spree. You figured Evelyn Nessbaum, the woman who lived with Ralph Hatch, knew too much, so in late December, you killed her. Then in February, you hired someone to kill Art Garrison, the bartender at the Dive Inn.

"In about an hour, we're going to do a line-up where three people will point at your sorry ass and say, 'Yeah, that's the guy.' So while the D.A. is still under the illusion that John McBride killed your father, I suggest you and your lawyer here discuss making a deal with him that will keep you alive."

Bacha looked at Victor Massey. "See there, five minutes is all it took. You've got ten minutes to convince this scumbag he can be smart and save his life before all the options disappear."

Bacha and Mendoza left the room. Victor Massey sighed, got up and stood in front of David. "I'm not going to be your lawyer. I'll let whoever the firm assigns know what the detectives have. Someone will be with you within a day or so."

"A day or so? What am I supposed to do today?"

"Keep your mouth shut." Victor Massey pointed at the door. "Those guys are cops. If the D.A. had a case, he'd be in here. So keep your mouth shut, and wait."

*   *   *   *

Four hours later, David walked out a side door of the courthouse, the sunshine warm and welcome on his face. His mother was waiting. She put an arm around his waist, and they walked toward the parking garage. He squeezed her shoulders. "No one told me anything. Do you know why they released me?"

"They dropped the charges after the line-up. No explanation, no apology, they just dropped the charges." She shrugged her shoulders. "I guess the person they did the line-up for didn't identify you."

David knew that was wrong. Judging by the banter as they waited to go into the line-up, the other four men were cops. Three times while he stood in the hot lights facing the mirror of the window, he was asked to step forward and state his name. As Bacha had said, three people had been asked to identify him. "Did I have a lawyer there?"

"Yes. A tall, young boy. He seemed too young to be a lawyer. He didn't say anything except they dropped the charges." Tears glistened on his mother's cheeks, but her voice sounded normal. "I don't understand. They're prosecuting John for the murder, and they arrest you for the murder. It doesn't make any sense."

"The District Attorney thinks Mac did it; the police think I did it. The police can arrest me anytime they want, but the District Attorney turns me loose."

"I can't stand it, David. It's all too hard. Do you mind if I go stay with Vivian in Atlanta? I know it's leaving you at a bad time, but with the trial starting this week, the reporters will be parked in front of the house. I don't want to go through all that again."

He squeezed her shoulders. "Don't worry about me, I'll be fine."

*   *   *   *

Just after three that afternoon, Victor Massey returned David's call. He couldn't explain why the charges had been dropped since all three witnesses had identified David. He said, "They obviously don't have enough evidence to secure an indictment."

At six the next morning, David took Mary to the airport and stayed until she boarded the airplane for Atlanta. He was relieved to see her go.

*   *   *   *

Over the next two days, David and Josh used the pagers to arrange meandering drives so Josh could screen David for tails. Thursday evening, Josh sent the code for a meet at ten that night. David shut off his bedroom lights at nine, and waited until 9:45. Dressed in black, he went out the back door, through the garage, and walked the driveway to the street. He walked in a long loop, watching for tails. At ten, he turned onto the street where Josh was waiting, and got into the Buick. Josh said, "We'll wait here. If they saw you walk this way, they'll start looking here. Then we'll know."

Josh had what looked like a small portable radio. "It's a scanner that seeks out the strongest signal. Assuming they'll use spread spectrum, we won't hear what they're saying, but we'll know if several people are using handhelds to talk to each other."

Slumped down in the seats, they waited silently for a few minutes. Illuminated by the mid-block street light, Josh's eyes moved constantly, watching both side mirrors and the rear view mirror. Finally he broke the silence. "Tell me what happened."

"Last week, they asked me to come in for a line-up, and I refused. Friday night, they arrested me and held me for a line-up Tuesday morning. After it was over, they released me. According to my lawyer, two women and one man identified me. I don't know who they were."

Josh was silent, so David told him about Bacha's replay of the murders of Frank and Hatch, and that he knew someone else had killed Art.

Josh said, "Jesus Christ, if they've got all that, why the hell wouldn't they have a case?" He suddenly grabbed David by the front of his shirt. "You aren't fucking wired, are you?"

David raised his arms, inviting Josh to frisk him. "You've got that tape and you think I'd turn you in? How fucking dumb do you take me for?"

Josh sat back, and searched the mirrors again. In a moment, he said, "Fuckin' cops got me spooked. I think that bartender had a letter." He watched a passing car. "So they know it all, but they can't prove it."

"They can prove I'm Dan Rhoades; they can prove I conspired with Ralph Hatch to kill my father, and they can prove Ralph bought the murder weapon. What more do they need? If they have all that, why did they let me go?"

"Only one reason you're walking around: they can't prove it." He turned toward David. "I'm sure that none of those people who picked you out of the line-up saw you with this Ralph Hatch, or else you would be in jail. They must be looking for a way to tie you together. Think hard: how are they going to do that?"

David tried to remember his meetings with Hatch. Other than Art, all the other faces were blank. The girls Art was hitting on were bodies without faces, the other men in the bar not even that. "I couldn't identify anyone who was in the bar during the first three meetings I had with Hatch. After that, I made sure we were never together where anyone might know either of us."

"Dead end, then." Josh rubbed his forehead as if it hurt. "They know you had to have an identical car. Are they going to find the guy you bought it from?"

"I don't see how. I bought it up in L.A., and I never registered it."

"The seller saw you?"

"No. Hatch bought it using his fake ID, the same day we picked up the gun."

"You know, the cops got all this information, they did the line-up, but the D.A. is going ahead with the trial. That means the cops aren't investigating."

"Somebody is."

Josh pointed a finger at David. "During the trial, I saw Mac's attorney give a note to some straight-up citizen. I saw her talking with him a couple of times. He wasn't the same guy who was tailing you in December. Maybe he's feeding this shit to the cops."

Desperation shook David's voice. "Then we have to take him out."

Josh said, "The trial starts tomorrow. If he's there, I'll find out who he is; where he lives. We'll go from there."

CHAPTER 25

▼

May 30, 1997, Friday

George knocked on Mac's door a little after seven. Just out of the shower, in his bathrobe, Gary answered the door. George shook his head at the bathrobe. "Some people have it very easy."

"And the wife's making breakfast. You eaten yet?"

The diminutive private investigator hadn't. As Mac put another place setting on the table, he asked Gary, "What'd you call me?"

"I don't remember. Probably Mac."

Mac put his arm around George's shoulders, pointing at Gary with a pancake flipper. "Guy does the dishes, vacuums, and does the laundry. You tell me, who's the wife?"

That was Gary's only success at levity. Mac cooked and served the breakfast without conversation. He finally got up, his plate almost untouched. "Can't eat." He turned and walked out of the room.

Both men watched him go. George took Mac's plate and added the contents to his own. "Guy's a great cook." Then he asked, "Wadda you got?"

"A conversation between David Kendall and a Joshua Strahm."

George revolved his fork, encouraging Gary to move it along.

"One thing they mentioned was that Ralph Hatch, using Rudy Hambly's ID, bought the car in L.A. on August 10th of last year. It was never registered."

"Holy shit, really?" George took out his cell phone and punched the speed dial. He shifted the phone to his left hand, and gathered a forkful of scrambled eggs. It was nearly to his mouth when he said, "Steve? .... Yeah, you ain't gonna believe this, but I got a hunch. I think Kendall's kid had Ralph Hatch use his fake ID to buy the car up in LA, same day they picked up the gun. ...Yeah, August

10th. …Right, Rudy Hambly. …For sure it was never registered. …Yeah, my cell phone."

George put the cell phone on the table, picked up his plate and walked it over to the microwave. He pressed Start. "Tie a car to the rat bastard, we can stop the trial. Any other nuggets like that?"

"Yeah, there's a few things. You have to listen to it on Mac's computer."

George retrieved his plate, picked up his fork and cell phone, and said, "Lead the way. I can listen while I eat."

They went to Mac's den, where the UHF transceiver was connected to Mac's desktop computer. Gary brought up the program to unscramble the sound files, showed George how to use the virtual tape player and handed him the headphones. While George listened to the conversation between David and Joshua, Gary shaved and dressed. When he returned, George waved his cell phone. "Steve called. He found the seller. He's on his way to do a photo line-up for the guy."

"Great."

George said, "I wonder what's on this tape Joshua has?"

"Tape? I must have missed that."

George rewound the display counter. "They were moving around some, took me twice before I got it." Satisfied with the counter reading, George handed the earphones to Gary and clicked Play.

Gary heard, "You've got that tape and you think I'd turn you in? How fucking dumb do you take me for?" The first part was almost lost in the rustle of clothes. Gary modified the parameters until the words were clear.

George listened to the clean playback and said, "Got to be something that nails David to the wall. I read about two cases where hit men had tapes implicating the mastermind." He added, "Strange, though. I think Joshua forgot he had it until David reminded him."

"So you think he's had it for a long time?"

"Who knows? What do you make of the part about the bartender's letter?"

Gary said, "He must have been blackmailing David, who didn't believe the old 'letter to the cops' bit, and did him anyway." After a moment, Gary asked, "You heard the part about me?"

"Yeah. Pissed me off. He knew I was tailing him in December. We could use you for bait, maybe nail them both."

"We'd know when he was close." Gary brought up the program that mapped the trackers. The Buick was still parked in front of Joshua's house.

"So we could tell if he came into the neighborhood, say late at night."

"Mac being here might complicate their planning. They wouldn't want to kill him."

Gary put that problem aside while he went over hours and expenses with George. He was writing the check when he thought of a solution. "I'll rent a motel room somewhere. Then I'll go to the trial when I know Joshua is there, and let him follow me to the motel. As an ex-con, we catch him packing a gun during a B&E, he'll be looking at serious time. He might give up that tape that David made."

*   *   *   *

That morning, Gary rented a motel room in San Ysidro, selecting the last unit in a rambling cluster of individual cabins. Surrounded by shrubbery, the boxy cabin offered an assassin a choice of hiding spots. Gary wanted Joshua to feel comfortable.

He returned to Mac's so he could find out where Joshua had parked his car. To his surprise, Joshua's car was still at his house.

At eleven, George called, sounding excited. The man who sold the car had picked Hatch from the photo lineup. Bacha would present that to Draper after the trial adjourned for the day. George said, "Man has to stop the trial now."

"I hope so, but if he won't allow the picture to be identification when eight people say it is, why is he going to allow it when nine do?"

"This is different. Ralph Hatch, whatever he looks like, now has a car identical to Mac's. He's connected to the murder by the use of Mac's ID to buy the gun."

"Not until Draper calls that picture a valid ID."

George said, "Guy's got to cave sometime."

"I'm losing hope. Anyway, I'm going to court. I'll give you a call if I see Joshua.

*   *   *   *

After lunch, Gary entered the Hall of Justice in downtown San Diego. He was leaning against a wall outside the courtroom when Joshua walked by. Gary hadn't seen him until he was close, and he wondered if the alarm had registered on his face. Joshua opened the door of the courtroom and went in. Gary keyed a number on his cell phone. When George answered, Gary said, "Joshua's here, carrying a motorcycle helmet. I'll give you a call when I'm ready to leave."

Julie and Mac came down the hall. Gary filled them in on Bacha's trip to LA, and the news that Hatch had bought a Ford Taurus. When he told them Bacha would present the new evidence to Draper after court adjourned, Mac leaned close to Gary and rumbled, "You mind I kiss you on the lips?"

Julie kissed Mac on the cheek. "I hope this thing is over." She grabbed Gary's hand and held it. "Is there anyway he can suppress this?"

"George had a hunch; Bacha followed it up. All legal."

*   *   *   *

When court reconvened, Draper continued his opening statement. He gave a minute by minute hypothesized chronology of the events of October 22nd, the detailed description supplying the illusion of truth. When Judge Perlin called a break at 3:30, Draper was still at the shooting scene, tracing blood spatter.

In the corridor, Gary called George. "I'm going to bail now. It might be easier to tail him before rush hour."

Just then, Joshua came out of the courtroom, walked toward Gary and leaned against the wall a few feet away. Gary sharpened his voice to help it carry and said, "Gee, thanks Darlene, but I don't think so. I'm bushed. I'm going back to the motel and try to recover from three days of no sleep."

George said, "Got it. The prick can hear you. I'll pick you up at the L street ramp. Run with your brights on."

"Okay, but don't try to phone me, I'm going to shut it off."

George said, "Yeah, I remember he's got that interceptor radio. Be careful walking into that parking garage."

"Oh, yeah baby, that does sound exciting, but not today."

As he walked toward the exit, Gary brushed past Joshua, fighting an urge to kick the shit out of the small man. He looked back as he turned to descend the stairs. Joshua was following at a respectful distance. Gary didn't think Joshua would try to kill him in public, but he was acutely aware that his gun was in his car on the third floor of the parking garage. Assuming Joshua had come through the metal detector at the courthouse door, he didn't have a gun either, but Joshua did his best work with a hypodermic needle.

Just in case he did work in public, Gary rushed to the ground floor and through the doors before he slowed his pace. As he turned north on Front street, he caught sight of the black motorcycle helmet Joshua was carrying a half a block behind him. Front Street was deserted, but not quiet. With the city's noise, he wouldn't hear Joshua run up behind him. Gary crossed the street in the middle of the block, wanting the excuse to look back. Joshua hadn't closed at all. If anything, the distance had opened.

He turned the corner at the Sheriff's Intake area. Two women walked toward him and he watched their eyes, looking for either to focus behind him. Both averted their gaze as he approached and passed them. He jaywalked toward the garage entrance, crossing the street and glancing back. Joshua wasn't in sight. That made sense. Motorcycle parking in the garage was near the exit. Joshua would exit the garage before he did, and since Gary could only turn right on the one-way street, Joshua would wait around the corner.

Inside the parking garage, Gary felt uneasy in the dim light. He hadn't seen David near the courtroom. Could he be inside the garage, waiting for Gary's return? David could step out, shoot him, and then escape on the back of Joshua's motorcycle.

Gary sprinted up the ramp to the second level, staying close to the cars. A car suddenly backed out. The driver had been looking the opposite way. Gary saw dark curly hair, David's hair. He was so sure he'd see David's face that it seemed almost surreal when the person who whirled to look at him was a startled stranger.

The man rolled down his window, but Gary skirted the rear of the car and ran on up the ramp. On the third level, he had his keys out when he reached the rental. He slid inside, locked the door, and took the Glock out of the glove compartment. He racked the slide to load it, and then searched the garage. No one in sight. He tucked the gun under his right leg, started the engine, and backed out of the parking space. As he drove down to the first level, he approached the row of motorcycles cautiously. Nothing.

He paid the fee, trying to see everything, expecting the blur of a motorcycle closing rapidly. As he drove into the sunlight, parked cars and passing traffic obscured his vision. Opting for speed to make a difficult target, his tires squealed as he slid into a small hole in the passing traffic. Ignoring the angry horns, he made a fast turn onto the cross street, heading for southbound Interstate 5.

At a stoplight, Joshua stopped his motorcycle one car back. Gary moved the gun into his lap, in case Joshua ran up beside him. At the green light, he moved slowly through the intersection, the rental in low range so the engine revs were well up in the power band, giving Joshua the opportunity to take a shot. Joshua stayed near the curb, and followed the car that impatiently tailgated Gary's.

Gary took the on-ramp to Interstate 5. Joshua was a half mile back, and seemed content to stay there.

Gary turned on his lights and flashed the high beams as he neared the L Street overpass in Chula Vista. He didn't see George's van, but that was the way George would play it.

In San Ysidro, Gary turned off the freeway and drove into the motel. Worried that he'd lost Joshua, he got out of the car, and opened the trunk lid. When Joshua rode by, Gary closed the trunk and walked to the cabin. The porch railing that fronted the cabin was overgrown with wisteria, so a person standing at the large window couldn't be seen from the parking lot.

Inside, a queen bed was flanked by fake wood nightstands. A mirrored dresser and one overstuffed chair were the only other furnishings. The bed cover, pillows, and towels were done in variations of chocolate brown. The green carpet looked worn, and the room had a faint odor of mildew.

He hung the 'Do Not Disturb' sign on the doorknob, closed, locked, and chained the door. As a defensible room, it wasn't bad. Other than the large front window, and a small frosted window in the bathroom, the door was the only way in. A heater and air conditioning unit mounted under the window left a notch in the corner of the room that wasn't visible from the front window. The notch was big enough to provide some cover from someone firing from the doorway, and the bed hid it from the bathroom window. He moved the nightstand to hide his legs.

In case Joshua or David kicked in the door and let go with a shotgun or a machine gun, he used two pillows and a rolled blanket to create a dummy in the bed. With the bathroom door not quite shut, a shaft of light illuminated the sleeping form. He arranged the chair cushions on the floor for comfort and opened the front drape just a crack. Holding the gun and his cell phone, he waited.

As the time stretched past an hour, the idea of a gunfight seemed silly. He looked at his watch: 5:42. By now, Bacha had told Draper about the car. Both Jank and the car seller had seen Hatch on the same day, once using Mac's ID, once using Rudy Hambly's. David had access to Mac's ID; Hatch had access to Rudy's, and that tied both men together. Hatch was dead, with a pick hole in his head, after telling the regulars at the Dive Inn he was going on a trip with Dan Rhoades. Two women had identified David as Dan Rhoades. It should be over. Mac would be free, so why the hell was he waiting to shoot it out with anyone?

Despite that reasoned assessment, he waited. Walking out the door could prove deadly. George would let him know when it was safe. Then he visualized George slumped in the front seat of the van, the hole above his ear bleeding down his neck. The image was so vivid, Gary started to perspire, as if death had crept into the room.

A few minutes later, the shaft of light from the bathroom blinked. He raised the gun. A light airplane passed overhead, breaking the breathless silence. Was it the shadow of the airplane, or had someone jumped from one side of the window to the other? Sighting down the barrel reminded him that he hadn't cocked the gun. Had he loaded it? Trying to be quiet, he drew the slide back. The bullet was there, its brass a dull reflection in the fading light. He sighted on the bathroom door, wanting to shoot, needing to do something to break the tension. His eyes began to water. The gun seemed very heavy. How long had he been holding his breath?

In his lap, the cell phone trilled. The gun didn't go off, a surprise since every nerve in his body had jumped. Still aiming at the bathroom door, he keyed the cell phone and put it to his ear. George said, "Hey, good buddy, the truck won't be in until late tonight. You might as well go home and come back later."

Evidently George was in range of the interceptor radio. 'The truck' was Joshua. Where was David? Outside, waiting with a gun?

Gary used a deep voice when he asked, "Could they have made a hand-off?"

"Don't know. Why don't you give him a call?"

Gary disconnected, and then called the Kendall's house. David answered, and Gary disconnected.

*   *   *   *

Gary drove to Mac's. When Gary asked if Draper was going to stop the trial, Mac shrugged. "Julie said she'd call after she meets with him."

Gary walked into the den and checked the tracker. Joshua's Buick was at his house.

An hour later, George called. "Joshua drove to David's. They're in the car talking."

"Great. Do you know where Joshua parked his motorcycle?"

"Little fenced-in side yard at the far end of the duplex. Why?"

"I want him to use the car."

In the kitchen, Mac was slicing tomatoes for a salad. He asked if Gary would join him.

"No, thanks. Will you watch the tracker on Joshua's car; give me a call if it moves toward San Ysidro?"

*　　　*　　　*　　　*

When Gary got to Joshua's duplex, he found two motorcycles in the brightly lit side-yard at the far end of the duplex, including the bike Joshua had ridden to tail him. After he unscrewed the floodlight, he used the automatic lock pick on the gas cap.

The lock pick made grinding noises. A large man appeared holding a magnum revolver at waist level. "I think you just fucked with the wrong bike."

Gary said, "This isn't your bike." The lock pick finished, and he removed the cap.

"What the fuck you doing? Why'd you put out the light?"

"I put it out because I'm fucking with this bike. The asshole doesn't want to pay me, then he doesn't get to ride it." Gary pointed to the bag on the ground. "You gonna get nervous if I get the sugar?"

The gun lowered. "You sold that asshole a bike on credit? That wasn't smart."

"Tell me about it. Can I get the sugar?"

"Yeah. Like I give a fuck." As Gary poured the sugar into the gas tank, the man said, "You gotta pay me for the flood light. They cost three bucks."

"I just unscrewed it." Gary pointed at the gun. "Ruger .357?"

The man looked at his gun as if surprised to see it in his hand. He uncocked it. "Yeah."

"Heavy. I'm a PI. When I need to carry, I pack a Glock 17, just a little over a pound."

The man held the massive revolver up. "Nine won't do the job every time. Get hit with a .357, you stay hit." He pointed the gun at Gary again. "You carrying now?"

The change in his voice made Gary look up. "I only carry when I'm working. This is personal." Gary pointed at the gun. "Besides, you forgot to cock it."

"Yeah. Shit. That's a mistake." He frowned at the gun.

Most of the sugar had gone in when the gas came up to the filler neck. Gary folded the bag, put the gas cap back on, then reached up and screwed the flood light back in. In the sudden glare, he asked the man, "We okay here?"

The man raised his left hand. "Actually, I'm happy about it. Asshole wakes me up every morning startin' that fuckin' thing."

Gary held out his hand. "Mike Smith."

The big man stuffed the gun in his belt and shook Gary's hand. "Jimmy Stack."

"Sometimes I need help doing jobs. Are you interested in doing some PI work?"

Jimmy Stack rubbed his chin. "Yeah, why not. You talking muscle?"

"Not necessarily. I like the way you handle yourself. It's hard to find help who can be cool when the situation demands that."

Jimmy Stack liked that assessment. Gary took his phone number and said, "I'll give you a call when I need help."

*   *   *   *

Gary got back to Mac's house just after eleven. Mac was watching the tracker data. Julie had called after her meeting with Draper. Mac said, "Same crap. It ain't a real picture, so it can't be used for identification."

After Gary stopped bitching, Mac pointed at the tracker log. "Drove back to his house about an hour ago. You think he might wait until the middle of the night?"

"Maybe they told us." Gary brought up the program, and they listened to the car bug. Joshua had told David, "The guy lives in this dump in San Ysidro. Probably rents the place by the month. If he was any good, they'd have put him up in a better place."

After a long silence, David had said, "I think Art did leave a letter for the cops. That's why they know so much, but they can't prove it."

Gary listened to the tape twice. They didn't make plans to kill him, so that threat seemed to be gone.

CHAPTER 26

▼

June 2, 1997, Monday

David had butterflies as he walked into the courtroom Monday morning. Mac's lawyer had made an issue out of his attendance on Friday. She had stared at him as he walked in, and found a seat. She said something to Mac, and he stood up so he could turn around and look. A bailiff was called, the court secretary left the room with a note, the D.A. came in and looked at him, then both he and Mac's lawyer left the courtroom. When the judge came in, he stared at David. Why had Mac's lawyer dropped him from her witness list if she didn't want him here?

He worried all weekend, but the court's convening on Monday was anticlimactic. He was ignored. The judge told the jury that Mac's lawyer would give her opening statement, and then the prosecution would begin to call witnesses. With a nod, he handed the floor to Mac's lawyer. She was so small the podium hid her view of the jury, so she stood to the left, almost behind the prosecutor's desk.

Her voice was clear in the quiet room. "We should not be here trying John McBride for a murder he did not commit. The police know who killed Frank Kendall, and when the trial is over, you will know who killed Frank Kendall. The man who killed Frank Kendall is not on trial, and he should be. He is not on trial because the prosecution has decided to try John McBride, based on evidence the killer arranged."

When she said that he would be identified during the trial, David wanted to get up and run out of the courtroom, afraid she would turn and point at him. It seemed hours before she finished. When the judge announced the morning break, David fled the courtroom, then fled the building, fleeing from that girl who wanted to kill him.

*   *   *   *

At six, David sat in the spa, letting the whirling jets massage the kinks from his body. He had just returned from a six mile run that seemed to have satisfied his need to flee. He picked up the cordless and dialed Josh's pager, sending him the code for a call to number five at 6:30. Number 5 was a pay phone a half-mile away, one of nine pay phones on a list of numbers Josh carried in his wallet.

At 6:15, David got dressed and walked to the pay phone, circling several blocks to arrive at the phone booth near 6:30. He was ten feet away from the booth when the phone rang. David suggested they use his spa for a meeting site, and told Josh how to count the boards in the fence to find the ones that rotated. Josh said he'd be there about ten.

*   *   *   *

David was in the spa when he became aware of an apparition. Josh, moving silently in dark clothes, seemed to appear from nowhere. He shed his clothes, and slipped his pale, thin body into the bubbling water.

When Josh was seated, he revealed an unusual anger. "Your leaving the trial today was a mistake, and with the cops as close as they are, we can't afford mistakes. I need you there because I wasn't at the shooting. On cross, Mac's lawyer asked a detective Steve Bacha about the cell phone in Frank's jacket pocket. She wanted to know if it was charged. What difference could that make?"

"If it wasn't charged, then that's another way they could prove he had my phone." David felt his headache intensify. "She's going to nail my ass, isn't she?"

Josh sounded cranky. "No idea. Another thing she asked each witness was if they realized that the cars weren't in the same place. An old guy coming out of the restaurant when you shot Frank said that the cars weren't there when he pulled in. He started to park where the shooting happened because it was close to the door, but his wife convinced him to park near a light. She said she saw some guy in a long coat near the dumpster at the back of the lot. Why is Mac's lawyer so interested in where the cars were?"

"Because the D.A. wants the jury to believe Frank and Mac were in the lot all that time arguing, and Mac got so mad, he shot Frank in a fit of rage. If the cars were moved, that scenario goes out the window."

"Who was this guy in the long coat? Was that you?"

"No, it was a guy wandering around casing cars. Remember? The guy I yelled at?"

"Oh, yeah. Did he see you?"

"No, he didn't know who yelled, he kept looking around to see where the voice came from." David sank under the water to let the bubbles work on his aching head. When he emerged, he said, "Sorry about running out. It spooked me when she said she'd identify me during the trial. I got an instant migraine."

"She was probably blowing smoke."

Josh slid under the water. In the underwater lights, David could see him massaging his forehead and temples. Maybe they both had headaches.

Josh surfaced and said, "Mac's lawyer and Draper went at it constantly. Rattled Draper so bad, he had to have a lot of the questions read back."

"You think she's good?"

"Oh, yeah, she's very good." Josh rubbed his face as if it hurt.

"She's going to get Mac off, isn't she?"

"I don't know. The judge doesn't like what she's doing. He warned her three times about it being a trial for Mac, not for anyone else. The third time, he said if he had to do it again, she'd be in contempt."

David reminded Josh about J D Jastillana, the CEO of The Jastillana Group of Insurance Companies. "J D might have Perlin by the balls."

"I hope so, because it doesn't look good," Josh climbed out of the spa and put on his clothes. He pointed a finger at David. "You gonna be there tomorrow, right?"

David said he would. Josh disappeared into the darkness. Feeling alone and vulnerable, David wondered if he could get drunk enough to drown in a spa.

*　　*　　*　　*

For the next three days, David listened to testimony from cops and forensic technicians, and wondered if the mind-numbing boredom of a trial was training for prison. For no apparent reason, Draper put a pathologist through an hour-long explanation of the damage to Frank's brain. He spent additional hours while his blood expert explained spray patterns at the shooting site, and the blood shadow of the killer, and an hour on the quantity of blood on the killer's shoes, and how fast it might have dripped off metal if the killer had flicked the blood off his shoes. Another long hour was spent examining where the limits of the search for blood spray were set. After the fifth day, David was convinced he'd rather kill himself than continue to attend the trial.

*   *   *   *

Friday morning promised more of the same. A blood dispersal expert was called to explain that single drop of blood on Mac's driveway. Two hours later, David had no idea what, if anything, Draper had proved.

Draper rested the prosecution, and the judge decided to call the morning break before Mac's lawyer began the defense. David felt sick as he left the courtroom. The bitch was coming for him next, and she knew exactly how he'd killed Frank.

CHAPTER 27

▼

June 6, 1997, Friday

Outside the courtroom, Gary used his cell phone to listen to his messages. The only message was from Andrea, in San Diego at a hotel in Mission Valley. He called the number. Vintage Andrea, she answered in a snit. "What took you so long? I've been hungry for hours."

Gary said, "Yes, I'd love to take you to lunch, or whatever meal it is for you."

"How long will it take you to get here?"

"Twenty minutes." Gary was already walking toward the stairwell when she disconnected abruptly. A hungry Andrea was a vicious and unpredictable animal.

*   *   *   *

Seventeen minutes later, Andrea opened her door wearing a towel. She turned and walked away. "I couldn't wait. I ordered room service."

Gary said, "Hello, Gary. Have I told you how nice it is to see you again?"

She shot him a malevolent look. "Give me a break. I was up at three, district time. The omelets on the airplane tasted like gasoline, so all I've eaten is one bag of peanuts. Then I waited for you to call. What the hell took you so long?"

Gary walked over and put his arms around her. She returned the full body hug, and said, "That better be a pickle in your pocket."

"No. I'm really glad to see you."

She pushed him away. "Don't be. I've found Mr. Right. If everything goes as planned, I'll be sporting a ring shortly."

The intensity of his disappointment surprised him.

She added, "He says he's deeply in love with me two-thirds of the time. He stays away for the other third. That seems to work."

Room service came. Andrea had evidently ordered when she was near death. While they shared the feast for six, she told him more than he wanted to know about Mr. Right. After ten minutes of that, he changed the subject. "Why are you here?"

She snickered. "Did I tweak your fragile ego? You can't stand even hearing about him?" When he didn't react, she made her contemptuous noise and resumed attacking her cantaloupe. "The newspaper is nervous about millions in liability payments if they print your story. I'm here to find out how much of it is factual. I want to look your D.A. in the eye while he reads the nasty things we're going to say about him. I have an appointment to see him at noon, outside the courtroom."

"The Post is going to publish the article?"

She got up, pulled a manila folder from a briefcase, and handed it to Gary. The article was a lead-filled truncheon directed at Draper's head.

"No shit, they're really going to print this?"

"If it's true. Can someone corroborate each of the facts?"

"Yeah. How much time do you have?"

"Until five tomorrow afternoon."

"That's not gonna be easy. We'll have to hustle. When are they going to print it?"

"Not until the trial is over. The lawyers say it could cause a mistrial since the jury isn't sequestered. Once the verdict is in, it goes on the front page."

"Holy shit. Front page?" He laughed. "Why would they do that?"

She finished a piece of toast. "My newspaper's parent corporation hates the San Diego newspaper's parent corporation. We try to scoop them."

He read the article again, made notes about witnesses and asked what she'd need for confirmation. Things he'd discovered with the illegal bug would become conversations intercepted with a long range microphone in a public place. He made a list of people she'd have to see, and then made phone calls to set up appointments.

*   *   *   *

At noon, they were outside the courtroom. Since David was attending the trial, Andrea had decided to get his reaction. In position to ambush him, she stood next to the wall facing the courtroom door. Opposite Andrea, Gary would be partially hidden by the open door.

The bailiff opened the door. Gary pointed as David came out, and Andrea walked into his path so rapidly that they collided. David grabbed her conveniently outstretched arm to keep her from falling. She played the shy, flustered female, getting his full attention, before she told him she was a reporter. "I'm doing an article for the paper. Would you look at it for me? Let me know if I've got any of the facts wrong?"

David said, "Over dinner?"

"Oh, it's just a little thing. Maybe you could look at it now? It'll only take a minute."

She led David out of the crowd and fumbled in her briefcase. She handed him the article and watched him while he read it. Other than the color rising in his face, he showed no emotion. He handed it back. "Whoever this Gary Charboneau is, he's suckered you. He's obviously an expert at drawing sinister conclusions from innocent facts. I will sue if you publish this article, because it isn't just going to hurt me, it's going to destroy my mother. You should be ashamed of yourself for believing this garbage."

"That's why I asked you to read it. Can you tell me what isn't true?"

In a voice that wasn't quite under control, David said, "He arranged the facts into cause and effect. If my father used my cell phone on certain days, that doesn't prove I was calling him back to the lot to be murdered. I lived with my father, so of course we're going to share things like cell phones. If I knew the bartender at the Dive Inn, that doesn't prove I murdered him. I never knew a man named Ralph Hatch. This Gary Charboneau has built a hateful piece out of rumors and associations, not facts. My mother has already suffered a terrible loss, and this is going to kill her." He turned and walked away.

Andrea stuffed the article into her briefcase. Gary said, "He just gave you something we didn't have. He said his father used his cell phone."

"I thought you knew that."

"We didn't have confirmation from David."

A few minutes later, Draper came out of the courtroom. Andrea gave Gary her room key-card and said, "Meet me at the hotel at two." An order, not a request. She hurried after Draper.

Gary decided to do his phoning from her room. He was there when she returned just after one, in a mood that was foul even by Andrea's standards. Draper had donned walking shoes and walked her down to the harbor at a furious clip, his daily exercise evidently. Not only did it smudge her dignity to run beside him in high heels, her one good suit was dirty. And to each slap at him she quoted from the article, Draper had replied, "Can't comment on subjects which might be addressed during an on-going trial."

After her second bath of the day, Gary drove her out to Silverlake Resort to meet Doris Hambly. The tall, slim, soft-spoken woman had invited three others who knew Ralph Hatch to her trailer. All four agreed that the modified picture of Mac looked exactly like Ralph Hatch. Doris told Andrea that although Ralph hadn't discriminated between fiction and reality, he had been a decent, kind and gentle man. An hour later, Andrea felt she knew Ralph Hatch.

By five, Gary and Andrea were inside the Dive Inn in Pacific Beach. Prodded by the offer of free drinks and $100, Smitty had gathered two other regulars who had shared an alcoholic haze with Ralph Hatch. They all liked the man. He was such a marvelous story-teller that they didn't much care that his stories weren't true. Andrea listened while the men outdid each other to impress the reporter from *The Washington Post*. She heard about the plot to have one partner get caught embezzling from the other, then the ominous turn when the gun was purchased. At the time, they all believed that Ralph had embellished the story far beyond the truth. Smitty thought Ralph might be telling the truth when he saw the half of the $100 bill, but he didn't tell anyone.

Andrea asked about Art, the bartender. He had been an intimidating character who had physically tossed each of them out of the bar when they'd exceeded their limit. No one was allowed to puke in Art's presence. They agreed Art was no angel, and he had heard all of Ralph's stories. If he knew the kid Ralph was talking about, Art might have tried to make some money with that knowledge.

That evening, Andrea took Gary and Steve Bacha to dinner on Shelter Island. Bacha read the article, and then told Andrea what he thought a prosecutor could prove in court. According to Bacha, they could prove Dan Rhoades was David Kendall. They could prove Frank had access to Dan Rhoades' cell phone by David's admission to Andrea, and they had strong evidence that Frank had used Dan Rhoades' cell phone that day. They could prove that the cars were moved between the end of dinner and the killing, and they could prove Dan Rhoades' cell phone received a call some five miles away from the restaurant during that time. They knew that call was made illegally, using an open cordless base in the apartment building across the street from the restaurant. The only logical inference for that call was that the killer had summoned Frank back to the restaurant, and who but David Kendall knew that Frank had Dan Rhoades' cell phone? And Dan Rhoades cell phone was never used after the night of the murder.

Bacha concluded his list by saying, "And if Draper were to put all nine people on the stand to testify that the picture is an accurate representation of Ralph Hatch, then it would all be over. We could tie the gun and the look-alike car and Frank's murder to David."

Andrea sounded astonished. "That's all it would take, just the agreement that the picture represents Ralph Hatch?"

"Sure. His use of John McBride's ID in purchasing the murder weapon connects David to the murder weapon, because David had access to Mac's personal data. The car seller puts Ralph Hatch, using Rudy Hambly's ID, in possession of a Taurus like Mac's. Rudy Hambly's ID establishes the connection to the body found in Arizona, so we have Ralph Hatch being murdered more than a month before the murder of Frank Kendall, and that means someone else had the weapon and the car at the time of the murder. David had the means to bring Frank back to the lot. David is connected to the car, the weapon, and the opportunity to murder his father."

As Gary drove Andrea back to her hotel, she used her tape recorder to prepare herself for the next meeting. Kissing her on the cheek at the door to her room, Gary promised to pick her up in the morning.

*　　*　　*　　*

Andrea met Julie in her office at eight Saturday morning. The two women talked for three hours. Later, Gary drove Andrea to the murder scene so she could take pictures. Gary took pictures from inside the dumpster, probably a useless exercise with the sun glaring from the lattice. They drove the route the killer might have taken to Mac's house, timing the trip. Twenty-nine minutes later, they arrived at Mac's.

Mac seemed to adopt Andrea. He pulled her into the kitchen while Gary booted the computer in the den. In the ten minutes it took Gary to arrange the sound files on the computer, Mac found his way into Andrea's heart. As Gary came into the kitchen, Mac said, "You tell this guy 'cause you got to trust the person you marry. He doesn't do the right thing with that, then you know he ain't the one."

Andrea tried to hide the tears. Gary looked at Mac, wondering how that had happened. Mac said, "Sandwiches ready. Whadda you want to drink?"

While they ate, Andrea asked Mac about his fights with Frank on that last day.

Mac said, "What Draper don't see is that the arguin' was both of us struggling to make the business better. We fought about how, but we both knew we was on the same side." His eyes misted, and he looked away until he could recover his composure. His voice stronger, he said, "We couldn't do it alone. We needed the other guy."

"And at dinner that night? What did you talk about if you didn't discuss the business?"

"Don't remember. Since it happened, I thought a lot about those dinners. We never talked about why we met every Tuesday, but for me, it was so I could find out how Frank was. Work is important, but it ain't real life. We talked about my wife dyin', Frank's prostate cancer, the tough stuff, to let the other guy know he ain't facin' it alone."

After lunch, Gary played the sound files so Andrea could record them. After she listened, she said, "No doubt about that. David did it. But I don't understand. If you picked up public conversations, why can't Julie use them to exonerate Mac?"

She caught Gary's 'get real' expression and shook her head in disgust. "If you'd do things legally, you wouldn't have this trouble."

"If I did things legally, you wouldn't have heard what they said."

✱   ✱   ✱   ✱

Gary drove Andrea to the airport. As he unloaded her baggage, Andrea asked if the article would help Mac.

"It'll be too late. If Mac's convicted, David will have to confess before an appeals court will overturn the jury's verdict."

"So it's all riding on the testimony of an alcoholic with a history of perjury."

"Afraid so."

"Shit." Andrea picked up her bags and walked into the terminal.

CHAPTER 28

▼

June 8, 1997, Sunday

David returned to the house with the Sunday edition of *The Washington Post*. He went into the kitchen and paged through the paper on the breakfast table, not drawing a full breath until the last page. No article. He felt no relief.

On Friday, the defense had put Mac on the stand to describe the day of the killing. He said that he hadn't been able to call Frank on his cell phone that Tuesday, and for several previous Tuesdays. The cell phone had become crucial to the defense.

Then the reporter had ambushed him with the article. Unable to eat, he'd returned to the courtroom with his stomach on fire. He'd sat through the afternoon, every muscle tense, waiting for his name to come up. The day ended with his name not yet mentioned.

Friday night, Josh had listened to David's description of the article. Josh thought it might be the cops trying to rattle him. David knew better. A wealthy investigator from Virginia bankrolling the investigation was so off the wall that it had to be true. David's nemesis now had a name: Gary Charboneau.

*   *   *   *

Monday morning, David gave an unsigned thank you card addressed to Gary Charboneau to the bailiff and asked him to deliver it to the defense desk. When Mac's lawyer picked up the envelope, she turned around and scanned the spectators, then signaled to the investigator sitting in the back row. He walked down to the rail, went back to his seat, opened the envelope, and smiled. David's nemesis now had a face.

That morning, Mac's lawyer called a blood dispersal expert to testify. He showed a video of Mac getting into a Taurus wearing a long coat spattered with phosphor-laced syrup. Then he projected photos of the interior of that Taurus, taken in black light. The interior lit up like a Christmas tree, each pinpoint of light showing where the coat and gloves had rubbed. She asked, "How can you explain the absence of any blood or gunshot residue inside John McBride's car after the murder."

"Mr. McBride wasn't covered with blood or gunshot residue when he got into the car."

Next, the expert projected black light photos of the residue on the door of the Taurus after Mac kicked pools of the phosphor syrup off his shoes. All the photos showed large clumps of debris. When he compared those pictures with the photo of the Taurus the night of the murder, the fine spray pattern looked very different from the experiment. He concluded, "The blood was sprayed on the car door through a small, round orifice from a distance of eighteen inches horizontally and twelve inches above the ground. The spraying pressure decreased over time so that the last drops impacted at a much reduced speed, exactly the pattern expected from a small rubber bulb."

On cross, Draper picked at the timing. The expert had done an analysis that showed the killer would have had to be at the car 24 minutes after the murder to have finished spraying and left the scene before the cop arrived. He gave a time analysis of the route the killer might have taken, which showed that if all the traffic lights were green, and the killer had driven ten miles an hour over the speed limit, he could have reached Mac's house in 22 minutes. After pointing out that the spraying would have to start before John McBride said he arrived home, Draper dropped the cross examination.

Next, Mac's lawyer called Fred Ehmer to the stand. After he was sworn in, she went through his record of arrests, past lies and false testimony, asking about each. Fred didn't remember most of the events. His testimony was a litany of 'I can't remember that at all.' He didn't deny any of it, he said he was sure the records were accurate, but he just didn't remember. She asked, "Why did you wait six months before you went to the police to report this murder?"

Fred said, "Well, there was no reason for me to tell the cops. They wasn't going to believe me, and I didn't want the killer to know I saw him."

"Do you know who killed Frank Kendall?"

"Yeah. David Kendall, his son, was the one who shot him."

David wanted to scream that the man was lying. His fury built into a massive migraine, and, afraid he would throw up and cause a scene, he left the courtroom.

*   *   *   *

Josh wasn't upset about David's leaving court early. In the hot tub that evening, Josh said, "Mac's lawyer had Ehmer walk through the whole scene, step by step. Even with pictures and charts, it sounded like bullshit.

"On cross, Draper got blindsided when the guy proved he wasn't drinking any more—he took a blood test every day to prove he hadn't had any alcohol—but that didn't slow Draper down. He knew the defense had put the guy up in a hotel. Ehmer lives in his car, and you could tell he liked that hotel. Then he made Ehmer admit that he knew Mac had money, and that he hoped Mac would be generous. Draper spent an hour going over all the times the guy lied during trials. Draper was brutal, man. He did a job on the guy." After a pause, he added, "Draper knows that somebody coached Ehmer. He kept asking the guy who had told him this or that."

"You think Charboneau coached him?"

"Somebody did; he wasn't there. Fuckin' Charboneau's got to be insane to pull that kind of shit. We've got to take him out."

"The newspapers will go ballistic. Draper will cave for sure."

"Not if it looks like an overdose. Besides, you'll have a great alibi."

CHAPTER 29

▼

June 14, 1997, Saturday

Julie spent the entire week having witnesses testify to Mac's character, responding to Draper's suggested motive that John McBride had been enraged and out of control. On Friday evening, the defense rested.

Gary had been uncomfortable in the courtroom with Joshua and David. Now that Andrea's article had revealed his role in the investigation, he was sure they would try to kill him. Aware of his vulnerability near the courtroom, he parked his car in different locations, and watched for tails.

According to the tracker, Joshua's car had been parked on the block behind David's house several times. Joshua was using the back route into David's house, yet the inside bug hadn't picked up anything. At Gary's request, Margaret Deville, the lady listening to the bug, did some sleuthing, and heard them talking in the hot tub. "With the noise of the water, I couldn't hear what they were saying."

Eavesdropping at hot tubs wasn't impossible, but Gary didn't have the equipment. So Saturday morning, he drove to the house behind David's. Flashing his DEA badge, he learned from a neighbor about the Takahashi's work schedule. He noted the hasp on the inside of their unlocked gate. He made a quick trip to a nearby hardware store, and installed a padlock on the gate. He wrote them a note: "Dear Homeowner, I've seen people I don't recognize going in and out of your gate. The enclosed keys fit the lock I purchased. Your neighbor." He slid an envelope containing the note and the keys through their mail slot.

That evening at Mac's house, the tracker on Joshua's car showed it parked on the street behind David's house. The next readout indicated that the car was parked on David's street. Joshua had decided to risk being seen.

*   *   *   *

Monday morning, Gary went to the courtroom to verify that Joshua and David were there. He stayed for a few minutes after court convened, time enough to hear that Draper intended to take the entire day for the prosecution's closing statement.

Gary left the court and drove to the Kendall's garage. He used the lock pick on the garage door, got a hammer from the tool bench, and smashed the glass protecting an underwater light in the hot tub. About half the water drained out. He hoped David would assume the glass had broken from stress.

*   *   *   *

That evening, when Mac returned from the trial, his haggard look said it all. Draper had created a hypothetical scenario to account for the cars being moved. He suggested the movement of the cars was proof of the rage gripping both men, as first Mac, and then Frank had tried to leave the lot, only to have the other man walk alongside the moving car, pounding on the window. He said the timing of the shooting was proof that Mac had donned heavy clothes to escape the wind chill. Again Draper had attempted to create the illusion of proof by associating exhaustive detail with unrelated facts.

Mac said, "I'm so tired of listening to him, I'm ready to plead guilty to shut him up."

Gary checked the trackers. Joshua's car was parked near his duplex. Smashing the light had kept them apart. Why were they reluctant to talk in the car? Had they found the bug?

CHAPTER 30

▼

June 17, 1997, Tuesday

Lying on the decking, David snaked a flexible retrieving tool through the broken light and down the outside wall of the hot tub. When the tool's fingers touched the concrete base, he probed until he felt something move. He pushed the plunger on the handle, and then moved the tool until the fingers grasped the object. He slowly extracted the tool through the light housing. Just as he saw the glass shard, it slipped and fell.

The head down position made his headache worse.

The trial was over, that was some consolation. Mac's lawyer had lynched David in her closing statement, telling the jury that they hadn't heard the case against the real killer. For three hours, she figuratively pointed the finger at him, telling the jury the killer had arranged the evidence, the killer had the motive, the killer had the means, but they hadn't been allowed to hear the evidence against the killer. Every time she mentioned "the killer," he felt the jurors looking at him.

The tool touched something that moved. Pushing the plunger, he extended the fingers, and then slowly closed them. A moment later, he had a piece of the glass from the underwater light. The glass was crushed on one end. The lens had been deliberately broken.

The new lock on Takahashi's gate, and now the vandalized hot tub had to mean that someone knew where he and Josh were meeting. David sent Josh's pager the code for a phone call at 8:30 to phone booth number seven.

*   *   *   *

David was too anxious. He got to the pay phone at the small convenience store on Morena Boulevard eight minutes early. He circled the block slowly to use up the time. He still had to wait before Josh called. When he heard about the hot tub, Josh said, "Your house must be bugged. I'll come over and look for a transmitter."

*   *   *   *

At ten, Josh knocked on the back door. When David opened the door, Josh motioned for him to come outside. David followed him to the sidewalk. Josh started walking, and David asked, "Where are we going?"

In a quiet voice, Josh said, "I used the Interceptor on the car. I didn't get anything for a couple of minutes, then I heard a quick buzz. I found something."

When they got to the car, Josh took a penlight out of his pocket and showed David the four wires hanging from blocks on the bumper supports. They moved away, and Josh said, "We'll leave the bugs there. We can use them to set the guy up."

David felt sick. "He had the fucking car bugged."

Josh put an arm out to slow David down. "When we talked last time, I'm pretty sure we discussed taking him out. When I tailed him on the bike? He drove weird: going like stink sometimes, then really slow. I ended up too close to him a couple of times. Then, on the freeway, he drove at a steady speed." Josh's voice sounded strained. "The motel was a setup. His room was off by itself with shrubbery around it. He was going to nail me when I made my move."

In David's driveway, Josh said, "We'll look for transmitters, but he may have used microphones. The Interceptor won't pick those up."

Inside the house, Josh and David talked about the CD's in David's collection, and then put one on at a moderate volume. The interceptor found the bug in David's phone on his bedside table. They went through the house, turning on radios, fans, televisions, and even the vacuum cleaner without finding another transmitter. In his mother's bathroom, Josh ran the shower, motioning for David to stand close. Speaking so quietly David had to strain to hear him, Josh said, "Make some small talk, then let's leave."

Outside, Josh choreographed the conversation they would have. When they were in the car, David asked, "Why do you think it's taking so long to publish that article? What are they waiting for?"

"Got to be waiting for the verdict. They probably want a guilty verdict so they can fry Draper's nuts about putting an innocent citizen away."

"When it does come out, the networks will be parked in front of my house. I'm going to bail, go to Oregon, hook up with my lady again."

"Best thing to do." Josh was silent for a moment before he asked, "What about this Charboneau? Should I take him out?"

"The TV guys would love that, film of the dead body at eleven. I'd probably be the lead story for a month. Besides, what's the point? It's all in that article."

Josh asked, "Do you want me to do anything while you're gone?"

"Why don't you come with me? My lady has a friend."

"Love to, my man, but my parole agent frowns on out of state trips."

*   *   *   *

Thursday afternoon, the jury announced it was hopelessly deadlocked at eight to four. No one was told whether for conviction or innocence. The evening news reported that Judge Perlin had sent them back into deliberation.

Friday evening, the news reported the jury still deadlocked eight to four. Judge Perlin ordered the jury sequestered over the weekend.

Saturday morning, David packed his car. He called his mother in Atlanta and told her he was going away for a few weeks. After he paged Josh to confirm his departure, he drove to Interstate 5 and pointed the car toward Oregon.

*   *   *   *

A week later, on a Friday afternoon, David returned to Jackie's home on the west side of Eugene with four bags of groceries. He put his purchases away, then opened the can of frosting and iced the German chocolate cake he'd baked earlier.

Jackie came home to the cake sitting on the counter, the salad on the table, the lit candle between two place settings, and David offering a glass of white wine.

She put her purse down. "This is not going to work, David. We're roommates. How do I repay you for doing all this?"

David knew exactly how she would like to repay him. The comely, overweight brunette didn't dare believe he was making the moves on her. David had picked her out as she browsed in the romance section of a bookstore in Eugene. After a discussion about authors, he took her to dinner. Two days later, she called him at the motel and asked if he'd found a place to live. Then she offered to rent him a room at her place. After tonight, he would be firmly ensconced in her heart, and her house.

He needed a hiding place. When the judge sequestered the jury, *The Washington Post* had printed the article in its Saturday edition. The Sunday edition of the San Diego newspaper carried it on the front page. The reporter had quoted him saying that he and his father had exchanged cell phones.

Monday, when the jury reported they were still deadlocked 8-4 for conviction, Judge Perlin dismissed them and declared a mistrial. Monday afternoon, Josh reported that Draper was on television defending Mac's prosecution, and vowing to try him again.

On Tuesday, Josh called and described the scene around David's house. The networks had camped out, believing David was inside. Charboneau was there, giving interviews to any of the bored reporters who would talk with him. He was the lead on all the San Diego news programs that night, pushing to have Draper removed, insisting another prosecutor would have arrested David weeks before.

David didn't want to kill Charboneau. The media knew it all, there was nothing more to learn, and another body would drive them into a frenzy. "All we have going for us is Draper. If the guy is pushed any harder, he'll cave."

Josh reminded him that Charboneau was doing the pushing, and if they removed him, they would also remove the source of funding for the investigation. Then he said, "The media won't use him if it looks like a drug overdose."

That afternoon, David drove up to Salem and asked around about buying a gun. He sat at a bus stop until a seller found him. For $300, he got a 9mm Glock 17. He intended to keep it with him at all times. He was not going to prison.

Wednesday, Josh called. "Charboneau was on a morning show yesterday, so today, they had Draper on to refute it all. He went through the whole bit about not trying the case in the media before he said that 60 Minutes wants to do a story."

"Sixty Minutes? Are you serious?"

"Yeah, man. Charboneau has pull out his ass. We have to stop him."

Friday, in a mid-afternoon call, Josh said the story had dropped off the front pages, although an editorial suggested that Draper should resign for prosecuting innocent people while a killer removed witnesses. "Fuckin' newspaper practically said you did Hatch, Evelyn, and Art."

David asked, "Would you do me like you did Art? A little roofie to put me to sleep, then enough heroin to end it."

Josh said, "Don't be in a hurry. We can still beat this."

*   *   *   *

By nine Wednesday morning, David missed Jackie, even though she had just left for work at seven. She had become his refuge, and her inventive lovemaking was a sensory overload. A romance novel fan, she had dozens of roles she longed to play. Why had he wasted his life hiding in his room when it was the simple pleasures with a woman that lifted his spirit?

As if to remind him that it was too late, his pager buzzed. When David called the number, Josh said, "I got it scoped out, but I'll need your help. Can you be at the airport in Oceanside by six tomorrow morning?"

"Yes, but I won't be worth a shit."

"I'll be in the motor home. Unless we get lucky, you'll have days to sleep."

David called Jackie and told her he was needed in San Diego. He paused for a moment to let her suspect the worst before he said, "If it's not too much trouble, I'd like to leave most of my stuff here. I should be back in a few days."

She sounded happy when she asked him to be careful.

*   *   *   *

Just after four the next morning, David reached the Oceanside airport. Among the parked cars, he saw the motor home. He made the left turn into the parking lot, wondering if the motor home was full of cops.

He took his bag from the car, clamped the gun into his armpit, and locked the car. His footsteps crunched in the gravel as he walked to the motor home, feeling freedom dissipate in the last few steps. He knocked gently, and then held the gun ready. A moment later he heard movement, and Josh looked through the blinds. He opened the door, saying, "Hey." David put the gun in his belt and climbed in.

Josh climbed into the bed over the cab. "Take one of the bunk beds and sack out. We'll be heading to Chula Vista about six."

*   *   *   *

David fell asleep as soon as his head hit the pillow. He even slept through the noise of Josh getting up and dressed. The motor home was on Interstate 5 heading south when he joined Josh in the cab. The noise of the motor home, loud in the back, was muted by partitions and the bed over their heads.

David asked about the odd fixture on the couch. The seat cushion had been replaced with a wooden box built of two by sixes. Heavy plastic nailed to the top of the frame sagged into the opening to form a tub.

Josh said, "Part of the plan." He pointed at the glove compartment. "I made a sap. Check it out."

Josh had filled a six inch leather pouch with small lead pellets. Complete with a leather strap and small enough to fit in a pocket, the sap weighed almost six pounds. Josh said, "I tried it out on a shelf brace. It broke the two by four in half." He grinned. "When it hits Charboneau's head, the pellets should spread the impact so it won't fracture his skull."

"You know how to find him?"

"He runs most mornings at the Chula Vista Marina. I thought about doing him there, but we'd have to be lucky. If somebody saw us, the harbor cops are right there, and there's only one way out. If we were parked at the best spot to take him without being seen, we'd still have to drive almost a mile just to turn around. We'd never make it out if somebody saw us take him.

"He usually eats breakfast at a coffee shop in Chula Vista. That's where we'll do it. We park the motor home beside his car. I'll stand behind the motor home, and you'll give me the signal when he's almost to his door. That's when I'll come around."

David said, "When he sees you, he's going to go for his gun."

Josh shook his head. "It's all timing. Someone approaches you with a big smile and their right hand out, you're going to shake the guy's hand, even if you hate him. That's the way people are wired. When I have his right hand, I'll hit him with the sap, and you'll open the motor home door at the same moment to hide us from the restaurant. Then you'll help me get him inside, and I'll shoot him with roofie so he stays asleep."

"I hate parking lots. I've been there and done that."

"If we don't get him today, and if there aren't a million joggers around, we'll try to take him tomorrow where he runs. If it doesn't look good there, then we'll wait to take him at the restaurant. That gives us two chances every day."

David asked, "So he's in here unconscious. Then what?"

Josh jerked a thumb over his shoulder. "We strip him naked, hang his clothes up nice and neat, put him in the plastic, and shoot him with roofie. We put the cover over the frame and it looks like an overstuffed couch. Then I drive you back to Oceanside, and you split for Oregon. I go back to San Diego, check into the RV Park in Rose Canyon, and wait for four days."

A siren wailed suddenly, silencing both men while they looked in the mirrors. An ambulance swept by. Josh said, "Then I'm going to drive to that park on Mission Bay after dark. I'll clean him up, get him dressed, and then shoot him full of heroin. When it's quiet, I'll drag him out and leave him lying on the lawn with the tubing and the needle in his pocket."

David said, "So he'll have a four day growth of beard, but his clothes will be clean."

"Right. He's been somewhere partying over the July 4th weekend. It's been such a good party, he didn't even need his clothes. Then he shoots too much, and the other members of the party, not wanting to fuck with the law, take him to the park and leave him." Josh pointed at David. "The death pulls the alarms; they go looking for you. When they find you in Oregon, your lady swears you were there on the day in question. Might be a good idea to take her out someplace that night, get a few more witnesses."

"They know about you. What are you going to do for an alibi?"

"My neighbors will have seen me working on my motorcycle on those days. I'll be in and out, getting parts, that kind of shit, annoying all sorts of people so they'll remember me. I'll go back to the motor home every couple of hours to check on sleeping beauty, and to give him his next shot of roofie." He grinned. "See? Piece a' cake."

CHAPTER 31

▼

July 3, 1997, Thursday

Just after six, Gary returned from his run, looking forward to a hot shower and then a leisurely breakfast at the Budget Cafe. Naked, on the way to the shower, he checked his messages. He heard Julie's worried voice say, "Gary, we have to meet with Draper and Fred Ehmer in Judge Perlin's office at nine this morning."

Gary pressed the button to speed-dial Julie's office. She answered immediately. She didn't know the subject of the meeting, but she had a guess. She told Gary he wasn't to say a word if Fred had admitted he was coached.

As he took his shower, Gary mentally kicked himself. In the rush after the article was published; doing the interviews and the talk shows, on the phone with someone from the media almost constantly, he had forgotten about Fred. The hotel had been paid through Sunday before last, which meant Fred had been back in his car for ten days. He hadn't received the $4500 Gary promised, nor heard anything.

＊   ＊   ＊   ＊

Just before nine, Gary met Julie outside Judge Perlin's office and followed her into a conference room just up the hall. Inside, near the end of an oval table designed to seat twenty, Fred Ehmer sat sandwiched between Judge Perlin and the D.A., Peter Draper. To the judge's right, a huge man with beefy fingers sat ready to type on a court reporter's machine.

Julie and Gary sat down and Judge Perlin said, "Ready," to the court reporter. While the man typed, everyone stated their names, and then each was sworn by Perlin. Then he announced that they were there to address an issue raised by Fred

Ehmer, namely that his testimony had been coached. Judge Perlin said, "Mr. Ehmer feels that he might have been mistaken in what was said, so he asked that you be present, Mr. Charboneau, so you could recreate the dialogue accurately."

Judge Perlin turned to Fred. "Mr. Ehmer?"

"Yeah, your honor." He looked at Gary as he said, "Mr. Draper told me I could be arrested if I didn't report any coaching that might have went on while I was talking to Mr. McBride's lawyer and her Investigator."

Julie said, "Excuse me, Mr. Ehmer." She asked Draper, "Mr. Ehmer was questioned by the police before anyone from the defense team ever met him. Is there something in his trial testimony that was inconsistent with, or went beyond, his statement to the police?"

Judge Perlin said, "That's what we're here to discover, Ms. Williams. Now will you please let Mr. Ehmer continue." He pointed at Fred.

Fred said, "Well, Mr. Draper scared me. I don't like being in jail, so I thought real hard and I remembered that Mr. Charboneau told me I shouldn't say 'Yeah' or 'Nah', like I do usually. I should use 'Yes' or 'No'."

Julie said, "I told you that, Fred."

Fred looked embarrassed. "Oh, yeah, that's right." He turned to Judge Perlin. "So it was her that coached me, not him."

Judge Perlin asked, "What other coaching did you receive?"

"Well, she said lots of things, but mostly how I should act, and dress. I don't..., well, she did say I had to call you, 'Your Honor.'"

Judge Perlin leaned forward so he could see Draper. "Did you specify what might be considered illegal coaching?"

Draper barked a sharp laugh. "With his background, I find it impossible to believe he isn't intimately familiar with the term."

"I ain't what?" Fred asked.

Judge Perlin hoisted his considerable bulk from the chair with a grunt. Everyone in the room except the court reporter rose. The judge said, "This meeting is over," and started for the door.

Fred, tailgating the judge, said, "Your Honor, please, you got to help me."

Judge Perlin stopped and turned with an astonished glare. Fred, evidently unimpressed, moved closer and said, "Mr. Draper took my car, and they want hundreds now to give it back. Every day, it goes up more. I been sleepin' on the street since he did that. Is that legal, what he did?"

Draper said, "It was parked on a city street for 72 hours. That's illegal."

Incensed, Julie said, "Oh that is petty. Is it your intention to push Mr. Ehmer out of town so he won't be available to testify the next time you try Mr. McBride?"

Draper spoke to Perlin. "It was a police matter. I wasn't involved."

Julie asked, "Could we get the impounding officer in here, under oath? In view of Mr. Draper's intention to re-try Mr. McBride, I think this is witness tampering."

Judge Perlin said, "Put the motion in writing." He turned to Draper. "If I were you, I'd pay the impound fee. The car is his domicile."

"Yes, Sir." Draper turned to Fred. "Go to the police impound yard this afternoon. They'll release it to you."

Gary put an arm around Fred's shoulders. "Come on, Fred. I'll buy you breakfast, then we'll go out to the impound yard. I'm sure Mr. Draper can get your car out by eleven."

*   *   *   *

In the car, Gary gave Fred the $4500, apologized, and explained that events had moved so fast, he'd forgotten his promise.

Fred put the envelope of money inside his shirt. "I stopped drinking because I was afraid of losing that car. After 10 days of sleeping in doorways, I had to do something to get your attention."

The precise diction surprised Gary. He said, "I am sorry."

Fred said, "I thought maybe we could negotiate something. I didn't get him off, so you don't owe me anything, but a hung jury isn't the worst that could have happened. And you do want me to be in town for the next trial."

"What do you want?"

"I sure could use a motor home. There was one in the paper. They were asking eight thousand. It's a lot, I know, but I'll put up this money you gave me."

*   *   *   *

They ate breakfast at Mac's house. Gary used the Internet to find a single-wide mobile home in a park near Fallbrook for the same money. By late that afternoon, Fred owned it. The previous owner had gone into a nursing home, leaving the place furnished and clean. With a home, a car, and off the booze, Fred thought he might have a chance to get a job and rebuild his life.

They made an appointment for nine Monday morning with a HUD representative in Escondido to register Fred for Section Eight housing assistance. According to the park owner, this would limit Fred's portion of the space rent to thirty percent of his SSI income. Fred decided he'd finally come into some money.

*   *   *   *

Friday morning, the fourth of July, Gary skipped his morning run, ate breakfast with Mac, and dressed to go see Margaret Deville, the lady listening to the bug. As soon as he had heard her voice mail, he realized he'd forgotten both of the people who could put him in jail. Margaret would have seen him on television, so she knew he didn't work for the DEA. When he'd talked to reporters in front of David's house, he didn't go see her, afraid of drawing attention to her. Then the talk show came up, one thing led to another, and he forgot.

She now knew the bug was illegal, and he wondered if the police would be waiting for him. He called her and asked if he could stop by in about thirty minutes. She sounded welcoming, inviting him to join her for tea. He offered to pick up some scones on the way.

Despite his dread, Margaret was alone. They sat at her dining room table, and she told him that David had stopped by his house early that morning, around two, in a motor home. By the sounds from the bug, he had picked up some of his clothes. Then Margaret said, "Something that happened before David left for Oregon has been bothering me. Would you listen, see if you can make any sense out of it?"

Margaret had the tape player queued. Having swept for bugs many times when he was working for the DEA, Gary recognized the squeals and pops. "They found the bug," he said. He listened to the noises of the search for other bugs until the two men left the house, and then backed the tape to a noise he didn't recognize. He asked Margaret, "Got any idea what that is?"

"It's Mary's shower, in the Master Bathroom."

Joshua and David had talked with the shower running, and then they'd gone to the car and talked there. He decided to revisit that conversation, now that he knew they had found the bug in the house.

"Margaret, about the DEA thing, I…"

She reached over and patted his hand. "Don't concern yourself. One thing about becoming an old lady, we lose all our powers of deductive reasoning." His chagrin must have shown, because she patted his hand again. "I thought Frank was a nice man. I would help the devil convict his killer." She sat back and sipped her tea, and put the cup down. "If the police ask, should I still say you're with the DEA?"

"Sure. That'll protect you." He stood. "Since David found the bug, I'll remove it."

While Margaret watched, he went to the Kendall's house. The lock pick got him in and he went to David's bedroom to take the bug out of the phone. He was putting the phone back together when his cell phone vibrated. It was Margaret. "Two police cars just pulled up. Oh, my, two more just pulled up."

Gary heard pounding on the front door. He moved to the window in the bedroom, there were two cops in the backyard. The pounding on the front door, interspersed with the doorbell, was now accompanied by shouts of, "Police. Open the door." Evidently, they weren't going to break anything to get in. He went into the kitchen and dropped the bug into the sink drain. He returned to the bedroom, and put his tools into the briefcase, then put it in David's closet.

The pounding stopped. He eased down the hallway, hearing voices outside. He moved to the door and listened. A male voice asked, "Do you have a key?"

Margaret said, "They have a house maintenance service. They'd have a key."

"You know the name?"

"Oh, dear, I've never paid any attention to that. Sometimes they come in private cars, but I know I've seen a brown van with writing on the side. What's the problem?"

"One of the neighbors said they saw a man go in here."

"Oh, yes, I saw him. He was in and out in less than a minute. I don't know who he is, but I've seen him here before."

"When was the last time the occupants were home?"

"Their boy, David, came by at two this morning in a big RV. The engine woke me up. He left it running while he got something out of the house." In a lower voice, she said, "The husband was murdered some months ago. Frank Kendall? The thing that's been in all the papers? They're accusing the boy of killing his father. Some reporters have been watching the house, trying to get an interview with the boy. Maybe he sent this other man by to get something he forgot."

"And where do you live?"

"Over there." After a moment of silence, she said, "Margaret Deville. Don't cap the 'V', it's all one word."

"Well, thanks Ma'am. You've saved us a lot of trouble."

Through a gap in the drapes, Gary watched three squad cars leave. One cop went to a house at the end of the block, evidently the reporting party, and knocked on the door. He talked to the person who answered the door, then departed.

Gary got his briefcase, and went out the back door. He followed a path to boards in the rear fence that rotated apart, and stepped through into the Taka-hashi's yard. He opened the padlocked gate with the lock pick, then went through and stood on the gas meter to close the lock. He circled two blocks and approached his car from another street. Once on the freeway, he called Margaret.

Her, "Hello," sounded worried.

"I owe you big time. Thank you."

"Oh, good. You're out safely?"

"Yes, thanks to you. Some other time, I'll pick up the recorder, and pay you for all your help."

"Visit after nine at night. She's usually asleep by then." Margaret knew the neighbor who had called the police.

*   *   *   *

At Mac's house, he booted the PC and opened the file of the last conversation in the car between Joshua and David. They had just swept the house for bugs and found one, and they weren't talking about it. They knew the car was bugged.

Joshua asked, "What about this Charboneau? Should I take him out?"

"The TV guys would love that, film of the dead body at eleven. I'd probably be the lead story for a month. Besides, what's the point? It's all in that article."

"Do you want me to do anything while you're gone?"

David said, "Why don't you come with me. My lady has a friend."

"Love to, my man, but my parole agent frowns on out of state trips."

Gary understood two things: David had gone to Oregon to establish an alibi, and they intended to kill him.

*   *   *   *

Gary was up early Saturday morning, trying to figure some way to wear the Glock under his sweats. He decided on an ace bandage to hold the gun against his right thigh. It wasn't comfortable, and hardly a fast draw, but it would have to do.

He drove to the Marina Parkway, trying to watch everything. On the land-scaped parkway, the turn along the shoreline of the Port of Chula Vista was crammed with cars, an early morning meeting at the Port Building, he guessed. He circled the two and a half mile course. No motor homes were parked there.

Outside his car, doing his stretching exercises in the cold, brisk breeze, he worried that a Harbor cop might see the gun bulge on his right leg. He bounced on the balls of his feet to see if the gun was going to chafe. He didn't feel it move.

He reset the lap timer on his watch, and began to run.

As he ran the concrete path that snaked through the swath of greenery edging the marina, he heard cheering. A crowd near the water was watching swimmers. That explained all the cars.

After the sidewalk ended, he ran to the railroad tracks, then crossed over to the other side and ran west. As the parkway curved to the north, the eight foot cyclone fence ended at an unused Little League baseball field. Metal pipe skeletons of bleachers behind home plate stood against the pie-shaped wedge of the eight foot cyclone fence.

Beyond the field's first-base line, the eight foot cyclone fence resumed. The half-mile of fence formed a tunnel with the line of cars parked on the street. If David and Josh were together in a motor home, one of them could step from the door just as Gary approached, shoot him, and drag him inside. His body would disappear into a hole in the back country, and his rental car would go to Mexico. With no body and no evidence of foul play, they might get away with it.

At the three-quarters mark on the first lap, Gary knew carrying the gun was a serious mistake. His thigh was on fire, a sure sign that the gun had raised blisters. Gary reached into his pants, pulled the gun from the bandage, and then held it under his sweatshirt until he reached the car. Not willing to run another lap unarmed, he got into the car and drove toward Mac's.

At Mac's, he took a leisurely shower, put antiseptic cream on the blisters, dressed, and then drove to the Budget Cafe for breakfast. With no plans for the day, he took his time, reading the newspaper through for the first time in weeks. When he finished, he realized that he hadn't thought about being stalked by killers for an entire hour.

Gary walked toward his car, the keys in his hand. The motor home parked next to his car was backed into the space, he supposed for the same reason he had backed in, to let the morning sun on the windshield warm the interior.

As he approached his car, Joshua walked from behind the motor home, holding out his right hand. "Mr. Charboneau, how are you?"

Joshua's left hand was in his pocket, no doubt holding a gun. Gary couldn't go for the Glock with the car keys in his hand, but dropping the keys would be the signal for Joshua to shoot. Gary backed away trying to look confused while he slid the keys into his front pocket, and then reached behind his back for the gun.

Joshua matched his steps, moved closer and said, "I just want to talk. I think we've had a misunderstanding."

The gun caught on Gary's belt, and it seemed like three years before he had it aimed at Joshua. Gary yelled, "Show me your left hand, right now."

Joshua acted like it was all some big fucking joke and kept his hand in his pocket. "I don't have to do anything. You're way out of line."

Gary put the gun against Joshua's nose and yelled, "You fuck, you don't hear me? Show me your other hand." Expecting Joshua to fire without taking the gun out of his pocket, Gary squeezed the trigger.

Joshua held out both empty hands and screamed, "Okay, okay, God damn, Man, take it easy, take it easy."

Rage replaced fear, and Gary needed to kill. He pushed the gun against Joshua's forehead, fighting the urge to pull the trigger.

Joshua's voice took on a pleading tone, "Jesus! Please! Don't shoot me."

The gun forced Joshua's head back, and he didn't see the kick that Gary aimed at his crotch. The impact lifted the small man off the ground. He fell to his knees and folded over, his forehead almost on the ground.

Gary took a step back and kicked Joshua in the head. Joshua fell over backwards, an arc of blood spurting from his face. Shifting the Glock to his left hand, Gary went into the man's pocket. Instead of the expected gun, he found a sap.

That threat gone, Gary became aware of the motor home. David was inside. Was he pointing a gun?

Feeling he only had seconds to live, Gary turned to his car to flee, the hidden threat so debilitating that he had trouble with the door lock. The expected bullet never came and he was a block away before the shaking began.

CHAPTER 32

▼

July 5, 1997, Saturday

David waited until Charboneau was out of sight before he got out of the motor home. Josh sat hunched over. Blood flowed from a cut that extended from his upper lip to just below his left eye. He smelled of urine, both legs of his pants were wet to his knees. David helped him to his feet. "I'll take you to a hospital."

Josh managed to mumble, "No hospital. Take me to my place."

In the motor home, the bleeding intensified until his shirt was covered with blood. Without asking, David drove to the county hospital and took Josh into the emergency room. A nurse grabbed a wheel chair, and took Josh into a curtained area. After David answered the questions regarding relationship and insurance, he was ignored.

David had worried that Charboneau might go for his gun, but he hadn't guessed that the P.I. would go berserk. Now he wondered if Charboneau had been playing with them, waiting for an opportunity to maim with impunity.

All the signs were there. After he hadn't shown up for two days, his appearance at the Marina this morning had been an answer to a prayer. Not only was the Marina unusually noisy, but all the harbor cops seemed to have joined the crowd watching the swim meet. To make it perfect, the few joggers that had been circulating ended their runs about the time Charboneau started his.

Parked on a side street, David had urged Josh to get in position to take Charboneau on his first lap. Josh said, "We'll have to drive by him if we go now. He'll see us park, and he'll expect to see people getting out. Let's wait until he's almost through with his lap, then we can drive around and park. Besides, on his second lap, he'll be tired. He won't move as fast when I go to take him."

"Does he always do two laps?"

"Watched him six mornings; two laps every time."

Just after that, the great situation took a turn toward perfect. An SUV pulled out, leaving enough space for the motor home to be fourth in line with a van, a small bus, and a Suburban. As Charboneau approached the motor home, he would be hidden from the Port building by the three tall vehicles.

Just before Charboneau finished the northbound leg, Josh drove from the side street onto the Parkway headed south. They made the 'U' turn at the southern end of the landscaped parkway. Charboneau crossed to the southbound side and David watched him through the side drapes as Josh drove to the open spot and parked.

To their dismay, Charboneau got into his car and drove off.

If Charboneau had been playing with them, maybe he hadn't liked that situation, so he decided to move the confrontation to a better spot.

Josh had decided Charboneau probably cut his run short because he was in a hurry. If he had someplace to go, he wouldn't show up at the Budget Cafe, but they watched the place anyway. They had almost decided that he wouldn't show when he drove into the parking lot.

David had waited until Gary went inside, and then drove the motor home into the parking lot. He backed into the space next to Charboneau's car, putting the motor home's side door next to the driver's door. Josh got out and stood behind the motor home, near the open window so David could signal when Charboneau approached.

Charboneau took his time. Almost an hour later, he came out. David held up three fingers. Josh watched as David folded the fingers in: Three, Two, One, Go. The timing was perfect, but Charboneau had been too quick.

*   *   *   *

Four hours and 35 stitches later, David drove Josh home. Nothing could be done for his scrotum; time would tell if surgery would be necessary. The only good news was that he would lose no teeth. He was to keep ice on his face and testicles for two days, then use heat on both for at least a week.

Parked near Josh's house, David scrubbed the blood off the seats and floor mats. When the motor home was clean, Josh said, "Go back to Oregon and stay there. You'll need the alibi because I'm going to kill Charboneau. The first time I catch him alone, I'm going to cap him."

There was no point in arguing. Josh was beyond logic.

CHAPTER 33

▼

July 7, 1997, Monday

Gary felt groggy and hung over as he began the trip to Fred Ehmer's mobile home at seven Monday morning. He hadn't slept much since Saturday's incident with Joshua. In restless dreams, he had pulled the trigger and felt the spray of Joshua's blood.

The drive to Fallbrook was therapeutic. Fred was ready, and they were at the HUD office in Escondido by nine. Completing the application for Section Eight housing took less than half an hour. The woman told Fred he should have an approval within the month. With his space rent fixed, and a job as a janitor that the landlord had offered, Fred had tears in his eyes when he thanked Gary.

*   *   *   *

Knowing Joshua would want revenge, Gary hired George to help him watch the shit. After a couple of weeks at home, Joshua was admitted to a hospital where he had a testicle removed. When he was released, he convalesced at home for almost three weeks before he took his first motorcycle ride. On his fourth ride, Joshua rode the freeways to Chula Vista and headed toward Mac's. George called the police, saying he thought he saw a motorcyclist holding a gun. The cop who stopped Joshua three blocks from Mac's didn't find any weapon.

The incident did seem to change Joshua. He found a job with a gardening service, and worked long hours, mowing lawns. Gary took over the daytime surveillance. He knew Joshua was biding his time, and watching him mow lawns began to work on Gary's mind. It would be so simple to drive up beside Joshua as he leaned on the noisy mower, and put one in his head. The noise of the mower would cover the gunshot, and Gary would be gone before anyone noticed that Joshua was on the ground. After two weeks of fighting those urges, Gary dropped the surveillance.

Not that anything was resolved. According to the private investigator he'd hired in Eugene, Oregon, David was sampling domestic bliss. The initial buzz over the newspaper article had died. Sixty Minutes would run the piece, but they were waiting until the case was resolved. Mac's conviction or David's arrest would supply the theme that would carry the story. The date for Mac's third trial had been set for the end of October. Draper didn't respond to the newspaper editorials, saying it was wrong to try the case in the media.

Draper had discovered Fred Ehmer's new living arrangements. He let Julie know that Gary's generosity would be part of the testimony in the third trial if she used Ehmer again. Judge Perlin wasn't going to change his previous ruling about Jank. Despite the evidence against David, Draper still had everything he needed to convict Mac.

*   *   *   *

Early in September, Gary visited Bacha at the police station. Seated at his desk in a four man cubicle, drinking coffee from a vending machine, Gary whispered, "I might have overheard David say that he would be an idiot to turn Joshua in, as long as Joshua has some tape. I'm guessing a videotape of David admitting to something illegal."

Bacha's eyebrows jumped. "Do tell. That's all the rage among scumbags recently. The idiots think it's protection for the hit man."

Still speaking softly, Gary said, "Joshua did the bartender at the Dive Inn."

"So if it's a protection tape for Joshua, it would have been made before that."

"Maybe in late December before Evelyn disappeared. Remember George was watching David during that time."

"So Joshua probably did her, too." Bacha dug at his ear. "You think Joshua did Frank?"

"David did Frank all by himself."

Bacha rubbed his chin. "So let's say that Joshua became a partner sometime between October 22nd and the end of December. Joshua knows he's hired to cover up Frank's murder, which is a first-with-special-circumstances offense. Were I Joshua, looking for the taped confession to keep David from even thinking about rolling over on me, or killing me after it's all over, I would choose Frank's killing."

Gary stopped with the coffee cup almost to his mouth. "And if it's protection, someone besides Joshua has it."

Bacha shook his head. "It's in a safe deposit box. Assholes like them. Whoever has the key doesn't know what's in the box."

"You think a lawyer has the key?"

"Assholes don't trust lawyers." Bacha looked at his watch and then stood up. "Duty calls. Was this going somewhere?"

"If you saw Joshua running around in the middle of the night with a gun, could you get him on a felony?"

"He's on parole, so that would be a felony. If he were to point the gun at someone, that could be two felonies, which would make Joshua eligible for three strikes. That might lead to some interesting plea bargaining."

*   *   *   *

In bright daylight, Jimmy Stack's size stunned Gary. When he had dumped sugar in the motorcycle, Jimmy's size hadn't registered because the .357 held Gary's attention. Now, as Jimmy stood in the doorway of his unit in Joshua's duplex, he was a glowering giant. Aside from a small belly, he looked very fit. A sleeveless T-shirt was molded to his pecs. His tattooed shoulders nearly touched the door frame on both sides, and his arms were the size of Gary's thighs. A bottle of beer was almost hidden in his left hand.

Recognition changed the scowl to a grin. "Hey, it's the repo man. You back to do another sugar deposit?"

"Actually, I need some work done. I was hoping you might be interested."

Jimmy turned sideways and motioned him inside. "Let's talk. You want a beer?"

Inside, the living area was a showroom. Decorator touches in earth-tones set off the rose and blue drapes. A gray Berber carpet was a backdrop to upholstered furniture with dark oak trim. Several mirror arrangements reflected plants that hid the corners, making the small room seem expansive.

"This is nice," Gary said, not sure it was the right thing to say.

"I'm an interior decorator." Jimmy pulled a bulging wallet from his back pocket, and handed Gary a card. "As you can see, I work for myself. You need your place decorated?"

"I live in Arlington, Virginia, in an apartment that's half this size. I'm there so seldom that it doesn't look lived in."

Jimmy Stack grinned. "So, then, repo man, come into the kitchen and tell me what I can do for you."

Sitting at a small, round wooden table in the kitchen, Gary explained his idea. When he finished, Jimmy grinned. "You're gonna pay me $10,000 for that? If it works, it's gonna be over in seconds."

Gary winced. "It's risky. If he comes out the door with a gun, that's one thing. If he isn't carrying, you'll have to convince him to go back in and get a gun. And after he goes out to his car, you have to piss him off without appearing to be threatening in any way. If you do piss him off, he's unpredictable. He might shoot you."

Jimmy Stack drained his beer in one long pull. As he set the bottle on a coaster, he asked, "You got anything I can use that might irritate him?"

"He knows me as Gary Charboneau. A couple of months ago, I yanked his chain pretty hard."

"You did that? He told me he dumped his motorcycle. Did you know he lost a nut?" After Gary nodded, Jimmy grinned. "Well, shit, Bro, you just handed me $10,000. When do we want to do this?"

*   *   *   *

Two nights later, at seven minutes after midnight, Gary, Bacha, and his partner, Able Mendoza, sat in an unmarked car parked just in front of Joshua's car. When the alarm on Gary's watch chimed, Bacha said, "Now remember, Able, we need this asshole alive. We don't shoot unless we are up against it."

"I'll ask permission before I pull on him." Able turned to Gary. "And unless Steve and I are on the ground bleeding, you don't ever have a piece in your hand. Is that clear?"

Gary said, "Let him shoot you both. Right. I got it."

Bacha laughed as they got out of the car. The detectives hid behind the shrubs nearest Joshua's car, and Gary stood in the shadow of a parkway shrub some thirty feet away, almost in front of Joshua's duplex. Gary wasn't able to get a full breath, and he thought about loosening the straps on the bulletproof vest. He was hyperventilating with good reason: The plan was stupid, and it wasn't going to work. The detectives were out here on their own time, and if Joshua didn't bite, they wouldn't try again. Even if Joshua did fall for it, some public defender would get him off on entrapment.

Jimmy Stack walked up to a window in Joshua's duplex and rapped on the glass. Gary heard the window slide. Seconds later, Joshua slipped out of his front door, wearing only jeans. Gary couldn't see Joshua's right hand, he held it behind his naked torso. In his left hand, he had some long black object. As he approached Bacha's hiding spot, Gary saw the flashlight. If Joshua caught the detectives in the spotlight, would they risk a bullet?

Inches from the detectives, Joshua tiptoed by the shrub. He approached his car and turned on the flashlight, stooping to shine it under the rear bumper. He extended a gun toward the car. Gary felt his heart leap. Felony number one.

Jimmy Stack ambled up, his voice carrying in the near silence. "You think it was Charboneau?"

Joshua jerked erect as if Jimmy had goosed him. "You know Charboneau?"

"Yeah. He hired me to do a few things. Like dump sugar in your gas tank, let him know when you left your house, what you were driving."

Joshua turned to face the big man. Gary held his breath. In a steely voice, Joshua asked, "Did he also pay you to fuck with me in the middle of the night?"

When Jimmy laughed, Joshua raised the gun and shot him. Jimmy roared, "You cocksucker, you shot me." He took two quick steps, grabbed Joshua's gun in his left hand, and hit Joshua in the face with his right hand. The blow was short and powerful. Gary heard a snap like a bone breaking. Joshua fell so rapidly, Gary wondered if the punch had broken his neck.

Jimmy staggered back a step, abruptly sat down, and fell onto his back. Gary got to him as Bacha rolled Joshua over and handcuffed him. Jimmy said, "Your cheap ass vest didn't even slow the bullet down. Felt the fucker go clear through me." The front of his shirt was bloody.

Bacha called for back-up and an ambulance. Using Joshua's flashlight, Gary located the hole in Jimmy's shirt just below his diaphragm on the right side. He ripped the shirt away and saw a long indentation in the vest, as if the bullet had hit and changed direction. He unbuckled the vest and carefully lifted it away, expecting to see blood spurting from a hole. There was only a large purple groove in Jimmy's skin. Gary looked at his hands, now slick with blood. What was he missing? He turned Jimmy's right arm and spotted a long groove on the underside that was bleeding profusely.

Jimmy stared up at the stars. "How bad is it?"

"The bullet ricocheted off the vest and took a hunk out of your arm."

Jimmy looked annoyed. "Fuck that. I can feel the hole in my side."

Gary played the light over the purple spot on Jimmy's side. Probing gently, he felt a knot forming over a rib. "Looks like it broke a rib, but that's it. No hole. You're going to be around to spend the $10,000."

"I want a bonus for getting shot."

Gary laughed. "See there? You feel better already."

*   *   *   *

When the ambulance carrying Jimmy Stack left, Bacha and Able put Joshua in the rear of a patrol car. Other than nearly drowning in the blood from a broken nose, he seemed to be lucid. Bacha said, "Now starts the hard part. Doing all the goddamn paperwork."

Able muttered, "Won't get into bed until four. Shit."

Gary felt ecstatic. "You think this finishes it?"

Bacha said, "I'll see the man. Joshua faces attempted murder on top of the other two felonies, so Draper's got all sorts of leverage to get that tape. It also means he won't have to face Mac's lawyer again. I think he'll jump at the chance."

*   *   *   *

Bacha didn't know the man well. A week after the incident, Mac's third trial remained on the schedule. Draper announced that he would not consider a plea bargain with a third strike felon who had attempted a murder. Draper's announcement hit Mac hard.

The next day, Bacha called and asked Gary to stop by. When Gary arrived, Bacha was sitting at his desk, observing the holes in the ceiling. His partner, Able Mendoza, was at an adjacent desk, talking on the telephone. Bacha motioned Gary to a chair, then reached into a drawer in his desk and took out a bottle of peanuts. Gary declined the silent offer, so Bacha dumped a handful of peanuts into his left palm, and then put the bottle back in the drawer. He ate a few before he said, "Draper isn't playing the game the way he should. I think we have to assume he has some serious career incentive."

That was very obvious. "And?"

"And that means the man isn't going to do the right thing until he's forced to do it." Gary waited for the punch line. Bacha finally added, "We have to get him that tape."

"How do we do that?"

"Joshua has a mother, a brother, and a sister. Only the sister comes to visit him. Cute girl. Name's Lauren. She's nineteen, goes to City College, wants to be a dental assistant."

Gary wondered what the man was trying to tell him.

Bacha said, "So who do you think has the key to the safe deposit box?"

Cops don't accept the obvious, people are too unpredictable. Thinking out loud, Gary said, "You know she's got the key."

Bacha popped a few more peanuts into his mouth. He grinned. "We were listening when she asked when she should do that thing for him. He answered, 'When I'm dead, or when I tell you.'"

"Can you get a search warrant?"

"It's not my case. I can't even talk to her." He ate the rest of the peanuts. "No law against you talking to her."

✱   ✱   ✱   ✱

Lauren wasn't just cute, she was stunning, with auburn hair framing an angelic and flawless face. She approached warily, looking from her mother at the door, to Gary on the front step. Gary asked, "Can I speak with you privately?"

"What about."

Gary beckoned. "Take a short walk?"

"Who are you?"

Her mother told her, "He's workin' with Joshua's lawyer. He thinks you can help." The tired, sad looking woman turned to Gary. "Lauren didn't hang with Joshua. I don't see how she can help."

Gary repeated his invitation. "Take a walk?"

"Just a minute." Lauren disappeared and returned a few seconds later wearing a baseball cap. She evidently avoided the sun to preserve her flawless complexion.

At the sidewalk, Gary stopped. "I didn't want your mother to hear about the key." She didn't respond. She looked around but not at him. He said, "Joshua's lawyer sent me for the key."

She squinted. "Joshua needs to tell me directly."

Bacha had been right; the tape was in a safe deposit box.

Gary said, "Look, I'm just a go-fer, but as I understand it, the D.A. is going to make an offer Joshua can't afford to pass up. To complicate the thing, the cops got Joshua in lockdown all day, and the D.A. says the offer is only good for 24 hours. The lawyer is going off his nut, but neither the cops nor the D.A. will budge."

"I'm sorry. Joshua has to tell me directly."

Gary mimed frustration. "Look, what's inside that box is a tape made by a guy named David Kendall. On the tape, he explains how he murdered his father. This guy, David Kendall, wanted Joshua to work with him. Joshua knew once he fixed things, this David Kendall would want to kill him to make sure he didn't talk. So Joshua had him make this tape to protect himself. That way, Joshua could do stuff for the guy without worrying the guy would pop him.

"Now everything is changed. Joshua's facing the rest of his life in prison for what he did, and all he has for a bargaining chip is that tape, which means that he can give the D.A. David Kendall. You've heard about the case. The D.A. has gone through two trials trying to convict the wrong guy. The D.A. doesn't believe Joshua has anything on David, so he's given Joshua today to put up or shut up."

She shook her head. "I'll be home this afternoon. Have the D.A. call me, and I'll tell him what I told you. I'll release it when I have a call from Joshua."

Gary's frustration was real. "You don't understand. If we tell the D.A. you refuse to release evidence that could convict David Kendall, he will arrest you for obstruction of justice. You will go to jail, and you will stay in jail until you do release it."

"I don't know what's in that box."

Gary was yelling at her. "Yes, you do. I just told you what was in that box." Tears formed in her eyes, so Gary made an effort to look calm. "Look, sweetheart, when Joshua told the lawyer what was in the box, he started the ball rolling. A tape like that isn't protected by attorney-client privilege because it doesn't have anything to do with Joshua's guilt or innocence. So Joshua's lawyer is obligated to tell the D.A. what's in the box, and he'll be obstructing justice if he doesn't. So who do you think is going to wind up in jail if you don't release it? The lawyer?"

She was crying, looking at her feet.

Gary handed her his card. "The lawyer has a meeting with the D.A. at four. That's my cell phone. Call me if you change your mind. If you don't, the D.A. will probably arrest you tomorrow morning."

Back in his car, watching Lauren plod back into the house, Gary called Bacha. When he answered, Gary said, "Have him call her now."

*   *   *   *

Bacha, waving an audio tape in the air, met Gary in a hallway just after he'd cleared check-in. Bacha pumped a fist. "Worked like a charm."

"Joshua called Lauren?"

He led Gary back to his desk; put the tape in a player, saying, "He made the call about ten minutes after you left her place."

On the tape, Gary heard Joshua's voice say, "Hello, Lauren?"

"Joshua? Is that you? You don't sound right."

"You know how my nose makes me sound, sweet baby. Why did you want me to call?"

"They said if I don't turn over that tape, they're going to arrest me."

"You idiot." With his nasal passages blocked, idiot came out 'idit.' "How did they find out about the tape? Did you watch it?"

Gary felt like leaping into the air. Joshua had confirmed there was a tape.

Lauren said, "I don't know what's in the box. Some investigator for your lawyer told me it's a tape, and then said the D.A. would arrest me if I didn't release it."

"Aw, sweet baby, he wasn't working for my lawyer."

A silence stretched until she said, "Joshua?"

"Listen baby, I just told them what they wanted to hear. Fuck!"

"What do you mean?"

"They're taping this conversation."

"Isn't that, like, illegal? Don't they have to tell you?"

"Listen, sweet baby, what's in that box is my ticket to ever being free again. I'll let them have it when they make me a deal. Meanwhile, you're going to hang tough. You do the jail thing for me, sweet baby. I wouldn't do this to you, but it's the rest of my life you have in your hands."

"I'm scared, Joshua."

"You hang tough. You don't want to see me die in here, do you?"

"No."

"It won't be long, sweet baby. The man is not going to put me away for the rest of my life, because he really needs to nail this other guy. He'll put the screws on you, hoping you'll cave, but he'll deal if you hang tough."

"All right."

"Love you."

"Love you, too, Joshua."

Gary asked, "Will Draper force her to release it? He doesn't want to hear David confess."

"He can't risk it. If that information gets out, he's dead meat. How long will it take you to get the recording where they talk about the tape?"

Gary did some quick calculations. "About an hour and half."

"Go do it. I'll give you a call when I get an appointment with him."

*   *   *   *

The conversation he'd recorded from the bug in Joshua's car contained damaging admissions from David. Since the bug was illegal, other facts discovered as the result of those admissions would be inadmissible. Gary inserted the sound of passing cars to blank all the damaging passages, leaving only the conversation about the tape. To make a single tape that might fool the experts, Gary used a microphone placed outside on Mac's lawn while he played the tape on a speaker in Mac's bedroom window. The sound quality of the new tape was barely audible. With any luck, the poor quality would convince Draper it was genuine without expert verification.

*   *   *   *

It was almost six that evening before he and Bacha were summoned into Draper's office. Draper listened to Gary's tape. He eyed Gary malevolently. "Will you testify to the authenticity of your tape?"

"I'd be delighted."

Draper listened to the tape of the phone call between Lauren and Joshua, and then told Bacha to give Lauren a choice of going to jail or giving up the tape.

*   *   *   *

Gary didn't sleep much that night, worried about his tape being used to force Lauren to release the key. If the tape was exposed as a phony, David's videotaped confession would be inadmissible.

*   *   *   *

The next day, Draper embraced his new cause by involving the media. He announced that in return for dropping one of the felony charges, Joshua had provided a videotape of David confessing to his father's murder. Draper had issued a warrant for David Kendall, who was now a fugitive. Almost as an afterthought, he said that the charges against John McBride had been dropped.

Since Joshua had volunteered that he had a videotape of David's confession, Gary's audio tape was no longer critical to the case. Bacha had Gary's tape returned to him, supposedly to see if he could enhance it. Gary reported back that, during a high speed rewind, that section of the tape had caught fire and melted.

CHAPTER 34

▼

Just after dark, David shut off his car lights and coasted down the hill. With the engine idling, he guided the car into the driveway, pushing the button on the remote. The garage door opened, and momentum carried the car inside. He stopped the barely moving car with the emergency brake so the brake lights wouldn't show, and then used the remote to close the garage door.

He reclined the seat back and listened to the tick of the cooling engine. Being here was dangerous, but he didn't have any choice. He'd returned from grocery shopping in Eugene and had seen the cops at Jackie's house. With four dollars in his wallet, he'd driven north into Washington, filling the car in Vancouver on his credit card. In Bellingham, he'd used his ATM card to empty his checking account. With the electronic trail pointing at Canada, he'd turned south.

He had come to San Diego for two reasons. If he was going to live as a fugitive, he needed the fake ID and the forty thousand remaining in the safe deposit box. He'd gone by the bank branch just before five, and despite a case of nerves that made him shake like a Parkinson's victim, he had cleaned out the box without any problems.

The second reason he'd come back was to kill Charboneau. The man was a specter that would haunt his every move. David could make a life in Mexico, or in South America, but he would never be comfortable until Charboneau was dead.

CHAPTER 35

▼

Booked on a noon flight to the District, Gary went to the Marina early for his last run in San Diego. He did stretching exercises, reset the lap timer on his watch, and began to run on the concrete path that edged the water. At the railroad tracks, he crossed the parkway and ran to the west, next to the eight foot cyclone fence.

As the parkway curved to the north, the cyclone fence that guarded the industrial complex ended, and a four foot steel mesh fence began, enclosing a weed choked area that had been a Little League baseball field. Tubing for bleachers rested against the tall fences behind home plate. The field had probably been abandoned because any ball going foul would clear the tall, barbed-wire topped fence that paralleled the first and third base lines. Little League teams couldn't afford to lose that many balls.

Beyond the first-base line of the abandoned field, the eight foot cyclone fence resumed, enclosing an acre or so of steel shelving arranged in rows. The rusting shelves held metal molds and dies. Leaving the metal exposed to the salt air seemed silly. If the dies might be needed, they should have been protected. If they weren't going to be used again, why not scrap them rather than expose all that expensive shelving to the elements?

The fence was topped with three strands of old fashioned barbed-wire supported on angle brackets that faced in. That, too, was strange, as if the fence were designed to keep people in, not out. Then he saw the logic. If people wanted to climb in, they could, but getting anything out wouldn't be easy.

In the distance, perhaps 300 yards beyond the shelving, a row of mismatched factory buildings stretched to the north, the tall window-starved metal construction suggesting an abandoned aircraft factory.

Gary dumped his sweatshirt on the hood of his car and began his second lap. He looked forward to going home, and getting back into the dating scene. Since he had been out of circulation for over two years, he would have to rely on the married women he knew to introduce him to their single friends.

He had crossed the railroad tracks again and was running west beside the chain link fence when a Corolla passed him. As it disappeared around the bend, Gary wondered if it was David's car, then dismissed that thought. David would have changed cars by now. Gary watched the overcast, hoping to finish his run before the sun burned through the thin mist. The Corolla backed into a parking space some 200 yards ahead, next to the yard that contained all the rusting steel shelving. He thought about crossing the street, and then chided himself for being jumpy. There was no reason for David to be hunting him.

The tall fence on Gary's right gave way to the weed-choked Little League field with its four foot fence. About a hundred feet from the Corolla, Gary was beside a motor home when David, holding a handgun, stepped onto the sidewalk. Blocked by the motor home, Gary couldn't dart into the street, and he'd be dead before he could reverse direction. David went into a shooting crouch, leaning his left arm against the tall fence for support. Gary vaulted the short fence and ran into the field. The shelving in the adjacent yard shielded him momentarily. Trapped in the pie shaped wedge, Gary ran toward the only cover, the steel scaffolding for bleachers.

He looked back as he ran, expecting David to rest his gun on the top of the fence to steady his aim. But David didn't stop. Using his left hand for a fulcrum, he vaulted the low fence in one quick motion. His easy stride said it all: no point in wasting energy or bullets. Gary was unarmed and trapped.

As Gary approached the scaffolding, he saw that the end framework formed steps. From the top step, it would be a four foot leap to the barbed wire bracket mounted on top of the tall fence. Since the bracket faced away into the industrial area, he could use it to jump the fence if he could leap high enough. Sprinting, Gary jumped onto the second step of the narrow pipe. His momentum carried him up the third step, but he reached the fourth almost stopped. If he didn't make it, he was a dead man. He jumped for the top of the fence, grabbing the barbed wire to pull himself up. Ignoring his barb-ripped palms, he felt the sole of his running shoe grab on the bracket and he was up, then pushing off to jump into the narrow space between two shelves, bending his knees and rolling sideways with the impact. When he hit the ground, his head bounced off the shelves. Dazed and hurt, upside down with his feet caught in the shelves, he heard running steps. Frantically, he yanked his feet free and stood up as David found a clear shot between two shelves. In the instant Gary was vulnerable, David took the time to push the barrel of the automatic through the links in the fence. Gary dodged around the end of the shelf just before a bullet hit a steel die with a horrific crack.

Gary ran through the rows of shelving, dodging left, then right, as David fired three more times. When the firing stopped, Gary glanced back to see David jumping from the top of the fence. Hoping the shit had broken a leg, Gary ran straight down a row, and out of the shelving. The nearest factory building was 300 yards away, and there was nothing he could use for cover. He was going to die on that endless plain of asphalt. He sprinted for the nearest building.

David emerged from the shelves and dropped into a shooter's crouch. Gary dodged to the left, the bullet a painful snap as it went by his right side. He counted to two, then dodged again to his left, then dodged right as the expected bullet didn't come. Still no bullet, so he glanced over his shoulder. David was running with that peculiar head-back form of a sprinter. He was gaining.

Gary made it to the corner of the building with a fifty yard lead. A door just beyond the corner wasn't locked. Gary pulled it open and rushed inside. He lost precious seconds examining the door for a lock that didn't exist, and then he turned and ran into the dim cavernous building perhaps fifty feet high and two hundred yards long. Parallel sets of railroad tracks embedded in the concrete floor seemed to fade off into the gloom. Painted windows high on the walls allowed some light. Along both walls, screened rooms provided the foundation for open mezzanines. Near the roof, catwalks had provided access to long gone overhead cranes, their steel rails still in place.

Where to hide? The wire enclosed rooms provided no hiding places, and the mezzanines were dead ends. Steel I-beams formed a long row down the center of the building, too thin to hide behind, but Gary chose the third one, and wedged himself into its recess. The beam felt like a toothpick. He heard the door open at the end of the building.

Time stopped. At the far end of the building, something scraped out a dirge-like beat, probably a wind driven ventilation fan. A narrow shaft of sunlight from a broken window pierced the gloom midway in the building. Somewhere outside, tires screeched. The stillness deepened and became oppressive. Gary's nerves danced. He knew David was walking the row of beams, ready to shoot. He could hear stealthy footsteps but they seemed to be in the steel of the beam. He wanted to yell, to go charging into the abyss, to run for the sake of running, hoping David would miss. His eyes tired of the constant scanning, his nerves threatened to collapse as twinkling lights filled his peripheral vision. The adrenaline made his heart skip beats.

Something rattled near the roof. Gary looked up to see David aiming at him from the overhead catwalk. Just ahead of the bullet that ricocheted off the beam, Gary whirled around to the opposite side. The catwalk was close to the beam and Gary had to keep David in sight to stay covered. He poked his head out from one side or the other, trying to guess where David would go next on the catwalk. David snapped shots as Gary exposed himself. One bullet tugged at his sweatpants as he jumped sideways.

David tired of the game. He ran some forty feet to the ladder and began to descend. Gary ran for the distant end of the building, moving right and left to make the shot tougher. David didn't shoot. When he got to the floor, he came after Gary in his weird, head-back sprint. Gary had a hundred yard lead but it wasn't enough. He couldn't see any doors in that end of the building.

Suddenly, a uniformed security guard stepped from behind a beam and leveled a revolver at Gary. "Freeze or you're dead." An overweight man, probably in his seventies, he looked frightened and nervous enough to shoot. Gary made an abrupt turn to his left, and yelled, "He has a gun."

David cut across the angle. Barely thirty yards separated them as David went into a shooter's crouch. Gary reached a set of stairs as David's gun fired. Surprised that he felt no pain, Gary ran up the stairs, turned right, and entered an open loft crammed with steel chairs.

Someone was screaming. Animal cries of pain echoed in the building. He heard David pounding up the stairs. Gary grabbed a metal chair by the back, and swung it at the opening just as David emerged. David looked surprised as the chair jammed the gun into his face. It fired, and a hole appeared where his nose had been, spouting blood. Grasping the chair as if it might keep him from falling, he disappeared down the stairwell.

Gary sprinted down the stairs. David landed on his back on the concrete floor. The gun fell from the chair, and David picked it up. Gary dove from the staircase and landed on David, driving his gun hand up over his head, the gun clattering away.

Kneeling on David's arms, driven by a fury that seemed to have no limit, Gary battered the hole in David's face, feeling bones break.

*   *   *   *

The next morning, when Gary walked into the cubicle, Bacha said, "You look like shit."

Gary held up his bandaged hands. "A tetanus shot; antibiotics, I'm as good as new."

"I was talking about your face."

"When I jumped into the shelving, I used my face to stop."

Bacha winced. "I saw the debriefing tape the harbor police made. That was quite a jump. You must be an athlete in your other life."

"Adrenaline and fear will do that to you."

"Not to me. He'd have nailed my ass while I was trying to get over the fence." Bacha laughed. "I tell people that jogging can kill them. When I get the urge to exercise, I lay down with a beer until it passes."

Gary's sweatpants were lying on Bacha's desk. Bacha picked them up with a pencil through the bullet holes in the leg. "You were wearing these when the bullet went through?"

It was hard to believe. The holes seemed to be centered in the leg. "I moved just before he fired. I guess the pants hadn't caught up with my leg."

Bacha shook his head. "If he'd hit you…" Bacha didn't have to complete the thought. After the paramedics had treated his cuts, Gary had walked through the entire scenario for the harbor police, and then again for the San Diego detectives. As he showed them where he was in relation to David, it seemed incredible that he hadn't been hit.

On edge from the hours of trying to explain what he couldn't remember, his racing mind kept Gary awake all night. What if that rusty barbed wire he grabbed to pull himself to the top of the fence had broken? Or he had sprained an ankle when he jumped? What if David had fired through the fence instead of poking the gun through, or the door to the building had been locked? And inside the building, what if he hadn't looked up in time to see David on the catwalk; what if the security guard had shot him, and what if David had ducked the chair? Gary's mind disliked being alive accidentally.

Now, adding more fuel to fry his shattered nerves, Bacha took him to a conference room with a television and VCR and asked him to watch the videotape made by the harbor police. Twenty three cartridges had been found. Counting the bullets remaining in the gun, if both clips David used had been full, there should have been 25 shell casings found. As they watched the tape, Gary tried to recall each shot. He only remembered thirteen. He did recall four as he dodged through the shelving, when David was still on the other side of the fence. That satisfied Bacha. He called someone and told them that only two cartridges had been found on the baseball field. He speculated that the other two probably ejected through the fence into the yard somewhere.

Gary asked, "The security guard all right?"

Bacha grinned. "To hear him tell it, he felt more embarrassed than wounded. He said he was lying there, screaming in pain, when you walked over, took one look at his leg, and said, 'For Christ's sake, it's a scratch. Go handcuff that asshole and call it in.' The guy said his leg hurt like crazy, but he figured you knew what you were talking about, so he got up, went and handcuffed David, and then called it in. Wasn't until the paramedics got there that he realized the bullet had gone clean through his leg."

"I thought the guy was going into shock. I was just trying to distract him."

"You did. He was still laughing about it when I visited him in the hospital last night."

"He saved my butt. David had me cold until he stopped to shoot at the guard." To change the subject, Gary asked, "How is David?"

"They did some surgery last night to put broken facial bones back in place, but he'll be walking today."

*   *   *   *

Nearly a year later, Alice flew out to San Diego to see Mac. Gary was in San Diego to testify at David Kendall's trial, so he drove Mac to the airport to meet her. Gary was amazed at the difference in her face when she saw Mac. She was almost reverent as she hugged him, and she had tears in her eyes. This tall, slim, serious woman never cried. The hug over, she whispered something in Mac's ear, and then he had tears in his eyes, too.

Alice turned toward Gary, wiped at her tears, and said, "You tell anyone about this, and I'll spit in your food when you're not looking."

As they rode toward Mac's house, Alice said, "I heard David testified that an insurance company paid Draper to convict Mac."

"Draper denies it." Mac grinned. "But I got their five million."

Gary said, "Since part of his plea-bargain forced Joshua to testify against David, David's going to return the favor. Joshua's been charged with first degree murder for killing the bartender."

Mac said, "Good. A guy like that should stay locked up."

Alice asked, "Will David get the death penalty?"

Gary said, "That's what the jury recommended."

Alice asked Mac, "Is that going to destroy Mary?"

Mac said, "She did her grieving when the article came out, when she knew he'd done it. She just hopes that she's not around when the automatic appeals run out."

Alice asked Gary, "So I don't have to avoid 60 Minutes any more?"

Mac touched Gary's arm. "How come you looked so bad when you was on there? Didn't recognize you."

Gary said, "Let me tell you about the 60 Minutes' makeup man. I wanted to disguise my face, but he wanted a challenge. He started by asking what sex I'd like to be."

*   *   *   *

That evening, Mac made an early Thanksgiving dinner with a turkey and all the trimmings. As they sat down, Alice asked why Mary wasn't there.

Mac rumbled, "Asked her, but she's got a hot date." Mac carved a slice of turkey and said, "I figured it couldn't be doing her any good to sit around the house, thinkin' about things, so I convinced her to come to work. She's good at sales, better than Frank was. Sometime after she started, she met a buyer. He's put roses in her cheeks."

He rumbled a laugh. "Mary and me go out Tuesday nights for dinner. We usually end up arguing." He grinned. "Last Tuesday, she flipped me the bird as she was driving off. Laughed so hard, I damn near fell down."

Read on for a look at another PI Gary Charboneau novel

COMING SOON

SET-UP

PI Gary Charboneau has made a horrible mistake, and the love of his life has nearly paid the ultimate price. She has physically recovered from her injuries, and with the help of two friends, she seems to coping with the mental trauma. Then she is arrested for murder, and she begins planning her final escape.

Knowing that he is racing suicide to rescue her, Gary vows to stop the prosecution even if it means killing someone. He has to, or the guilt will rip him apart.

PROLOGUE

Her legs trembling, Deborah Morgan leaves her car and walks toward the white van parked at the bus station in Salinas. With the bars inside the van's windows reflecting sunlight, she can't see if he's there. A uniformed prison guard walks to the back of the van, opens the padlock with a key, lifts the hasp, and then opens the rear doors. The slim, dark-haired man who gets out is short, maybe only 5–8 or so. He reminds her of a kid on his first outing: his clothes too new and too big, carrying a gym bag that is too empty. The guard shuts the door, climbs back into the driver's seat, and drives away.

Deborah walks into the small man's space. "You Michael Castellanos?"

Startled, he looks up at her, his expression wary. She's aware of what he sees: a pony-tailed Amazon in hiking boots with a face devoid of make-up, wearing denim bib-overalls over a man's plaid cotton shirt.

In a soft voice, he asks, "Who are you?"

"If you're Michael Castellanos, I need to talk to you."

"You parole?"

Without warning, Roger's face replaces Michael's. It's not real, she knows that, just some part of her damaged mind trying to warn her away. She can't look, so she nods toward her car. "No, I'm not parole. Get in for a minute so we can talk."

Not looking to see if Roger has disappeared, she walks to the car and gets in. When she looks through the windshield, Michael has his own face. She raises her eyebrows, her expression asking if he's going to get in. He shrugs, ambles over and joins her in the car. While she's pulling the keys from the bib pocket of her overalls, she asks, "You still want Sharon?"

He reacts to his ex-wife's name quietly: A narrowing of the eyes; a ripple that runs across his jaw, but nothing more. He asks, "Who are you?"

She carefully slides the ignition key into the lock as she says, "I'm a good friend of Jackie Switzer. A very good friend."

Jackie's name doesn't provoke him. His voice is even when he asks, "What do you want?"

She talks to the driver's side window. "Jackie knows you're going to come looking for her and Sharon, so they both plan to run." She turns toward him. "Do you have to get even with Jackie?"

"Who the hell are you? Why is any of this your business?"

Softly, she says, "I'm in love with Jackie. She's in love with me. I don't want her hurt."

"She shattered both my elbows." He raises his permanently bent arms. "I owe her."

"Sharon and Jackie work at a women's shelter in Santa Maria. They help battered women disappear. They know how to stay hidden. After they leave tomorrow morning, you won't find them."

His cheek twitches.

When the silence stretches, Deborah says, "If you'll forget about Jackie, I'll put you alone with Sharon tonight."

Other than a fleeting sneer, he doesn't react. Desperation breaks through her fear. "Jackie would be with me right now if you weren't in the picture. Sharon uses you to keep Jackie from breaking up with her. When I offered to run with them, Sharon got hysterical and accused Jackie of abandoning her. I need Jackie; Jackie needs me. I'm offering you a chance you'll never get again if you'll just leave Jackie alone."

"And where will Jackie be tonight?"

"She'll be in Santa Barbara having a farewell party with friends. She's going to stay over. Sharon doesn't like that crowd, so she'll be home packing."

He continues to look at her. When the silence becomes agony, she says, "I can have you back to your parole office in San Jose by tomorrow morning. They'll know it was you, but they won't be able to prove it if you don't leave anything at the scene."

His voice is strained when he says, "I think this is a fucking set-up."

She looks at her hands. "I can't think of any other way to keep Jackie with me."

"Bullshit." His sudden yell makes her jump. "It's a set-up to nail my ass. What's the plan? They'll be waiting to blow my head off?"

She watches his hands, ready to block a swing at her face, her other hand on the door latch so she can roll out of the driver's seat. Her voice warbling, she says, "They don't even know you're out. I told them that the prison called and said your release got moved back to tomorrow."

"And I'm supposed to swallow that? You think I'm fucking stupid?"

The failure crushes her. When she trusts her voice, she points at the bus station. "You haven't missed your bus to San Jose. Forget I talked to you, okay?"

He gets out of the car. When she prepares to drive away, he puts up a hand, asking her to wait.

*   *   *   *

After midnight on Sharon's street, Deborah parks one house away. She's been cool most of the day, now the fear is back. Her trembling is so bad her clothes are vibrating. As the car goes dark, she points and says, "That window's lock is broken, and it slides easy. Close it after you get in. You don't want to wake the neighbors."

"Does she have a gun?"

"Yes, but she's been taking Valium and drinking; so she's usually wrecked by now."

After a pause that lasts a lifetime, he gets out of the car. As she uncocks the tiny gun in her pocket, the shakes ease. On the cell phone, she keys RCL and One, lets it ring once, and then turns it off. She waits until he's in the shrub below the window before she unlaces her boots. He's still looking in the window when she gets out of the car, so she holds the latch while she rests her weight against the door to close it quietly.

From behind a tree in the parkway, she watches the dark outline as he raises the window. He seems to get larger and then the upper half of his body silently folds into the opening. She hurries across the driveway and goes in the side door of the garage. Inside the dimly lit garage, she's pulling off the boots when she hears Sharon scream. Then, as she steps out of the bib overalls, Sharon's screams are cut off by five evenly spaced gunshots that rattle a rake hanging on the wall. In the silence, Deborah lifts her shirt over her head, wads it with the overalls and drops both into a laundry basket. Opening the dryer door, she gets her pajamas and puts them on. Her bathrobe is hanging from the clothesline. She puts it on, then steps into her slippers. As she walks into the house, the shakes are gone. The dread has been replaced with an infinite emptiness.

James M. Murphy, II
1340 Glen Ellen Lane
Lompoc, CA 93436-8243
805-735-5201
oreilly@concentric.net

0-595-32753-2

Printed in the United States
22594LVS00006B/61-204